## "HOLD M[E]"

"No. I care about yo[u]." [His voice] was husky with needs he was fighting to suppress. "I could do you more harm than good. You deserve a man who will stand beside you, who belongs to your time and who has a life you can share. You need a future, and I can't give you that. All I have is the past."

She wanted to lash out at him, accuse him of being blind to everything good the present held out to him, but instead she did something quite different. She wrapped her arms around his neck, reaching up to kiss him.

He tangled his hand in her hair. "You need someone to tame you, woman. You don't know when you should be afraid." He drew back, struggling to stay in control.

"Tell me you don't feel anything for me, and I'll move away," she whispered.

"I can't lie to you." He shuddered, desire coiling around him. "I've wanted you and needed you for a long time. For more than a lifetime."

Dear Reader,

Those who read our stories know of our love for New Mexico and the Navajo people. What you may not know is that David, my husband of thirty-two years, was raised on the Navajo Nation.

From the stark beauty of that ancient land comes our inspiration. Here in the Four Corners, the old and the new live side by side. Massive red-rock cliffs and great sandstone spires that have stood for aeons reach up to the sky and cast their shadow on the new highway that runs beside it. Images like these may be viewed at our Web page, http://www.comet.net/writersm/thurlo/.

Despite the relentless encroachment of modern civilization, the land remains sacred to the *Dineh* and, with quiet dignity, they continue to live their lives between their sacred mountains.

In *Timewalker*, a powerful Navajo medicine man travels from the past to the present. We invite you into a world where dreams and reality mingle—a place where magic, hope and courage exist side by side. Our characters are fictional, but the spirit that drives them is as old as the desert itself.

*Timewalker* has long been one of our favorite novels. I hope you'll enjoy our story and that the characters will live on in your memory.

Walk in beauty,

# AIMÉE THURLO
# Timewalker

## Timetwist

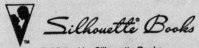

Silhouette Books

Published by Silhouette Books

**America's Publisher of Contemporary Romance**

To Mary Elizabeth Allen, for hours of kibitzing

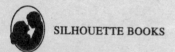 SILHOUETTE BOOKS

ISBN 0-373-51243-0

TIMEWALKER

Copyright © 1994 by Aimée Thurlo

Visit Silhouette at www.eHarlequin.com

Printed in U.S.A.

# *Prologue*

*June 1864*

Benjamin Two Eagle crouched low behind the big rock and looked toward the east. The night was dying, and so were the fortunes of the Navajo people. Soon *Jóhonaa'éí,* Sun, would rise above the canyon, and Green Eye's calvary would come forward once more. For fifteen dawns it had been the same— rifle fire, arrows flying and hoarse screams as warriors and soldiers in turn tumbled to the ground, their lives extinguished like burning twigs cast into the river.

His life meant nothing to him now, except as an instrument to avenge the deaths of those who'd followed him on this futile attempt to escape. The last to die had been the women and children of his tiny band. Bullets had even less conscience than the soldiers who sent them blindly into the scarce cover of the box canyon. He had fought on alone with captured ammunition, arrows and illusion for three days more, but the last cartridge had been spent at dusk yesterday, and magic alone couldn't turn back a heavily armed troop of soldiers.

A week ago, he might have been able to slip away, but he couldn't have abandoned the ones with him. Instead, he'd tried to help some of the others escape, but all attempts had failed, and now he had but one chance left.

Turning his back to the rifles and sabers just a hundred feet away in the darkness, Benjamin took sacred corn pollen from his medicine pouch and spoke a blessing for safety. He touched the pollen to his lips, then released the yellow life-giver to drift away on the breeze.

Clearing his thoughts, he brought out the amulet of their god, known as Slayer. The turquoise amulet representing Child-of-the-Water was no longer in his possession. He'd been forced to relinquish it in payment to the man who'd offered them safe passage—the man who had betrayed them. Now he only had the one, but its magic would still be enough. He stared deeply into the man-shaped agate. Like his father and his grandfather before him, he felt the great powers known only to Navajo *hataaliis*—medicine men. The amulet took on the subdued glow of a hot coal, and he began the chant that would take him to safety. Later, he would return and extract his revenge.

Benjamin could no longer sense the cold of the desert morning. All his energy was focused on the warmth of the stone lying in his palm. As the heat passed up his arm and into his body, he continued the ritual chant, realizing the magic was happening now. His body was fading, and the stone took on more light as his spiritual Wind Breath, his essence, passed into the tiny figure.

Suddenly, Benjamin sensed a coldness wrapping around his arm. He fought a surge of panic and maintained the chant. Yet the magic was changing somehow, in a way he couldn't explain or control. Benjamin stopped his prayers, gazing down through transparent eyes. It was too late. He couldn't reverse the process he'd already started. His spirit poured into the stone, like a broken pot losing water to the sand.

As Benjamin Two Eagle's body disappeared into the stone in a flash of light, one last anguished thought filled him. He'd sought escape, but what he'd actually found was a trap more powerful than any he'd ever known. Not even death would be able to find and release him. The agate amulet dropped to the sand and faded to darkness once again.

Footsteps approached tentatively, but no living Navajo was there to stand and defend their homeland.

# Chapter One

*June 1993*

The temperature inside the cinder block trading post was only slightly cooler than the searing heat of the New Mexico desert outside. If it hadn't been for the extremely low humidity, it would have felt like the interior of a pressure cooker. The swamp cooler, a Southwestern-design air conditioner whose effectiveness depended on the evaporative cooling of water, barely seemed to make a difference today. The owner blamed it on a broken-down water pump.

The trace of a breeze that wafted through the screen of the open window smelled of sun-scorched earth and wilted grasses. FBI agent Julia Stevens found herself wishing she were on a shelf inside the walk-in freezer.

Restless, she strolled through the small store. Waiting was the worst part of her job, and she hated it. She glanced around, studying the place for the umpteenth time. Shelves stacked high with fabrics, linens and Navajo rugs lined one wall. The back was cluttered with rolls of baling wire, shovels, tools and other hardware. Against the opposite side, beneath the thick glass of the battered oak counter, was a huge selection of squash blossom necklaces, rings and watchbands, crafted from silver and inlaid with turquoise and coral. Tables placed in the middle of the emporium were crowded with sacks of flour and sugar, and with every imaginable variety of canned food. Walking space was at a premium, and she found herself hemmed in by dry goods as she went around the store searching for a cool spot.

Her partner, Bobby Sanchez, a dark-haired man in his late twenties, stood just behind the door of the adjoining stockroom, watching through the door via a one way mirror. Bobby was an excellent agent, but at a glance he looked more like a misplaced accountant. With wire-rimmed glasses, short-cropped hair and the shuffling gait of someone who always appeared to have something else on his mind, he never attracted much attention during field operations.

"Bobby, you're positioned so that the camera will catch everything from the moment he enters, right?" Julia asked, adjusting her loose cotton top over the pancake holster.

"Stop worrying," came a voice from behind the door. "Just don't let him get too close to this mirror, or he might want to take a look inside."

"I'll make sure he doesn't go behind the counter," she said, then glanced over at the proprietor, a man in his sixties. Charlie Miller had been here as long as anyone remembered. "Mr. Miller, you're confident you can identify him?" she asked.

"You bet. I may not know anything about Eddie except his first name, but believe me, he's hard to miss. The guy's shaped like a Coke machine with a head and always follows the same pattern. He comes in alone, flashes a big roll of bills and buys everything that interests him. He's very cunning, too, like a coyote. He knows precisely what he's buying and gets only the best pieces. Someone's taught him well."

"It looks like we're ready for him, but let's go over our strategy just one more time. Once he pays for something, we'll check out the bills. If the serial numbers match, it'll tie him to the bank robberies. Then, after that, I'll let him see the amulet. If you're right, and he's particularly interested in Indian-made antiques, he's going to be very eager to buy this."

"You can count on it," Charlie said.

"Then I'll just wait for him to make an offer and force his hand by insisting on more money than he's got. Hopefully, when he goes for more cash, he'll lead us to the bank loot, as well as to the other members of the gang.''

"Got it! But there is a question I've been meaning to ask. Those robberies have taken place all over the Southwest," Charlie said thoughtfully. "You don't really think the gang's robbing banks so they can buy Indian art, do you?"

"No, that's just their way of laundering the money," Julia replied. "By purchasing things that will increase in value as time passes, they're counting on making even more money in the long run."

"They almost pulled it off, too. How'd you figure out what they were doing?"

"Some of the stolen bills were marked. They turned up in one of your competitor's deposits. He told us what was going on, and that's when we checked with you." Julia smiled. "The Bureau really appreciates what you're doing, Charlie."

"I'm glad to help out," Charlie said, rubbing his chin pensively. "But I must admit, I'm surprised you'd risk that beautiful amulet of yours on something like this."

"I figured it would be effective bait, and besides, I have no intention of letting it out of my hands." She fingered the turquoise amulet, a two-inch carving in the shape of a man, hidden for now inside her blouse. The piece had been in her family for generations. There was no way she'd allow anything to happen to it.

Julia stood by the window hoping for another breeze, but none came. Impatient with the curtain of shoulder-length brown hair that framed her face, she fastened it back with a scarf.

A moment later they heard a car pull up. Charlie Miller walked to a counter near the window, then glanced back at her. "This is the man," he said quickly, then returned to his chair and began to whittle on a piece of cottonwood branch.

"Hey, Charlie, how's it going?" A tall, muscular man dressed in blue jeans, a tan cotton shirt and bolo tie entered the room.

"How ya doing, Eddie?" Charlie said, glancing up, then back at his whittling.

"You got anything interesting for me today, old man?"

"Don't I always?" He brought out a small whetstone and started sharpening his jackknife. "My niece will help you. She's running the store today, learning the business," he said, and feigning pride, beamed her a wide smile. "Julia, this is Eddie. You take good care of him, okay?"

"You bet, Uncle Charlie," she said brightly.

"She's mighty sharp and cuts a hard deal." Charlie grinned at Eddie. "Watch out for her."

Eddie's gaze shifted, and he eyed her with the same pensive speculation a snake might show a curious rodent.

Julia tried to see herself through his eyes. She was five foot two with small, delicate features that men found appealing. But there was an unshakable self-assurance etched permanently in her expression that intimidated some. It was a quality that spoke of hardships overcome and the tenacity those had instilled. Although that hard edge was nothing more than facade, she used it often to her advantage, and it was seldom challenged.

"I've got several things you might be interested in," she said, trying to appear friendly and non-threatening. Using the glass top of the counter, she unfolded a Navajo rug woven in white, black, navy blue and red. "This pattern is called the Old Chief's design because it was traditionally worn only by the chiefs. It's in excellent condition, and we estimate it to be about one hundred years old."

"What else?"

"One more item." She then brought out a horse's ornate bridle. "This is Navajo-made and about sixty years old. It's crafted out of a very pure grade of silver."

He studied both items for a long time, inspecting the weave of the rug, then the details forged on the bridle. Finally he glanced up. "I'll take the rug. How much?"

She quoted him a high price, expecting him to bargain some, or at least make a show of it. He never even blinked an eye. Pulling out a thick roll of bills, he counted out the amount she'd asked in hundreds and fifties. "I guess that'll be all for me today then, Julia."

"I'll wrap up the rug for you in just a minute." She rang up the sale, then took several bills back out of the register. "Uncle Charlie, could you put these big bills in the safe?" She gave him the cash, knowing he'd step into the next room and hand them to her partner.

"Sure. I'll be right back." He opened the door to the store-room, then went inside, closing the door behind him.

She moved back around the counter and folded the expensive rug carefully, wrapping it in brown kraft paper. A moment later, Charlie called out to her. "Do you need any change while I have the safe open?" It was the signal that some of the numbers had matched.

"Not right now, thanks." She casually reached down and readjusted the amulet so that it now rested outside her blouse.

Eddie's reaction was all she'd hoped it would be. His eyes became riveted on the turquoise man. "Where did you get *that?*"

"This?" She held it up, feigning innocence.

"I have one almost like it," he answered. He reached into his shirt pocket and pulled out a leather pouch. Inside was the small figure of a man, only his was carved from agate. "May I take a closer look at yours?"

She held it out, still attached to the leather band that kept it around her neck. His nearly identical amulet had taken her by surprise. She hoped it wouldn't lessen his interest in buying hers. "The turquoise is as close to flawless as you can find," she said, trying to point out its merits. "And it's older than the rug you just bought."

"I want it," he said flatly. "How much?"

"I'm afraid this isn't for sale. But I could have a Navajo artist I know make one up for you in a week. You'll like the price of that much more, too."

"I'm not interested in a reproduction. I think yours and mine belong together. There's a story about these, something to do with the Hero Twins of Navajo theology, but I can't remember the details.''

Julia nodded slowly. ''I know the tale,'' she answered. Maybe telling him would serve her purposes by making his interest even more pronounced. ''When Sun was convinced the Twins were really his children, he gave them each a gift that would identify them as his and make them invincible. He gave Monster Slayer a small agate man, and to Child-of-the-Water, one made of turquoise.'' She studied his amulet. ''I'd been told that mine was part of a set that had been broken up long ago, but I was never quite sure if that was true.''

He made her an offer of five thousand dollars, then doubled it when she shook her head.

She forced herself to remain very calm, hiding her growing excitement. Now it was time to push. ''Double that to twenty thousand, and you've got yourself a deal.''

''I can come up with the cash,'' he assured, ''but I don't have that much money at the moment. Reserve the amulet for me, and I'll come back in a day or so.''

''Sorry. No promises and no guarantees. It's cash-and-carry around here,'' Julia replied.

''I've done quite a bit of business with Charlie, and I've never asked for credit. I can give you three-fourths of your asking price right now, fifteen thousand dollars cash. Let me take the amulet, and I'll be back tomorrow with the other five thousand.''

''You can leave the deposit if you want, but the amulet stays with me until I'm paid in full. No offense, but that's the deal.''

''Lady, that's too much money to hand over without getting something in return. I've done business with your uncle, but I don't know a thing about you. How do I know you won't take my deposit and head for Mexico?'' His eyes narrowed with suspicion. ''I'll tell you what we can do. I'll leave fifteen thousand with your uncle, and you and the amulet go with me to get the rest of the money. We won't be long.''

Charlie appeared from the next room. ''I heard the last part of your deal. I'm not sure that's a good idea.''

"Charlie, she'll be perfectly safe. Think about it. You can identify me, and so can several other businessmen on this reservation. I've been a steady customer for weeks now. If anything happened to your niece, I'd be out of business, and half the cops in New Mexico would be out looking for me."

Charlie nodded. "Yes, that's definitely true, but I still want to know where you're going," he said, maintaining his role as her uncle. "I thought it was going to take you a day to round up the rest of the cash. Why rush through that process now?"

"The more I see that amulet, the less I want to risk it ending up in somebody else's hands. My business partner is back at a motel in Shiprock. I think I can persuade him to loan me the cash. If not, and I'm still short, I'll have the rest wired. It's not the way I would have preferred to do this, but Julia's given me no other choice."

"Have her back in two hours, or I call the Navajo cops. That's plenty of time to make a round-trip to Shiprock."

"She'll be back, Charlie. My interest is in the amulet. If she was willing to part with it for fifteen thousand, I wouldn't need to go through this at all."

Charlie glanced at his niece, and she shook her head. "It's my amulet. I want the cash, full amount, before I hand it over to anyone."

Charlie chuckled. "Hey, she strikes a hard bargain, what can I say?" He shrugged. "Just remember—two hours."

"You've got it." Eddie walked outside with her and waved to someone parked at the gas station about a hundred yards away. "Here comes our escort. He'll be following us."

"An escort? Why do you need something like that?" She forced herself to weigh the unexpected development calmly.

"You can't carry around as much cash as I do and not have someone else ride shotgun. A little security pays dividends."

She saw the other vehicle pulling up. Although the Bureau knew there were several thieves in the gang, this was the first indication she'd had that the buyer worked closely with a partner. As his face became visible, she felt the icy touch of fear. It was Luther Burns; she knew this guy. She'd sent him to

prison for armed robbery four years before. He'd escaped custody as he was being transferred from jail to prison and was
now listed as a dangerous fugitive.

"Hey, I forgot something. I'll be right back." Before she
could turn away, the car skidded to a stop beside them.

The driver stuck a shotgun out the passenger's side. "It's a
setup! She's FBI!"

Julia dove toward the door of the trading post, but before
she could get out of reach, an arm snaked out and grabbed her
by the shoulder. Eddie swung her up against the wall. Pinning
her there, he lunged for the thin leather cord that kept the amulet around her neck, and tugged until it snapped.

Julia stepped down hard on his instep and spun away, as she
reached for her gun. Eddie staggered back, bending to retrieve
the revolver inside his boot.

Before either of them could aim their weapons, Bobby
stepped out from the doorway. "Stop! You're under arrest!
FB—"

A shotgun blast cut through the air. Luther's shotgun peppered the wooden door frame, but some of the buckshot managed to find its target. Out of the corner of her eye she saw
her partner go down. She fired off three quick rounds, trying
to draw attention from Bobby, and was successful. But the
shotgun blasts continued. Wood splintered and showered over
her, as she returned fire blindly from behind the large soft-
drink machine where she'd crawled.

Stealing a glance at Bobby, she saw him escape into the
trading post on his hands and knees, clutching his side. Blood
trickled through his fingers. "Stay down, Bobby. I'll take it
from here." Great words, but she had no idea how to do anything more than defend herself at the moment.

BENJAMIN WOKE SLOWLY and opened his eyes, squinting
against the brightness of the sun. He sat on the warm ground,
a sturdy piñon supporting his back. It had been dark when he'd
last seen the world, but that felt like an eternity ago. He looked
around. The sun was high in the sky, and from its angle he

knew it was midday. Stretching mightily, Benjamin noted his muscles were still strong and flexible.

The breeze in his face felt good, but it smelled different somehow. He walked around, trying to clear the fog that surrounded his thoughts. He was on a small hill where several stones had been placed one upon another. He recognized this place. It was a shrine close to where he'd fought his last battle.

Suddenly, the crack of gunfire echoed across the river valley and up to where he was standing. Benjamin looked in the direction of the shots and saw a white man's building in the distance. That hadn't been there before. Perhaps soldiers, instead of the People, occupied the area now.

A startling realization abruptly flashed in his mind, jolting him considerably. His amulet was gone! What had happened to free him from the agate carving? It had to be magic, the power contained within the amulet of the Hero Twin. But who had released him, and what did they want?

AT THE SOUND OF SLAMMING doors, Julia peeked out from behind cover and saw Burns's car pulling away with both men inside. Julia stepped clear of the red-and-white soda machine and aimed carefully at the right rear tire. The two rounds she had left in the clip would have to do the job, because there would be no time to reload.

She held her breath and squeezed the trigger. The tire exploded and the car fishtailed wildly in the gravel. At least now they wouldn't get far. "Bobby, how you holding up?"

"I'll make it," he yelled. "Get that scum. I'll radio for backup."

She ejected the spent clip while on the run, and by the time she reached her car, she'd reloaded. The sedan was still heading out across the open desert, riding on the rim of the wheel. They couldn't go very fast with a flat. She'd catch up in no time.

Her optimism vanished the second she realized exactly where they were headed. The grove of cottonwood and brush near the San Juan River would make passage by either car impossible, and that's what they had in mind. They'd take away her advantage, and she'd have to pursue on foot.

Backup would arrive soon, but a lot could happen in fifteen minutes. If only she hadn't insisted the tribal cops stay well away from the trading post! Her fear that the suspect might have become familiar with the local officers seemed pointless now.

Julia knew that despite her training and experience, the odds were against her. She was outnumbered and outgunned, but there was nothing else she could do. If she held back now, she'd lose them. She quickly radioed her location to the Navajo units converging on the trading post.

A half minute later, she saw the fleeing pair slide to a stop beside a wide arroyo. They jumped out of the car and dropped down over the edge, out of sight.

From where she was, she couldn't estimate the depth of the wash or see what direction they were headed. She stopped a safe distance behind their car, reached for her shotgun and ducked out.

Julia ran to the arroyo, crawling the last few feet, and peered over the edge. It was a good fifteen-feet deep, meandering toward the river like a snake. It would be tough to find them in there, but she had to try.

She slung the shotgun across her chest by its nylon sling and scrambled over the edge. As she slid down the side, she kept the barrel up and out of the sand. A quick breath later, she hit the dry sand at the bottom and raced behind the cover of a large calved-off section of arroyo wall.

She waited there, listening for the slightest sound. She hated the violent part of her job. There were some in the Bureau who loved to mix it up this way, coming alive facing life-and-death challenges. But she preferred to deal with criminals who used their brains instead of brawn. Victory, when it came that way, was more satisfying. Situations like these, where you either killed or were killed, proved nothing except man's mortality.

She eased forward cautiously, listening and noting the two sets of footprints. They were up ahead somewhere, waiting for her to show herself. Keeping her back pressed against the dirt sides, she moved slowly, half expecting gunfire to erupt each time she took a step.

The silence, disturbed only by the drone of insects, unnerved her. Just ahead was a stretch with no cover except the natural overhang of the arroyo walls. She'd have to make it past there quickly. After that, the arroyo took a wide bend that would allow her to move about more freely. Hopefully, her caution wouldn't cause her to lose time if they were trying to outdistance her in a dash to the river.

She took a deep breath and, leaving cover, sprinted forward in a zigzag. Rapid-fire rifle blasts cannoned in the walled confines, and several rounds impacted against the arroyo sides dangerously close. She heard two of the bullets whine as they whizzed past her ear. They had an assault rifle—she recognized the distinctive sound. Cursing her luck, and blessing the aim which so far had been off target, she reached the bend.

Her heart froze as she edged around the dirt wall and saw what lay ahead. Although the man was being careful, she'd spotted the very tip of a shotgun or rifle barrel thirty yards away, trained in her direction. If she went any farther, he'd have a clear shot. As she started to move back, she saw a shadowy figure covering her only exit. The second man had gone around fast, blocking her escape.

Pressing against the arroyo wall, she looked up at the vertical overhang. The top was at least ten feet straight up. She might have been able to climb it under different circumstances, but as it was, she'd only be making herself an even better target. She glanced around, her spirits sinking. She was trapped in that curve. There was no way out.

Fear cascaded down her spine, and she took a deep breath, forcing herself to think clearly. She wasn't ready to die, and definitely not like this, trapped like a rabbit between two predators.

"God." Her whisper was more a prayer than a curse. Backup was still ten minutes away. What she needed was a miracle. She could hear the men advancing on her position.

She took a step back, but succeeded only in bumping into the wall of sand and rock that boxed her in.

As the sounds grew closer, she thought of her life and found she only regretted one thing: she had no family. There would be no one to truly mourn her passing, no one to remember her name. If only she'd had more time!

Suddenly, a thin stream of dust trickled down on her and a stout branch appeared inches in front of her face. Startled, Julia glanced up and saw her rescuer. He was crouching low on the ground above her, but even on his knees, he was a live, powerful figure. The air itself seemed supercharged with electricity, as eyes blacker than a moonless night caught hers. Julia's body tingled as if she were standing out in the open in the middle of a lightning storm.

The Navajo man smiled and wiggled the branch, urging her without words to take hold.

# Chapter Two

She holstered her handgun quickly and grasped the branch up as high as she could reach, intending to climb fast. As her legs coiled around it, the man pulled her up in one fluid, continuous motion. Together at the top, a few seconds later, they moved quickly and silently toward an outcropping of jagged boulders.

Safe behind cover, they stood face-to-face for one breathless moment. An unexpected rush of fire coursed through her as she studied her rescuer. Judging from his clothing, he was either coming from or going to a tribal ceremony. Her gaze drifted over him, taking everything in. He had shoulder-length black hair tied back in Navajo fashion. His partially open hide shirt barely contained the man's broad, powerful shoulders. A medicine pouch and sheathed knife with an elaborately carved bone handle hung from his leather belt. Deerskin leggings encased slim hips and long, muscular thighs.

Her mouth felt dry. "Thank you for your help, but it's best if you go now. I don't want to endanger you any more than I have. The men—"

"Will come searching for you. Then once they find you have disappeared, they will proceed to the river. If they follow it far enough, they will reach a settlement and escape."

His voice was like a velvety caress that soothed and excited at the same time. His English was flawless, though his choice of words was a bit formal. Maybe he'd studied abroad. "You really should leave," she said, her eyes dropping to the opening of his shirt. His chest looked as if it had been carved from stone. It was smooth, and accentuated with muscles that rippled as her gaze took him in. He was distractingly sexy, and the last thing she needed now was a distraction.

"Woman, we must catch up to those men before they get away."

"That's *my* job," she replied in her best authoritative tone. "You can't take part from here on. Those men are willing to kill, and you're not even armed."

He unsheathed his knife. The slightly curved blade was long and looked deadly in his grip. The cutting edge had been carefully sharpened and left little doubt as to the damage it could do. It was a weapon, not a carving tool. Judging by the natural ease with which he handled it, she had no doubt he had drawn that knife in defense before.

"Okay, not completely unarmed," she admitted, "but that won't do much good against a rifle."

"A silent man can slit the throat of any opponent, even an armed one."

The age of the Navajo warrior was long past, but she suspected that this man would have been one of the best, had he lived then. It was more than his courage—he possessed a definite charisma that commanded a power all its own. "I'm FBI agent Julia Stevens. Who are you?"

"I am called Benjamin Two Eagle."

"Well, Benjamin, I think you should know that these fugitives would like nothing better than to take a hostage. I've got enough problems on my hands without risking the life of a civilian. What you can do to help, if you're willing, is go to the trading post and lead the tribal police back here. They should be arriving anytime now."

"No. I'm staying. The turquoise and agate amulets are nearby and they belong to me. They fell into the hands of others a long time ago, but I'm going to get them back."

"How do you know about the amulets?" He'd piqued her interest. She would have liked to know more about him. There was something very compelling about this man. But there were more important things that needed her attention at the moment. ''Never mind. Just do as I've asked,'' she said, glancing back at the arroyo. ''I'm going to try and head them off at the end of the wash. Hopefully, I'll be able to collar them there.''

''Collar them? With metal bands—like slaves?''

Although her thoughts were racing ahead to her strategy, his words made her smile. ''No. It's just an expression for making an arrest. Now, please, go back to the trading post. I owe you one, and I don't want you hurt.''

She jogged toward the river, moving parallel to the arroyo and staying behind the cover of brush as much as possible. Reaching the end, she lay flat on the ground and crawled toward the rim to look down.

Benjamin appeared unexpectedly, standing casually beside her. ''That is not necessary.''

She gasped, then kicked out, sweeping his legs out from under him and forcing him to tumble to the ground. ''Stay down! Didn't you understand what I said? These guys are armed, and they mean business!''

He lay on his side, staring at her in surprise. It never occurred to him that she would attack. ''I know, I saved *you,* remember?'' He sat up slowly. ''The men who tried to gun you down have moved off. While we were talking, they went to the spot where you were ambushed, whispered to each other, then ran toward the river.''

''How do you know that?'' she asked pointedly.

''I heard them. Didn't you?''

''No, and you couldn't have, either,'' she snapped.

''Go down into the arroyo and track them yourself. You'll see I am right,'' he answered calmly. ''But you'll be wasting time if you do that, and you have none to lose. They are heading for the water, and if they get into the river, it will be impossible to track them.''

She glanced down into the arroyo. Two sets of tracks led where he'd indicated. ''Okay, let's go find them. You're obviously from around here and know the terrain. Maybe you'll give me the edge I need.''

He moved so quietly along the dry sand in his leather moccasins that she felt like an elephant stumbling along in comparison. He had the grace of a skilled hunter, and his prowess made her envious. She was supposed to be the expert. Of course, this *was* his home. She consoled herself with that thought.

"They are heading for the thicket of salt cedar along the water's edge."

"How do you know?" she asked pointedly.

"It's what I would do if I were them." Suddenly he stopped and signaled her to do the same. He crouched by a branch on the ground and brought it to his lips. "They were here just a short time ago," he whispered.

"And you can tell that from a branch?" she challenged, matching the softness of his tone.

"The sap within is still fresh." He gave her a puzzled smile. "Are you always this ill-tempered, woman, or do I bring it forth in you?"

"I prefer the term *skeptical*," she whispered back.

He continued along with her for a few more minutes, then motioned Julia aside. "The men are directly ahead. Stay here."

"Hold it, buddy boy. I chose this job, and this is my case."

"But you are a woman."

He'd said it as if convinced her fighting capabilities couldn't possibly be on a par with his. The attitude rankled her. "I can take care of myself. Now, I appreciate what you did, but I've got a job to do, so stay out of my way." She started to go past him.

He blocked her path. "You did not do so well alone before."

"I work for the Federal Bureau of Investigation. We're not invincible, but we're well trained. Unless you're in law enforcement, you're not equipped to deal with a situation like this."

"I am not a lawman, woman, but I know how to fight, and I know how to use the desert as my ally." He moved off before she could stop him.

Julia started to follow, but he vanished in a matter of seconds. Great. If a civilian got injured, the Special Agent in Charge would have her head on a platter.

As she approached the shallow river's edge where the muddy water splashed and bubbled, she studied the tracks. The men had split up. She decided to trail the one who'd chosen to head downriver toward Shiprock. The other tracks were too indistinct for her to follow.

Hearing footsteps ahead, Julia crept forward quickly, keeping her head low. Hopefully it would be Eddie, and she'd get the amulets back. As she moved closer, she recognized Luther Burns struggling through the willows beside the bank of the river. A moment later, he passed around a large salt cedar, and she lost sight of him.

Julia pressed on and started to close in, when she suddenly spotted Benjamin out in a small clearing about twenty yards away. He was stalking someone else; undoubtedly he'd managed to pick up Eddie's trail.

When Burns emerged from behind the salt cedar, Julia turned her attention toward him. She saw him look around trying to get his bearings, then suddenly grow rock still. His gaze was focused straight ahead on Benjamin. Before she could react, Benjamin ducked down, as if warned by some sixth sense. Burns fired off a shotgun round, but her unofficial partner had already disappeared.

Taking advantage of the diversion, Julia brought her own shotgun to bear. "Set it down easy, Burns!" She advanced toward him as he slowly complied with her order. "Now, face down on the ground. Move it!"

He spat out several explicit oaths as she frisked and cuffed him. "Do us both a favor and shut up," she said, hauling him to his feet. "It's a hot trip back to the trading post. Keep it up, and I'll handcuff you to the door handle and let you walk while I drive. You shot my partner, so don't test me."

Without warning, Benjamin Two Eagle emerged from behind the stand of junipers to her right. Julia instantly lowered the barrel of the shotgun she'd raised in his direction. "Don't *ever* do that! I could have shot you!"

"The other man is wading across the river. Leave this one manacled to that cottonwood tree over there. We will go after the one who has the amulets."

"I'd like nothing more, but I can't. I've got a wounded partner, and civilians at the trading post to protect. Eddie might just decide to double back and try to rescue his buddy. The best thing I can do is brief the tribal police as soon as possible so they can give us backup. We'll have plenty of manpower then." She gave Burns a hard shove forward. "Keep moving."

Her attention shifted to her prisoner for only a second. Yet by the time she turned back to Benjamin, he was gone. "What is it with this guy? He does more disappearing acts than Houdini!" she muttered sourly. "And how does he know about the amulets?"

"Don't ask me," Burns answered sourly. "He's your Indian scout, not mine. Where *did* you dig him up?"

"None of your business. Now keep walking."

Julia secured her prisoner in the back seat and drove to the trading post, radio mike in hand. Navajo Police Chief Franklin Roanhorse was eager for details, and she filled him in quickly. "We'll need several good trackers to pursue Eddie," she added. "Although I figure he'll go toward Shiprock, it's also possible he could return for his partner, or backtrack and head toward Aneth, Utah, or maybe even leave the river for Teece Nos Pos, farther west."

"I'll also have a unit check out the motel at Shiprock in case the associate he mentioned is still there," Roanhorse said.

"Chief, what about Agent Sanchez, my partner?"

"He's already being transported to the hospital. The paramedics said the buckshot didn't cause any permanent damage."

She breathed a sigh of relief. At least that was one less worry. Bobby had a wife and two kids. She arrived at the trading post a few minutes later. Several vehicles with the Navajo tribal emblem were parked outside a yellow, taped-off perimeter. Walking to the closest officers, she turned over custody of Burns.

Julia started walking toward the trading post when she saw

the chief's assistant, Pete Bowman, coming toward her. He was a large, barrel-chested Navajo, broad-faced and broad-shouldered. She'd met him once before and had been impressed with his cool efficiency.

"We've got roadblocks being set up," Bowman said, pointing them out on the small map he was carrying. "I know the trail the suspect is following, so I've covered the areas where he's likely to connect with the main highway."

"You should tell your men that there's a civilian—a Navajo—tracking him now," Julia said. "He's very good, like someone who'd served in Special Forces. He hauled me out of an ambush in that arroyo."

"Did you catch his name?"

"Benjamin Two Eagle. I figure he has something to do with whatever ritual is taking place." She described Two Eagle's clothing and appearance.

Bowman gave her a puzzled look. "There are no rituals going on now—I'd know." He shrugged. "But some of the People come in now and then from the remote regions of the rez. Out there, they tend to stick to traditional ways. Was Two Eagle an older man?"

"I'd put him in his late thirties."

He rubbed his jaw pensively. "Then it beats me. Are you sure of his age?"

"Meaning, am I underestimating by twenty years?" She knew what he was referring to. It was hard for Anglos to accurately gauge the age of any Navajo. A Navajo's youth seemed to last far longer than it did for others off the reservation. "I think you'll find my guess accurate, or close to it. I spoke to him face-to-face." She watched as several Navajo officers worked the crime scene, which included Eddie's abandoned car. "Maybe his clan or religious group is having a sing."

"I assure you, we'd know about it, even if it wasn't supposed to be common knowledge." Bowman smiled. "The rez might seem big, but in many ways it can be very, very small."

"Maybe he was wearing the ritual clothing to make sure it

fit for a future ceremonial, or perhaps he was on a personal spiritual journey," she said in a clip, annoyed with Bowman's attitude. She had been trained to observe. "Just ask your men to keep an eye out for this guy."

While Bowman was busy on the radio, she went inside the trading post. Charlie looked as if he'd aged ten years in the last few hours. "Are you okay?" she asked gently.

"Yeah, but this peaceful little corner of New Mexico sure came apart at the seams."

"You're right about that." She described Benjamin Two Eagle and asked Charlie if he knew anything about him.

The Anglo trader mulled it over. "I know lots of people here, but no one who wears clothing like that as a matter of course. I'll ask around, if you'd like."

"Do that, but don't worry if you don't find out anything. He's one of the good guys," she assured, deciding to trust her instincts for now. His actions spoke well for him. For a split second, she wondered if the attraction she'd felt might be swaying her judgment, but she dismissed the thought.

"What about Eddie?" Charlie said. "He knows that *I* turned him in."

"He also knows we're on his trail. If he was going to come back here, he would have tried that before the tribal police responded. My guess is that he's trying to put as many miles between him and this place as possible."

Bowman came to the doorway and waited there until she joined him. "We have our best trackers working both sides of the river now," he said. "We'll get him soon."

"I'm going to head over to the roadblock running south toward Shiprock, keeping my eyes open for hitchhikers," she said.

He nodded. "That one should be set up already."

"Good. My bet is the suspect will try to steal a vehicle and make a run for it. In the meantime, ask your officers to go over those abandoned cars and question Burns. He'll know where this Eddie person is likely to go. I don't think you'll get any answers, but you never know."

As Julia drove slowly down the highway, her gaze followed the brush and cottonwood *bosque* lining the San Juan River. Although the amulets were very much on her mind, one of her biggest worries at the moment centered on Benjamin Two Eagle. He was smart, and he definitely had courage, but she was still afraid he might get hurt in the manhunt. Eddie would be more dangerous than ever now, and that assault rifle was a formidable weapon. She owed Benjamin more than to let him face that alone.

As her thoughts focused on him, she felt a disturbing tingling sensation coursing through her. There was something compelling about him. Maybe it was charisma, or animal magnetism. Whatever it was, she would have loved the chance to explore it at leisure. But she was on a case. She shook her head as if trying to dislodge any distractions before they became too firmly rooted. She had a job to do right now, and that was the only thing that would be allowed to occupy her mind. Her only interest in Two Eagle was to find out what he knew about the amulets.

She arrived at the two-car roadblock twenty minutes later. Two officers wearing the tan uniform of the tribal police stood behind the front hoods of their cars. One held a shotgun, the other a rifle. The officer with the shotgun approached her car slowly while his companion watched her.

Julia pulled out her badge and identified herself. "Have you seen any sign of the suspect?"

"No, ma'am, and we have his description. We'll also have a photo soon. Your partner got him on video, and a print from that will be delivered the moment it's available. In the meantime, it'll be easy spotting anyone who doesn't belong here," he added with a shrug. "There's not much traffic right now. It's the hottest part of the day, and people tend to hole up."

She saw the perspiration that covered his forehead despite the billed cap. It was over ninety, and it was supposed to go even higher. Standing out on the asphalt had to be punishing. "You guys have enough water to drink?"

"Yeah, and it helps a bit," he said with a grin. "We don't

get out of the shade of our cars unless we see someone coming."

"I'm going to drive back to the area where I last saw the suspect and take a look around. Do you know where the search teams are now? I don't want to mess up the trail they're trying to follow."

"They're already a mile or so past the arroyo in each direction."

"Okay, thanks."

She drove back northeast on the Teece Nos Pos road, then slowed down as she passed the trading post. A police car was still outside in the parking lot, and officers were going over Burns's car, which they'd retrieved after changing the flat.

Knowing the arroyo began a short distance beyond, she turned off, following her earlier tire tracks. A few minutes later, she stopped the vehicle near a big cluster of boulders and glanced around. Except for the trading post visible in the distance, there was nothing around. Leaving the windows down so she wouldn't return to a miniature version of hell, she went to the arroyo and scrambled over the edge.

Julia felt uneasy coming back here, but it had to be done. There was a chance, admittedly slim, that Eddie might have dropped one or both of the amulets as he'd tried to make his escape. She searched the ground, hoping for a break. She had so few things to remember her mother by! The thought of having lost the amulet made her feel sick to her stomach.

Julia went into the section where she'd been trapped and looked around. A shudder passed like a wave through her body. She'd never come quite so close to dying. She remembered the emptiness that had filled her when she'd realized that in a year, maybe less, she'd fade completely from people's memories. She'd faced the prospect of death as alone as she'd lived her life. Regret had made it almost unbearable. Then, suddenly, just as she'd desperately wished for another chance to know life and be lucky enough to find love, Benjamin Two Eagle had appeared.

Odd the way that had happened—not that she believed the

incidents had anything to do with one another. She was a person who thrived on facts and logic, and to imagine connections where none existed wasn't her style at all.

As Julia moved farther into the arroyo, her thoughts continued to focus on Benjamin. He'd seemed to come out of nowhere. She still wasn't sure how he'd known about the amulets, let alone why he thought they were his. That worried her, too. But she brushed those thoughts aside to concentrate on the task at hand. Eddie and Burns's tracks led her along the arroyo, then down the banks of the river. Grasses and scrub brush made the search for the tiny stone carvings difficult.

She didn't give up easily, but after a long while, it became clear that her efforts were futile. Disappointed, she started back. As she approached the outcropping of rocks near her car, she spotted the faint outline of a man in the shadows.

# Chapter Three

Benjamin Two Eagle saw the government woman approaching the machine slowly and carefully. Aware she had seen him, he stepped out into the sun so she could identify him with certainty. He'd startled her by being there, but it had seemed pointless to go back into the arroyo when there was nothing there to find. Better to conserve his energy for the times it would be needed.

He watched her curiously as she drew near. She was short, but womanly in shape. Any man, white or Indian, would have called her pretty. Her eyes were the green of raindrop-laden pines, drawing his gaze there for embarrassingly long moments. A woman warrior, sidearm at her hip, and as proud as any man or woman he'd ever known. Yet she was a *bilagáana,* a white, and experience had taught him how costly it could be to trust those outside the *Dineh,* the People.

Unfortunately, he couldn't go to those of his tribe for help, so he had avoided the uniformed men who'd come earlier. The *Dineh* feared the *chindi,* the evil side of a man that remained earthbound after death. If he went to any of them with the truth, they'd be convinced he was from the grave. None would remain near him long enough for him to explain he was not a ghost, but as real as they were.

On the other hand, he was certain this woman did not believe he was a ghost. He'd felt the way she responded to him. And the amulet had been in her possession. Something told him that his fate was linked to hers.

The warrior woman approached, hand still on her sidearm. Satisfied no one else was there, she focused her attention on him. "What are you doing here?"

"The Navajo men tracking the one who escaped seemed to know what they are doing. But you need help, so I thought I would stay with you."

"With me?" She stared at him aghast. "You are *not* part of this investigation. You can't help." She slipped into the driver's seat. "But I'll be glad to give you a lift." She motioned for him to get in the car.

He stared at her. What portion of him did she wish to lift? "Explain." He sat in the padded seat and pulled the door closed, following her lead. Suddenly her machine lurched forward at an incredible speed. He gripped the soft, padded bench with both hands and concentrated on keeping his face expressionless. He wouldn't show fear, even though they were riding like the wind itself! That would give this woman an advantage over him that his pride would not allow.

"Is my driving that bad?" She glanced down at his hands.

He released his hold immediately. "I am not concerned about it."

"Where do you want to go?" she asked as they neared the highway.

"I told you. I wish to remain with you."

She exhaled softly. The thought had more appeal than she wanted to admit. "I think it's time you and I had a talk."

"About what?"

"Start with the basics. For instance, who are you? No one around here knows anyone called Benjamin Two Eagle."

He stared at her in mute surprise. No one remembered his name? How could that be? "My name is Benjamin Two Eagle. I am a *hataalii,* a medicine man."

"Then why hasn't anyone heard of you?"

"I cannot answer that. Perhaps I've been forgotten."

"I know Navajos don't speak for one another, but don't rely

on that to dodge questions. It won't work. Something's wrong with your story. Why don't you try being honest with me? I'm not trying to nail you, not after you helped me out of that jam.''

"Nail me? Jam? What dialect of English do you speak? I was instructed by missionaries from California, yet I hardly understand you.''

"Sorry. Maybe it's my slang.'' She paused, then started again. "Your story simply isn't believable. There are things about it that don't add—that don't make sense. If you are a Navajo Singer,'' she said, using the term she'd heard Navajos use around the reservation, "then people would know you.''

He grew serious. "Yes, you would think so.''

Perhaps legends and stories were not passed on from generation to generation anymore. Had his people lost that ability, or had they been so defeated they'd stopped caring? He was a *hataalii* with powers, a man traditionally well respected. If his own people didn't remember, then why had fate and his gods finally released him now? Maybe it was a punishment for the way he had failed those who had chosen to follow him.

He glanced down, lost in thought. As he did, his gaze fell on some papers filled with handwriting that was even worse than his. They were attached to a thin board by a piece of metal and placed on the floor of the trackless locomotive. The date at the top startled him. 1993! Almost a century and a half had passed! He had been within the agate much longer than he had imagined. Perhaps it shouldn't have surprised him. Women warriors and locomotives that could be driven anywhere—the world had certainly changed! Yet people remained the same. There was still evil and those who chose to oppose it.

"You haven't answered my question,'' she insisted. "Who are you?''

"I have told you the truth. I am Benjamin Two Eagle.''

"My question remains.''

"I have no answer other than the one I have given you. But I *am* a Navajo Medicine Man, and I need the amulets. Both of them.''

"Why? And how do you even know about them?''

He hesitated. The white woman was strong and intelligent, and she would not accept anything but an explanation that made sense to her. Even though he knew she would never accept the truth, he had no desire to lie to her. He did, however, have a desire to lie *with* her. "I know about them because they are a part of my heritage, part of me. And I need them for spiritual purposes," he said, wording his reply carefully.

"The *turquoise* amulet belongs to *me*."

He shook his head. "It may have passed into your hands, but both amulets are rightfully mine."

"What makes you so sure? I mean, you couldn't have possibly carved them yourself," she challenged.

"No, both of them were crafted long before either of us was born," he answered patiently. "I was never told how they came into being, but I know with certainty that they were meant to remain with the *hataaliis* of my clan."

"If you can offer proof, then you might be able to gain ownership of both amulets legally. But I want to tell you, I won't part with mine easily."

"You have already done that, woman. Though maybe together we can still track both of them down." He saw the pain his words had caused and regretted them. She was as strong willed as any warrior he had ever known, but she wasn't as hard as she tried to make herself appear.

She was a woman who balanced fierceness with softness, and he couldn't decide which drew him most. He recalled the way she had treated her enemy. Despite her anger, her outrage, she had held herself in perfect control, using only as much force as necessary to subdue him. And that was when his attraction to her had deepened.

She challenged everything male in him. Her strength was a match for his own. She tempted him to haul her in his arms and smother her mouth with his own until she surrendered to him.

But these thoughts were too dangerous for him to contemplate. He was here to fulfill a task.

"Yes, I lost the amulets," she admitted at last, pain lacing through her words, "but I *will* get them back."

Her voice revealed her stubborn resolve. But there was vulnerability there, too. He saw the way she was gripping the wheel—her knuckles were white under the strain. A sweet ache pierced him. He reached across, wrapped his hand over hers and squeezed lightly.

The gesture took her by surprise. She knew his people disliked touching strangers. His touch was warm and filled with tenderness. It soothed and excited all at once. A shiver ran through her, leaving a myriad of tingling sensations in its wake. Then, before she had a chance to gather her wits, he took his hand away. An inexplicable sense of loss swept over her.

"I can help you," he said softly. "You're unsure of my value to you, but in time you'll learn to rely on me and my word."

"Convince me." Through some miracle, she managed to keep her voice steady.

"The man you search for escaped in a damaged blue locomotive. It had firewood in the back. He took it from a squaw."

She gave him a perplexed glance. "You think you have trouble with my English!" she muttered. Slowly comprehension dawned over her, and she smiled. "You mean a pickup. He stole a pickup from a Navajo woman."

He planned to remember the words she spoke. "Yes, a pickup. Blue. The woman was very angry, but there was nothing she could do, and I was too far away. She started to walk back."

"Good lead," she admitted. "I wish you'd told me sooner." She picked up the mike and called it in. "Are you from a remote area of the reservation? Is that where you trained to be a Singer?"

He watched her use the telegraph without wires, wondering how she made the letters just by pushing with her thumb. Benjamin hoped she had not seen him jump when a voice came from the box. "I was born in a place where there were few families. And yes, that is where I learned. I have been away from everything and everyone for a very long time,'' he admitted.

"Learning."

He considered it for a moment. "Yes."

"And you made your own clothes as part of your education?"

"Yes."

"That explains quite a bit," she said slowly. "Okay, supposing I believe you…"

"You do," he answered simply. "Trust your instincts."

She scowled at him. "You read minds?" The thought made her uneasy and oddly excited. She glanced at him quickly, wondering if he'd read that!

A ghost of a smile played on his lips. "Some minds are easier to read than others."

HE WAS VERY HANDSOME when he smiled. The gesture eased the lines around his eyes—eyes that seemed to look right through the toughness she tried hard to project. Nothing she did or said fazed Benjamin Two Eagle in the slightest. He had the quiet confidence of a man who knew precisely what his capabilities were and didn't need to prove himself to anyone else. She admired that.

At least his answers had helped her understand the odd way he was dressed. It also explained his speech. If he'd spent years preparing to be a Singer in some remote area of the reservation, there was no telling how intensive his studies had been. Her guess was that he'd had very little contact with the outside world. It was amazing how he coped with technology, especially the late-model car with a modified engine, something he may never have experienced before. He *did* react to the radio, but covered his surprise immediately.

What puzzled her most was that all her instincts were telling her that he could be trusted. And some were telling her to do more than trust. Things were so much easier when she relied solely on facts and logic.

The desert gradually became a mass of sloping hillsides, me-

sas and canyons. She focused on her surroundings, staying alert
for any surprises. This was a great place for an ambush, with
narrow arroyos and high brush right next to the highway.

"There, up ahead, moving away from us," he said, calling
her attention to a spot near the top of the next rise. "That's
the loco—the pickup he stole. I recognize the way the back of
it is damaged, though it no longer contains the firewood."

"You've got great eyesight," she muttered, barely able to
make out the details, as the truck, nearly a mile ahead, sped
away from them. She pressed down hard on the accelerator.
"We'll catch him, but if bullets start to fly, get down on the
floor and stay there. Understand?"

He stared at her in disbelief. "You want me to cower in fear
while *you* protect *me?*"

"What I want is for you not to get shot. Give me your word
that you'll do exactly as I asked, or I'll stop right here and
make you walk."

He weighed her request, then finally nodded. "If the floor
provides protection, then of course. When you catch them, you
may need my help. I won't be of much use to you if I'm
wearing bullet holes."

Julia fought to suppress a smile. Though he was practical,
he was also worried about her. That knowledge pleased the
womanly part of her. Old-fashioned gallantry was rare nowa-
days.

She glanced furtively at him. His eyes were glued on the
truck. What on earth was she thinking? He was just worried
about the amulets. And her own thoughts should have been
focused only on business, too.

Julia picked up the mike and radioed in her position, making
sure a roadblock was going to be established at the next highway junction. "He can't get away, not in that old pickup. We'll
catch him, or he'll run into the tribal police. Either way, he's
ours."

As she headed down the hill, she saw smoke curling up from
the small bridge they'd have to cross. Eddie had set fire to the
wood he'd dumped in the center! "Now we know what he did

with the firewood.'' She cursed softly. ''If the bridge has been weakened too much, we won't be able to cross.''

She saw the truck motoring away at a more leisurely pace and imagined Eddie was having a good laugh. The thought rankled her. She picked up the mike, apprising the others of her problem, but assuring them that she'd find a way around it. She wanted all their manpower directed to that roadblock.

''The fire is not very big yet, but the center will be hot,'' he said. ''Can you push it aside?''

''You mean with the car?'' She considered it as she slowed, then came to a stop in front of the bridge. ''No. If a piece of burning wood gets caught beneath us, the gas tank in this thing could ignite. It's too chancy.'' Her gaze drifted over the field fencing that partitioned off a section of rangeland to their left. ''But there might be another way. Come on. Give me a hand.''

She jumped out of the car, took some pliers and the lug wrench from her trunk, then headed for the fence line. ''We'll cut down about fifty feet. Then we'll tie the wire at one end to the front bumper, loop the fence around the fire and fasten the other end to the opposite side of the bumper. Once we make that U-shaped scoop, it'll just be a matter of backing up the car and pulling the wood right off the bridge.''

They worked quickly. Without gloves, the wire cut into her hand more than once as she worked the pliers. Although she muttered several well-deserved curses, Benjamin remained silent. She assumed that he was simply more adept with the tire iron and was managing without the cuts that crisscrossed her hands. Minutes later, however, as they headed back to the car, she saw blood trickling from the back of his hand. ''Why didn't you tell me you were having problems? We could have traded tools.''

''What good would it have done? We both had a task to complete.''

''Well, okay, but it might have made you feel better if you'd complained a little,'' she said. Then, with a sheepish grin, she added, ''I know it would have made *me* feel better.''

He glanced at her quickly. "Why?" In this age, did women like men to show weakness as easily as *they* did sometimes?

"Haven't you heard the saying, 'Misery loves company'?"

"No."

She scowled at him. "Never mind."

"Now you're angry," he said, totally perplexed.

"You trying to show me up?"

"I was not trying to show you anything. You needed my help with the fence. I gave it. Why are you angry? Are you disappointed because I didn't choose to mutter angrily like you did whenever the wire cut my skin?"

She glared at him. "Pardon me for being human," she snapped.

"Why do you apologize? I'm not angry with you! You're angry with me."

"That wasn't an apology. Obviously, sarcasm escapes you."

"I don't understand you."

"No kidding. Now help me with the fence."

Dragging one end of it, now separated from its poles, Benjamin circled around the fire, forming a mesh loop. They moved quickly, noting the flames were scorching the asphalt roadbed.

"Ouch!" he complained as he tugged the fence back toward the car.

She glanced over at him with concern. "Are you okay?"

"Yes, but since you wanted to know when it hurts, I thought I'd try to please you."

She couldn't help it. She wanted to be angry, but the hopeful look on his face was her undoing. Theirs was an odd partnership, but an interesting one. She began to laugh, despite the frenzied pace they were taking.

He smiled at her while he attempted to attach the fence wire to his side of the front bumper. "That's much better. Anger is not good. I'll remember to say ouch more often so you can see I'm only human, too. Then it'll be easier for us to work together."

"We *are not* working together. For the moment, you're unofficially assisting me. Clear?"

"We are together and looking for the amulets. That is all that matters to me. Please phrase it any way that makes you comfortable," he agreed calmly.

She stared at him, all the time winding a strand of wire from the fence around the bumper. He was patronizing her without even trying. "You are the most exasperating man I've ever met."

"But a useful one," he reminded, moving over to help her.

His partially exposed, sweat dampened chest gleamed in the sunlight as he finished attaching the end she'd been working with. He grunted with the effort, as he took up the slack and pulled the fence tight.

The sound fueled her overactive imagination, and a hot awareness, almost equal to the heat from the nearby flames, swept over her. Did he sound like that when he made love to a woman? Did he have a woman? When he looked at her, did he wish she was his woman?

She saw him look up at her. There was something enticingly sensual in the way he captured her gaze. For an instant, she pictured herself stepping into his arms and feeling his naked chest against her. The vivid fantasy made her body throb with imagined pleasures.

He turned away and gave the fence one last tug. "We're as ready as we ever will be."

She glanced at him quickly, then realized half a second later he'd only meant it was time to try and drag the firewood off the bridge. "Oh. Okay. Let's put our work to the test then," she said, refusing any more distracting thoughts.

Julia got into the car, then put it in reverse. As she pulled the burning firewood off the bridge, several smoldering pieces worked their way through the holes in the fencing and remained behind. Benjamin ran over to them. Julia saw him kick the burning wood off the side and into the dry arroyo below. The pieces would harmlessly burn themselves out in the sand.

She joined him in the center of the bridge a moment later

and studied the road surface, examining the fire damage. The structure didn't sag or make any ominous creaking noises as they moved around. So far, so good.

She then inspected the sides, searching for hidden trouble spots. "I think it'll hold the car. Eddie set this fire in a hurry and didn't plan very well. If he'd set it more toward the edges, he could have ignited the wooden rails, which would have carried the flames down under to the support beams. We got lucky."

"Can we still catch up to him?" Benjamin asked as they dashed back to the car.

"Yeah. He lost time by stopping and setting the fire. We lost time dealing with it. I figure we're about even. But once we get past the bridge, I'll set some new speed records."

He started to get back into the car with her, but she shook her head. "Wait. I have a better idea. Cross on foot now," she said. "We know the bridge will hold you. After you're safe on the other side, I'll drive over."

"You're not really certain it's strong enough to take the weight of the car," he concluded.

"I can't be one-hundred-percent sure until I try. That's why I want you to be in a position to help if something goes wrong."

His jaw tightened and his lips were pursed, but he nodded curtly and did as she asked.

He didn't like it, that much she could tell, but the situation left them with no other options. Julia waited until he'd jogged across, then she drove back down the road. When she crossed over, she wanted to do it quickly.

Turning around, she accelerated. Her hands were moist with perspiration, as she gripped the steering wheel. Every muscle in her body screamed with tension. Then, just as she reached the halfway point on the bridge, there was a deep scrunching sound somewhere below the tires. The bridge sagged in the blink of an eye, and the structure began to collapse beneath her.

Without hesitation, she floored the accelerator. She'd need that momentum to make it to the other side now.

# Chapter Four

The car hurtled through the air, as the engine screamed from the strain of maximum acceleration. Her fingers were curled around the steering wheel in a death grip. A second later, the vehicle bounced onto solid ground with a hard, bone-crushing thud.

She took her foot off the gas and gradually braked to a full stop. For a second or two she could scarcely move. Feeling her breathing start up again, she put the car in reverse and carefully backed up to collect her passenger. Behind her was a tangled mess of wooden beams, splintered like matchsticks, among thin chunks of asphalt. In the center, a thin curl of smoke slowly grew in size.

Benjamin approached her side of the car warily. "Cars don't normally fly?"

She started to laugh, tension washing out of her. "No, but in a pinch, I can work wonders."

He smiled back, and the worry lines framing his eyes gentled. "I believe that."

"Get in." She cocked her head toward the passenger's seat. "It's time we gave Eddie a very unpleasant surprise." As Julia raced down the highway, heart still thumping overtime, she made a brief radio report on the condition of the bridge.

When they approached an intersecting dirt road minutes later, Benjamin leaned forward and gripped the dashboard hard. "Turn here. I have a feeling that's where we'll find him."

"Your hunches have been pretty good so far," she conceded. Julia slowed and pulled off the road a quarter mile past the turnoff.

"Do you want to go on foot from here?" Benjamin asked.

"No, I have to check something first." Julia got on the radio and learned that the roadblocks were still not in place. "We'll have to come back later," she said, pulling out onto the road. "I've got to stay in pursuit and follow the most likely route for now. That side road leads back to a natural gas well, and that's not exactly a ticket to a fast getaway."

He pursed his lips, and the skin over his cheekbones grew taut. "My intuition is reliable."

"Sorry, but I can't take the chance that Eddie will stay on the main highway and confront the tribal police before they're set up. If that happens, those cops are going to need all the backup they can get. That assault rifle is a fierce weapon."

They continued down the highway, but failed to spot the blue pickup anywhere. After ten minutes, they arrived at the roadblock, which was now in place. Benjamin hadn't said a word, but his silence spoke volumes. She could sense his disapproval as clearly as if he'd voiced it.

Julia left the car and approached the patrolmen manning the junction of the Aneth, Utah, turnoff and the main highway. "Any reports of the blue pickup I've been pursuing?"

"We've been on the lookout ever since you put out the call, but nothing matching that vehicle's description passed us on the way here," the senior officer replied.

"The suspect was heading right this way. I'm certain he wants to make it to Cortez or Farmington. Both cities are fairly large and off the reservation. There are plenty of non-Indians to hide among."

As Benjamin walked over, she saw the officers' attention shift to him. Even though it appeared they had never met him, his bearing alone commanded their respect. He carried himself with the same self-assurance of a military officer.

"Have you seen a man on foot, even at a distance?" Benjamin asked the Navajo policemen in English.

"There's been no one around," the oldest of the two answered.

"You think he abandoned the pickup and continued on foot," Julia observed, weighing the matter. "You know, it's possible. If he knows the reservation, walking to Shiprock from here wouldn't be that difficult. Then, to get off the reservation, all he'd have to do is follow the river until he reached Farmington."

"I think he expected the barricade in the road," Benjamin said. "Hiding the pickup on that dirt road back there would have been a reasonable choice for him to make."

She shot him a hard look. "Let's go check that out now." Suspicion crowded at the edges of her mind. He was showing remarkable insight for an untrained civilian. She glanced back at the patrolmen. "If the truck is there, we'll need one of those search teams here as soon as possible."

"Our best trackers are still near the river. They continued working the area until a few minutes ago in case the report of the blue pickup happened to be incorrect. But one of our officers talked to the vehicle's owner and confirmed that the suspect took the truck." He checked his watch. "The men are heading back to their vehicles by now. Shall I tell them to stand by?"

"Yeah, do that. I'll go check this out and get back to them as quickly as possible."

The drive back to the side road was short, mostly because she rocketed down the empty highway. With the bridge out, there were no oncoming cars. As they turned off and drove down the sandy track, Benjamin called her attention to an area about thirty feet from the road. She followed his gaze, but all she saw was a cluster of stunted junipers. As she pulled over for a better look, she spotted something blue that didn't belong there. She cursed under her breath. If that roadblock had been ready fifteen minutes ago, she would have been here instead.

"I'm going to go over there for a look. It might be a trap, so stay down and be careful." Julia retrieved her shotgun, then crept forward cautiously. She studied the ground for tracks, but it was too rocky to be able to tell much. Eddie had chosen the place well.

She approached the pickup from the rear, listening and looking everywhere. She peered inside. It appeared to be empty. Warily, she reached the door and yanked it open. There were no surprises. She started to call to Benjamin, when he emerged from around the other side of the truck. "You were supposed to stay back," she snapped.

"You never asked me to do that." He gestured toward the rise just ahead. "He went in that direction, and he's still carrying the rifle."

"How do you know that?" she demanded.

"His right foot made more of an imprint in the soft sand at the base of the hill."

"I'm going to call for a search team then," she said.

Benjamin walked back to the car with her. "The way you drive, we can easily overtake him."

"No, not across country. It's too rocky. We'd either puncture a tire or knock a hole in the oil pan and be stranded. We'll have trackers come in with either horses or four-wheel-drive vehicles designed for off-road use."

"This could have been avoided had you relied on my word instead of your need for caution."

She could have argued the need for sound police procedure, but instead she said nothing for several moments. "There's one thing you can do that will make it easier for me to trust you," she answered at last.

"What is it?"

"Let me take your fingerprints," she said, watching his reaction.

"You're welcome to whatever I have, but what are fingerprints?"

"You know…" She held up her hand and wiggled her fingers.

"I know footprints. What good will it do to press my fingers against the sand?"

Though the confusion on his face was evident, she found it

almost impossible to believe he didn't know what she was talking about. "*Where* did you go to school?"

"I was taught Navajo ways by my family, then I learned other skills from the missionaries."

"Oh, a boarding school on the reservation?"

"It was a long time ago," he answered with a shrug.

"And you never heard of fingerprints?"

"Is it important to me, to what I do and who I am? My time was better spent memorizing the healing chants that help the *Dineh*."

Julia couldn't argue with that one. She explained the process and retrieved a kit from the trunk of her car. "Once I have these, I'll do a background search on you."

"What will that tell you?" Benjamin turned and looked behind him.

"Well, for a start, I can make sure you don't have a criminal record." Julia could barely keep from smiling at his reaction.

"You believe I am a criminal?" His voice was suddenly as cold as steel.

"No. If I did, I wouldn't have allowed you to come with me. But I may yet have to justify my decision to bring you along. To do that, I'll need some hard facts to back me up. So far no one seems to know you."

"The soldiers knew who I was," he muttered.

For a moment she saw his eyes cloud over with sorrow. The pain reflected there tugged at her heart with an intensity she wouldn't have thought possible. Perhaps it was easier to empathize with someone who felt alone if you'd been there yourself. "Were you in the army once?" she asked, remembering his stalking skills and familiarity with the knife as a weapon.

"No," he said abruptly. "I have enough responsibilities without becoming a part of the way of death in your world."

So much for that. She thought of his job as a Singer. His primary duty was to work for the well-being of his people. Hers was to protect the public. They had much in common, even their intense dislike of violence. Though it was part of her job, it was a side she'd hated from the beginning. But she had no time to ponder further.

Benjamin stepped closer and offered her his hand. "Take what you need," he said softly.

For an instant, his words wrapped themselves around her. A powerful sexual awareness sparked the air between them. She took his hand, determined to keep her thoughts on business, but then his fingers brushed her palm. Her entire being opened to powerful and delicious sensations.

"This won't take long," she said, struggling to keep her voice steady.

"No hurry. I'm always a patient man with things that don't need to be rushed. And I do believe in being very thorough." He saw the color that flushed her face. She responded to him with an ease he found pleasing. "You aren't married," Benjamin concluded.

"You can't tell that by the absence of a ring," she challenged good-naturedly.

"I know." Benjamin smiled, seeing her avoid his gaze. He knew about the white man's custom of exchanging rings when they wed. Some of the dead officers he had seen wore them on their left hand. Navajos never touched a dead man's personal possessions, except for taking his weapons and cartridges.

As cars began coming up the road, he noted the relief on Julia's face. She was more at ease in her world of hard facts than in one of feelings. The observation only made him want to know even more about her.

The policemen were soon gathered around. He stood back and watched the white woman as she unfolded a map and began giving orders to the others. The Navajo men, all in uniforms and carrying guns, accepted it without question. How things had changed! But then again, in a more fundamental way, perhaps they hadn't. He'd always known that women could be fierce warriors, given the chance. Julia certainly proved that beyond any doubt. She feared nothing, including him.

That fact, in particular, drew him. Although he had never

displayed his power openly unless absolutely necessary, people would always sense it and respond to him with wariness and respect. Even now, the lawmen around her seemed to take special care not to offend him. Yet Julia did not appear to be intimidated by him in any way.

He smiled to himself. Maybe her own power, though certainly very different, was equal to his. He'd always trusted his instincts, and those were clearly urging him to act on the attraction between them. He wanted to know Julia in every way a man could know a woman. But his mind warned him of another danger. His actions would have consequences. After his task here was complete, he would be gone forever, and she deserved far more than the few hours of pleasure they would find in each other's arms.

"Let's go, Benjamin," she said as the others left to begin their search. "I want to fax these prints in." Julia glanced at him and sighed. "You don't have to ask." She explained as they drove east to link up with the north/south road, then made a right turn toward Shiprock. "With the equipment I have in the trunk, I can send a fax transmission from anywhere there's a telephone line. You *do* know about telephone lines?" Julia asked.

"I have heard of telegraph lines. I assume these are similar. Are they the wires on the forest of peeled trees which follow the roads?"

"Correct." Julia hadn't thought of it that way.

Benjamin continued with his questions. "And then, many days to get the information you need?"

"If there are priors, meaning a criminal record on file, then it's a matter of minutes. If not, then an extensive search will have to be done, and that could take hours." As her radio crackled to life, she picked up the mike and depressed the button. More than the usual amount of static crowded the transmission, but she couldn't contain her relief. "That's our first lead."

"You were able to understand *that?*" he asked, surprised.

"It takes a little practice," she admitted. "There were some prints taken from Eddie's vehicle. The Navajo police chief had them faxed in, and we now have a positive ID. The man's full name is Eddie Conway. He's got a criminal record a mile long, having served time for assault and armed robbery. We'll check out any known associates and try to get a lead on him through that, if he manages to elude the search.''

''You *will* find him,'' Benjamin said, ''if you accept my help.''

''What exactly do you want me to do now?''

He saw the suspicion in her eyes. ''I have done nothing except help you, yet you refuse to accept that I *am* your friend. How can I prove that to you?''

She took a deep breath. On a personal level she already trusted him. But she couldn't risk a federal investigation without more facts to support her decision. ''Complete trust takes time,'' she admitted. ''Sorry, but that's the way it is.''

A moment later, she turned off the highway into the parking area of a small diner, south of the Colorado state line, on Navajo land. ''Come on. I'm going to use their telephone and transmit these prints. Afterward, I'll question the customers. Maybe they've seen something that can help.''

The place was small, with just enough room for ten tables and a counter, but it was filled with Navajos. From the moment they entered the room, all eyes turned to her. He noted a few curious glances in his direction, since he was the only one not dressed like a white man, but the interest was clearly focused on her. The presence of an outsider made them uneasy—Benjamin could feel it in the air.

''I'll be right back,'' she said, indicating that he wasn't to accompany her any farther. She disappeared into the next room, carrying the small fabric case by a handle.

The eyes following her mirrored suspicion. At least that hadn't changed. Outsiders among the People were still not trusted. Good. Bitter experience assured him that attitude would serve them well. He had to remember that even if a *bilagáana* claimed to have the tribe's best interests at heart, their words could not be relied on. What they believed was best for the

Navajos and what would actually benefit the tribe were two very separate things. He had learned that at the expense of many whose blood would remain on his hands forever. And that was one of the reasons he just couldn't understand his feelings for this woman. Intuition continued to assure him she could be trusted.

Julia emerged from the other room a short time later. Benjamin watched her approach one of the Navajo men and ask him a question. The man stared at her, not saying a word. She repeated the process with two others, but they also refused to speak with her. She finally went over to the Navajo woman working behind the counter. "I was sent here to find and arrest criminals, but I can't do that without some help and cooperation from the public." The woman shrugged and asked Julia if she wanted to place an order.

Benjamin stood by the door, watching. After a moment, he made his way across the room and approached one of the young Navajo men with hair as long as his own. *"Yah'eh-teh,"* he greeted, then began to speak in his native tongue.

"Uncle," the young man said quietly, showing respect, "I just know a few Navajo words."

For a moment, he could not believe what he had heard. So the whites had even stripped some of the *Dineh* of their native tongue. "I, too, need your help," he said in English, an infinite sense of sorrow seeping through him. He spoke softly and asked about the *bilagáana* man they were searching for. The answers came, but they were not very helpful.

He could feel Julia's eyes on him as he made his way around the room. When she finally stepped outside, the tension dissipated, but the answers he received stayed the same. No white man had entered the restaurant or been seen along the state-line area lately. Finished, he joined her back at the car.

"Nice work. What did you find out?" she asked.

"No one here has seen him." He met her eyes with a long, direct look. "I am dressed in the old way, but I still belong among my people. They will never accept you. What happened inside is proof of that. Will you *now* admit that you need me to help you?"

"You're useful, yes, but not necessary," she said flatly. "The tribal police could have easily done what you did."

"If they had enough men, which they do not. That's why they are not here, but I am." He saw her gaze remain stony. "And not everyone will speak to a lawman," he reminded her, further emphasizing his point. Still, she didn't relent. "You are a very stubborn woman." But a beautiful one, too, he added silently.

TIME PASSED SLOWLY AS the miles stretched out before them. Julia had no idea what to do with Benjamin Two Eagle. If this power he claimed to possess was a sham, then he had to be connected to the gang in some way. Until she knew for certain which it was, she needed to keep a close eye on him. For now, having him along seemed as good a way as any to do that. As much as she hated it, he'd become her best lead.

"What's your family's connection to the amulets?" she asked him at last. "You told me that they rightfully belonged to you."

"During the time of Kit Carson and the war of the rebellion, those amulets were in my…ancestor's possession. It was well-known then that the amulets belonged to the *hataalii* called Two Eagle."

"Can you prove it?"

He thought about it. "Perhaps. Do any journals or newspapers remain that tell the truth about battles fought during that time?"

"Maybe there are some in the archives at the state library. We can check it out."

"It's possible the proof you want is there. My…ancestor resisted Kit Carson and his soldiers for a very long time. Many thought the amulets made that possible." His eyes drifted over her face with the gentleness of a soft breeze. "Why is the turquoise amulet so important to you, if you don't believe in our ways?"

Julia hesitated. ''It's the only inheritance I received from my mother,'' she said softly, hiding the tremor in her voice.

''I understand now. Keepsakes become very important when only memories remain.''

''Yes, exactly.'' She avoided his gaze, afraid he'd see the pain and sense of failure that had filled her ever since she'd lost the amulet.

He said nothing for a moment, though his eyes remained on her. He could feel her struggle against the darkness that weighed her down. Compelled to do something that would show her he cared, he took her hand from the steering wheel, and brought it to his lips. With infinite tenderness, he brushed the center of her palm with a feather-light kiss.

His gentleness bathed her soul in a warm golden glow. She touched his cheek with her fingertips, feeling the smoothness of his copper skin, and she heard him suck in his breath. She knew then that she had the power to affect him as deeply as he did her.

Yet nothing good could come of these longings they were stirring to life within each other. Slowly, and with marked reluctance, she disengaged her hand and brought it back to the wheel. Clamping a firm hand on her thoughts, she grew determined not to give the attraction between them any more power than it already had.

''I can't take something you've treasured away from you, but I will need it for a few hours. It's a matter of honor. There was an oath taken a very long time ago, and I have to carry it out.''

''What kind of an oath?''

He hesitated. ''It involves a ritual that has to be finished.''

She nodded, sensing he wouldn't say more. He was a complete enigma. The clothing he wore, especially the knife at his waist and the medicine pouch, looked like genuine antiques. When she considered his apparent lack of knowledge about twentieth-century technology, she could almost make herself believe that he'd stepped out from the past.

Hearing the radio call for her, she picked up the mike. Latent prints in Washington reported that Benjamin Two Eagle had no record at all, criminal or otherwise. That included the military as well, so his reference to soldiers still remained unexplained.

"Now you know I am not a criminal," he said quietly.

"Yeah. But I'm still a ways from explaining *you*," she answered, with a ghost of a smile.

"You're the kind who has trouble accepting even the truth, unless you've worked the answers out yourself," he observed, a gleam in his eye.

"Okay," she admitted with a chuckle. "That's a good point. But—"

She heard the all-units call over the radio, followed by a specific transmission to her. She picked up the mike and identified herself. "What's going on?"

"There's been a report of a break-in at a house northwest of Shiprock. A Navajo family returning home heard someone inside, so they left immediately. They knew about the Anglo fugitive and the shoot-out from a news broadcast on the radio."

"How do I get there?" As she listened to his directions, she felt like tearing her hair out.

"Just look for the flock of churro sheep," Police Chief Roanhorse told her, "then drive down that dirt road. Keep going until you pass a holding pen and a water tower. You can't miss it."

Julia wished she'd been someplace where all the streets had names. "I'll find it," she said. If they could, so could she.

"You might want to hold off and wait for one of our units to join you," the chief said.

"What would be the ETA on that?"

"Thirty minutes minimum. We've got most of our officers manning roadblocks or out searching farther west."

"This can't wait that long. In twenty minutes, Eddie could be halfway north to Cortez or all the way to Shiprock."

"Okay. Be careful and stay in radio contact."

She racked the mike. "With directions like the ones he gave me, we'll be lucky to find the place at all," she muttered.

"The directions were clear. What was it that you did not understand?"

Julia rolled her eyes. "Never mind."

She rocketed south, scarcely noting the beautiful sculpted rock formations east of the highway. Speed helped her relieve some of the tension gnawing at her. As they neared a large, fenced-in section of land, Benjamin gestured. "There."

She slowed and glanced over. "What's there?"

"The sheep."

From what she could see, the herd consisted of about twelve shaggy beasts that had decided to cluster around the meager shade from a stand of junipers. She might have missed them completely if Benjamin hadn't pointed them out, although she wasn't about to admit that.

She drove down the dirt track and, minutes later, saw the isolated wood-framed house. It was nestled among several juniper and piñon trees.

Julia pulled to a stop and parked about fifty yards away, behind a low hill. "Stay behind cover. Remember that assault rifle can fire thirty rounds as fast as he can squeeze the trigger."

Leaving the car, she drew her weapon and approached the home from the back, where there were no windows. Making sure she stayed low to the ground, she checked it out visually first. The rear door was wide open. People seldom locked doors in the rez. Undoubtedly, Eddie had known that, too.

Julia approached silently, then ducked inside. Hearing a rustling noise inside what appeared to be a storeroom, she smiled. She'd arrived in time. With any luck, it would turn out to be Eddie looking for food.

Julia crept across the room and stopped beside the doorway, her back pressed to the wall. Listening carefully, she tried to pinpoint the intruder's location before going any farther. A low groan, almost a growl, sounded to her right. Fear eroded her confidence, as she tried to identify the source of the sound. Maybe Eddie had come up with another trick, or found a dog to keep watch for him.

From her position, she could see a large foot locker to her left, near the wall. It would provide perfect cover. And if she reached it in time, there'd be no problem at all.

# Chapter Five

Julia crouched low, pistol ready, and slipped silently around the corner. What she saw in the room made her freeze instantly in her tracks. An enormous, shaggy-looking, three-hundred-pound black bear stood on all fours over an open sack of grain, its head raised, eyes trained on her. It growled a low warning as she waited, rock still, scarcely breathing. After an eternity, the animal ducked its head down for a mouthful of grain, looked up again, then chewed its food, watching her all the time.

Pistol clutched in both hands, she wondered if it was safe to retreat. If the animal charged, she wasn't sure if 9 mm rounds would do the job in time. Her bullets weren't meant to stop an animal that size in its tracks.

Hearing someone by the rear door, she turned her head slowly. Benjamin was about to come in. Calling out would startle the bear, but she had to warn him!

Benjamin caught her gaze and held up one hand, gesturing for her to remain quiet.

Julia saw the bear shift his position. The animal looked directly at Benjamin, then lowered its head again to eat.

A thought flashed in the back of her mind. The beast hadn't seemed quite so casual about her. Perhaps it sensed the pistol was dangerous. Out of the corner of her eyes, she saw Benjamin step silently into the room and slowly place himself between her and the animal. She knew that in most instances

Navajos considered bears evil, and she wondered if *hataaliis* had a specific method of dealing with them. Benjamin hadn't even drawn his knife.

"Don't be afraid," he whispered, glancing back at her. "You may leave now."

"What?" she mouthed. He was unarmed—there was no way she could leave him there alone.

"Go. I can handle this."

"Forget it," she said, in a barely audible voice. "If you know how to deal with this animal, by all means do it. I'm staying to help."

He gave her a look that could have reduced the desert temperature by fifty degrees. She smiled back at him calmly, refusing to be intimidated.

He glared at her, exasperated. "Just don't *do* anything," he warned.

Benjamin spoke to the animal, using words in Navajo or some other language she didn't understand. The beast seemed quite calm, which was a very good thing since she had another problem. She couldn't shoot now if she had to, because Benjamin had positioned himself in her line of fire. Worst of all, she couldn't swear that he hadn't done it on purpose.

As she watched and listened, she could see a strange affinity developing between the two. It was almost as if the animal understood what Benjamin was saying. Though the bear continued eating, it glanced up at him with the frequency of someone listening to a conversation. After a few minutes, the beast yawned lazily. The only tension in the room seemed to be hers.

"Move away from the door and let him pass," Benjamin said a second later.

"How do you know he's going to…"

Before she could complete the sentence, the bear walked toward the door. She moved aside slowly, giving the animal plenty of room.

Without so much as a glance toward her, the animal made its way to the rear door, jumped off the step and disappeared into the tall brush.

Feeling her knees grow weak, she leaned against the door frame for support. "That was too close."

He shook his head. "He had no intention of harming you, not unless you interfered with his meal."

"I suppose he told you that," she said in a shaky voice.

"Not in words."

She couldn't stand it. He looked totally composed, as if nothing major had happened. She, on the other hand, felt as if a herd of elephants had danced on her stomach. "Let me guess. The bear used sign language."

"In a way," he answered with a tiny smile. "And understanding it is one of the gifts I've been given."

"Part of your training as a *hataalii?*" Julia walked outside with Benjamin and closed the door behind them.

"No. Once when I was a child, I became very sick. Since I had seen a bear earlier that day, my mother asked for a *hataalii* to heal me. It was believed that I had fallen victim to the evil the bear brings. A bear impersonator came to our hogan, and after the ritual was performed, I was cured. The ceremony, from that day on, granted me immunity from any danger the bear poses. I can even invoke the bear and count on him for protection."

She might have debated that with Benjamin an hour ago, but there was no arguing with what she'd seen. His confidence was absolute. She would have sworn under oath that Benjamin had actually communicated with the animal. Then she pictured the expression on the face of the Special Agent in Charge if she put *that* in her report. She'd rather face the bear again.

The moment Julia reached the car, she picked up the mike and made her report. After advising the tribal police to continue their search, she glanced over at Benjamin. He was leaning back against the seat, his eyes shut. His face had grown pale and his breathing was shallow.

She watched him for a second. "Are you ill?" Maybe the encounter with the bear had taken more out of him than he'd admitted.

He opened his eyes. "I am all right." He hesitated a moment

before continuing. "You have seen what I can do. If I told you that I am also able to sense where the man you are searching for has gone, could you accept that?"

"Where is he?" If Benjamin knew something, she wanted answers, and she wanted them fast. They'd discuss the *how* later.

"I don't know his location exactly, but he has yet to reach shelter. He is out in the open, walking up a small hill."

She gave him an incredulous look. "No offense, but that's not much of a tip. You've just described three quarters of the reservation!"

"You don't believe me."

"I'm willing to listen to any solid leads you think you can provide. But I'm going to need something more than a landscape with hills to go on."

"I will tell you more when I can," he answered.

As they reached the highway, he glanced at two teenaged boys walking down the side of the road. "I will need that kind of clothing. Mine is too different and sets me apart from the other *Dineh*."

She glanced at the young Navajos. "If you want blue jeans and a cotton shirt, I passed a dry-goods store on this road yesterday. But I don't know what kind of prices they charge."

"I have no money."

Somehow it didn't surprise her. "Then how do you plan on paying for what you need?"

"Trade." He glanced over at her. "I have provided you with a service. Surely that is worth something. And it will be to your advantage if I blend with others more easily. It will allow us to get closer to our enemies without creating attention."

"I didn't realize that you'd attached a price to your services," she countered.

"I need money for clothing," he said with a shrug. "I helped you with the bear, and had you followed my suggestion, you would have found the pickup right away. Is that worth the price of…jeans and a shirt?"

She smiled. He hadn't mentioned that he'd saved her life.

Her respect for him grew. "All right. I'll cover your expenses. For now."

He nodded. "Then the matter is settled."

When they entered the store about fifteen minutes later, the young Navajo owner stared at Benjamin curiously. "Nice outfit. What can I do for you, Uncle?" he asked.

Benjamin studied the man's clothes. "I would like jeans and a shirt like yours."

The man responded to his request by bringing him a pair of blue jeans and a work shirt. "These aren't fancy, but you'll find they'll wear well."

Benjamin stepped into the adjoining dressing room, and emerged a few minutes later. "These will do," he said.

She stared at him for a moment. She missed the wild individuality of his old clothes and the openness of them that had exposed him to her gaze. Yet the partially unbuttoned chambray shirt still accentuated his lean, powerful build. She had to fight the inexplicable and annoying urge to slip her hands inside the cloth and caress his smooth, bronzed chest. Determined to banish those thoughts, she dropped her gaze.

Julia realized, a split second too late, what a mistake that had been. The jeans that encased his lower body teased her imagination. The cloth was stretched taut across the area where the metal buttons were, revealing an uncompromisingly male physique. In either traditional dress or modern, he packed a sensual wallop like no man she'd ever known.

Benjamin raised an eyebrow, a trace of a grin playing on his lips. "Do you approve?"

He was teasing her, and she found it irritating. Had she been staring in a way that had revealed her thoughts? She saw his expression and figured she had. "I'll pay the bill, and that will settle my account with you."

"For now." He tied his old clothes into a bundle, then fastened the medicine pouch, knife and sheath to his belt.

As soon as they returned to the car, Julia checked in with the tribal police, but there was no further news. "Eddie Conway's got to be holed up someplace. He's been doing business

for a while on the reservation and probably knows lots of people. He could be availing himself of someone's hospitality as
we speak. Some areas of the rez have no electricity, so news
might not have reached everyone.''

Benjamin closed his eyes for a long moment. ''The man we
want is in a hogan near a place where big wires cross the road
on metal towers.''

''How do you know this?''

He exhaled softly. ''You have done your check with Washington. Think! I would not be helping you if I was one of
them.''

She held his eyes. ''You want me to trust you, Benjamin,
yet you don't trust me.''

''There are things I don't believe you are ready to accept,''
he answered. ''Such truths may conflict with your own beliefs.
And remember that the *Dineh* have always suffered when they
trust outsiders.''

''And a cop never trusts anyone who has something to
hide.''

''Then we will have to judge one another by our actions.
Words alone can never be relied on. They can be twisted too
easily.'' He glanced over at her. ''Do you know how to find
the hogan I told you about?''

''The big power line you mentioned will help.'' She called
it in and waited as the signal was patched through to the chief's
office.

''The hogan you want has been abandoned for years,'' the
chief's assistant, Pete Bowman, told Julia. Then he gave her
directions. ''One of our deputies goes camping near there. It's
about five miles east of Beklabito, near the Teece Nos Pos
power grid. The dwelling has a hole punched in its side. That
means there was a death there, so no one from the tribe would
ever use it.''

''I'm going to check out a hunch and take a look at the
place. If I find out that someone's there, can you send
backup?''

"Our people are dispersed right now, but I'm sure I can find someone to respond."

"Okay. Just give me a chance to take a look around first. No sense in sending any officers on a wild-goose chase."

"It won't be that," Benjamin answered softly.

Somehow she suspected he was right, but there was no way she was going to give that assurance to the tribal police without some solid facts to base it on. As it was, she'd already stuck out her neck.

Thirty minutes later she pulled off the highway and followed a bumpy and dusty dirt track that seemed to wind nowhere. After five minutes, she began having second thoughts. "Maybe I took a wrong turn. There's nothing out here except sand, rocks and sagebrush."

"This is the right road," he assured, pointing out the tire tracks just ahead.

She clamped her mouth shut. She wouldn't ask him anything more until she saw for herself what, if anything, was waiting at the hogan. After another five minutes of trying to avoid massive holes that would certainly destroy her tires, she caught a glimpse of the hogan off in the distance.

Pulling behind a cluster of sage and stunted piñon trees, she switched off the engine. "I'm going over there. If you hear any trouble, call for help." She handed him the mike and showed him how to transmit. "Don't follow me. Not until I signal you."

"I am quieter moving through the brush than you are, and I can stay out of sight. Let me scout out the area first. I will be able to tell just from the tracks if someone is hiding there or has already moved on."

Julia weighed the plan carefully. "All right." Considering how long it would probably take backup to arrive, she could certainly use his help. "But don't get too close to the hogan."

Benjamin left the car and moved across the desert terrain as silently as she'd expected. She was gaining confidence in him and his abilities. With Bobby sidelined for now, she couldn't have asked for a better partner, even if he was a very unusual one.

Julia held back for a few more moments, then circled around to the west side of the hogan. As she approached the rear, a clump of brush that had been mashed down caught her attention. Tire prints clearly indicated that two vehicles had been driven through there, and both sets led directly to the hogan. Her best guess was that Eddie had managed to steal another vehicle and had met with one or more members of the gang here.

She looked around, trying to figure out where Benjamin had gone, and if there were any cars still hidden nearby. She searched slowly, hoping to minimize the sound of her passage through the tangle of sagebrush. Suddenly, she felt a hand on her shoulder. She whirled around, kicking out for the groin.

Benjamin slipped aside quickly, eluding her foot. "Easy, woman. I meant you no harm."

She'd never seen anyone fast enough to dodge that particular move. "Don't *ever* do that again!" she muttered through clenched teeth.

"The danger here is past. Now only death remains."

"You mean Eddie is dead?" she asked, and saw him nod.

She walked over to the hogan and stepped inside. The hard dirt floor contained only wind-scattered tumbleweeds, a few hundred flies and the body of Eddie Conway. "Maybe the amulets are still here somewhere."

"No."

She turned her head and saw Benjamin standing just outside the doorway. "Did you look?"

"No, but I would sense them if they were close by."

"We'll discuss *that* in another minute." Julia tried to remember to breathe through her mouth, as she quickly surveyed the shaded interior. The sweet-sour stench of blood mingled with the stomach-churning smell of flesh bloating in the desert heat. Choking back her revulsion, she knelt by the corpse. Eddie was lying facedown, and caked blood marked the entry of two bullets just at the base of his neck. A clean and neat execution.

She checked around for anything the killer might have left behind. The circular dwelling was no bigger than a small bedroom, but despite her thoroughness, she found nothing that would help her track down Eddie's killers. From the sweeping trail on the sandy floor, she knew footprints left by the killer or killers had probably been obliterated with a branch.

"You have no need for me here," Benjamin said, moving away.

Julia knew about the Navajo fear of the *chindi*. Elaborate rites were said to insure protection from the dead, but there was no time for any of that now. Julia glanced around once more, then left the hogan.

She returned to the vehicle, called in and asked for an investigative team to be dispatched. "We'll have to wait here until they arrive," she said at last.

Benjamin stood by the car, watching her curiously. "This place is unclean," he said. "Why stay?"

"The murder scene has to be preserved and searched. This helps us build a case. Those tire tracks, for instance, might eventually tell us what type of vehicle was used. If there's anything distinctive about the treads, it'll provide incriminating evidence. Bullets also have distinct markings that can link them to a specific gun."

"But the longer we stay, the farther the amulets will travel from here."

"Do you have an idea where to search next?"

"No."

She watched him for a moment. Her instincts had assured her that he wasn't involved, but logic now made other demands. She bit back her disappointment. Despite her arguments to the contrary, the attraction between them had definitely swayed her judgment in his favor. But now it was clear she couldn't go on fooling herself. There were only two plausible explanations for how he'd known to come here. He'd either belonged to the gang once and knew their methods, or he still did, but had balked at having a federal agent killed. In either case, there was no way she was going to let him out of her sight now. He was her key to finding the others.

The units arrived sometime later, accompanied by the medical examiner and Chief Roanhorse. Julia returned to the hogan with them and watched as the medical examiner, a cadaverously thin Anglo man with salt-and-pepper hair, studied the body. "I know it's much too soon," she said, "but we really need some new leads. Anything you can tell me would be appreciated."

The man nodded. "Not much I can say yet, except that it's a professional hit. The killer knew precisely where to place his shots."

"I'd like to check the contents of the victim's pockets. Do you have any objections?"

"We can catalog them right now."

The doctor reached inside Eddie's trouser pockets, and extracted two quarters, one dime and several pennies. "That's it. His wallet's not here."

She mulled it over. "After decomposition set in, positive ID would have been delayed even more if the victim had no wallet. I think Eddie's killers were counting on the body not being found for a long time. This is a very remote area. That's why they didn't bother to bury him."

"How *did* you think of checking here?" Chief Roanhorse asked.

"A tip," she said, and saw Roanhorse nod slowly.

As she walked back outside, she braced herself for some pointed questions about Benjamin, but none came. She had a strong feeling that the Navajo police chief knew something about him he wasn't discussing with her. Yet his acceptance of Benjamin's involvement in the case assured her it wasn't something she had to worry about.

The moment the chief emerged from the hogan, a tribal patrolman approached him. "There were two other men here, sir. One must have weighed around one hundred and sixty pounds and was wearing boots. The other wore soft-heeled shoes and was careful about his tracks. He left no clear impressions for us on the ground. We also saw evidence that two vehicles arrived here from the same direction, then were driven back to the highway.''

''Did you find anything around the area where the vehicles were parked? Cigarette stubs, food wrappers, matches?'' Chief Roanhorse asked.

''I bagged some roasted piñon shells that looked fresh. They were on the ground by the first set of tire tracks. If they were in the killer's mouth, we might be able to link him to this with his saliva.'' He held up the brown envelope, and the chief and Julia looked inside.

Julia nodded her approval, but she knew they could also have been Eddie's, and that wouldn't help them at all. ''Where can you buy piñon nuts around here?'' she asked.

''Almost everywhere. But the closest place would be Clyde Neskahi's gas station, about four miles down the road. You can't miss it—it's the only thing for miles.''

''I'll go check that out,'' she told Chief Roanhorse. Julia returned to the car and found Benjamin leaning against the door on the passenger's side.

''You are ready to leave?'' he asked, his voice taut.

''Yes.'' She told him about the piñon nut shells. ''If I have difficulty getting answers, see what you can do.'' He could still be of use to her, as long as he helped her track down the gang.

''I will continue to do my best to help you.''

The ride took less than ten minutes. She started to pull into the gas station, when she noticed a public telephone at one end of the small building. Julia parked beside it, went out to check the number, then returned. ''I'm going to have all outgoing calls made from that phone traced.'' She called in the request, then racked the mike. ''Okay. Let's go inside and find out who the employees have seen around here lately.''

AS THEY WALKED INSIDE what she called a garage, Benjamin saw the polite stares the two Navajo men, busy putting a rubber wheel on a car, gave Julia. He knew by their expressions she'd get no answers here, either—not without his help. The thought pleased him. They needed each other, so the arrangement was a balanced one.

When she tried questioning the employees, both claimed not to remember anything. With a glance at him, Julia walked back outside, noting the only food or candy for sale were bags of piñon nuts set on a shelf near the office.

Benjamin questioned the men in their own language, then joined her several minutes later. Once inside the car, Benjamin told her what he'd learned.

"The description of the man who bought the bag of piñons fits Eddie," she said. "But where's the tan car they saw him driving?"

"One of the men said he saw the same car going in the other direction about a half hour later with another white man driving. A pickup was following close behind, and the driver of that one wasn't Navajo, either." Emotions too complex to define suddenly flickered across his face at lightning speed. "One of those men has the amulets. We've got to find them."

She started the car and got underway. "We'll stay on the highway for now. We know the direction they were traveling in, so we'll just follow the trail to the next roadblock. There aren't that many places to turn off." She called in her location and relayed a message to Roanhorse, updating him on her plans and what she'd learned. As she placed the mike back, she glanced up at Benjamin. "Can you come up with any more brilliant leads, like the one that took us to the hogan?"

He closed his eyes for a long minute, then finally shook his head. "No."

"You want me to follow my instincts and trust you, but why won't you do the same thing? Don't your instincts tell you it's okay to trust me? For us to really work together, you've got to stop withholding information. Tell me how you knew where to find Eddie."

He considered what she said. "I know that if you continue to distrust me, your energies will be diverted away from the amulets. I don't wish for that to happen." He paused. "You already know that I can do things most people find hard to accept." He saw her nod and continued. "The key to a Singer's powers lies in knowledge, but the process of learning is one that has to be developed slowly and requires complete dedication to the Navajo Way. As a *hataalii*'s power increases, so must his inner strength, or it leads to self-destruction. Yet once that balance is achieved, nothing is impossible."

"So through the Way, you are able to make your predictions?"

"The Way is part of it," Benjamin admitted, "but not all." He pursed his lips, and his eyebrows knitted together, as if he were searching for the right way to explain. "The amulets are a part of me, part of my Wind Breath, my soul. It's through them that I can see what I have."

"You can link yourself to them somehow, is that what you're saying?"

He took a deep breath. "Did you ever watch a bird in flight and imagine yourself to be soaring with it?"

"Yes, when I was younger and things crowded in on me," she admitted.

"It's like that in a way. When I close my eyes and envision the agate man, I can see through its eyes."

"But not through the turquoise amulet's?"

"No, not that one, though the essence of both is part of me."

"How do you explain the restriction of your power, then?"

"I cannot—not yet—but I can tell you this. It is dangerous for me to continue seeing through the eyes of the agate Twin. I suspect that the man who is wielding both amulets becomes more aware of us each time I do that."

"Why would the amulets help him?"

"I don't know."

It was his tone, emotionless and factual, that bothered her the most. "Then don't link with the agate man—we have enough problems. We don't need to give those guys any more of an advantage than they already have."

"So you believe me, then."

"I'm not sure what I believe. Not anymore. But I can't afford to take any unnecessary chances." The risk to him, if he'd turned against the gang, concerned her, too. These men were playing for high stakes. They wouldn't allow him to remain a loose end.

The terrain began to change as the desert rose toward the Carrizo Mountains. Slowly, the canyons became more rugged and covered with junipers and piñon trees. Although the road hadn't narrowed, their passage was confined, as a solid wall of earth and rock pressed in on her right, while a steep drop-off to the canyon floor marked the left.

"Don't slow down," Benjamin said, sitting up until his seat belt dug into his shoulder.

"Why?"

"The amulets are near. I can feel them."

An old pickup, barely visible in her rearview mirror a minute ago, suddenly began to narrow the gap between them. It rocketed forward, closing in at an alarming speed.

"Hang on!" She gunned the accelerator, increasing the distance between them by pushing the powerful engine for everything it had. But as she cleared the rise of the hill, she saw an old sedan parked across the road with several men behind it. "They're trying to trap us between them! I'd say your hunches have been too accurate for their tastes."

"If we die now, then we are no longer a threat," he said, completing the thought for her.

"Yeah, but don't worry. I've got a few tricks up my sleeve." She slammed on the brakes. The vehicle fishtailed, and she whipped the steering wheel to the left, completing a one-hundred-and-eighty-degree turn.

As the pickup behind them was forced to brake, she reached for the shotgun beneath the seat. "Get out! We're making a run for it." She picked up her hand-held radio. "Head right for the pickup. They won't be able to shoot until we get close, because their partners are in the line of fire, too. The second you reach the halfway point, slide down over the embankment. We have a better chance down there."

She started to move forward, but Benjamin suddenly grabbed her arm and pulled her toward the drop-off. ''Here is better. Trust me. Evading capture is something I do very well. Jump over the edge and slide down on your backside. Hurry!''

# Chapter Six

They slid down the incline, a spray of bullets whining just over their heads. Rounds impacted in the sand and ricocheted off the rocks around them. Benjamin scrambled to a crouch and led the way into the roughest terrain, an area thick with tumbled-down boulders, sage and rabbit brush. Wheeling around behind cover, she fired off several rounds, forcing their attackers to drop to the ground.

"We must distance ourselves from that road. They will expect us to try and find another path back there so we can get help."

"We can't risk flagging down another driver. Stopping anyone might just get them killed," she answered.

"Agreed."

They pressed hard until they could no longer see the highway at all. Then Benjamin slowed his steps slightly, his expression one of rapt concentration as he listened to the breeze flowing past them.

She stayed very still, but all she could hear was the nerve-racking silence that normally came after a gun battle. "What's wrong?" Julia glanced in the direction of the highway. "I know we've outdistanced them. We were already over the hill before they got the nerve to come down the highway embankment."

"To elude, you must think like your enemy. They won't be eager to pursue us down here, but eventually they will come after us. We will have to make that as difficult and tiring for them as possible. They have an advantage. They are men, and their stamina will be greater than yours.''

''Wanna bet?'' Julia said, anger spiraling through her. ''Back at the academy, they didn't give the women any breaks. We were expected to fight hand-to-hand with men who were twice our size and compete in every kind of physical activity, from running cross-country on. Don't you *dare* underestimate me.''

Benjamin studied her for a second as if making up his mind. ''I don't doubt that you have heart, and that will serve us both well,'' he said at last. As the breeze stilled, his face tightened. ''They are coming now.'' He motioned to her, and they picked up the pace again.

''How do you know that? The only sounds I heard were trucks way over on the highway somewhere.''

''The Wind People speak to those who know how to listen,'' he answered softly. ''Wind People tell only the truth, but sometimes what they say isn't what we want to hear.''

''Like what, for instance?'' she whispered, wondering if those pursuing them also had hearing as acute as Benjamin's.

''Our enemies don't know how to cross the desert in silence. The Wind People carry their sounds to me. From their voices, I also know they are afraid, but they won't give up easily. They want to kill us because they fear us. They worry about the intuitions that continue to lead us to them. We are an even bigger threat now, because they have no idea where we are or what we'll do next. The biggest thing in our favor is that they lack patience.''

His movements across the ground were quick, but he was so quiet she wondered how he managed it. ''And you're hoping to outlast them, since we can't fight them directly, right?''

He nodded. ''Once we have exhausted them, they will begin to see things in a different light. They will talk themselves into believing that they can lay another trap, one where the odds will be more in their favor.''

As they reached a thicket of junipers, his footsteps became

harsher and he motioned for her to stop. As she watched, Benjamin walked into a bramble of sturdy trees and continued for several feet. Then he leaned forward and broke off a thin branch that marked his way even farther into the thicket.

She watched him as he prepared the false trail. "Good move," she whispered. "If they try to follow that, all they'll get is scratched up and frustrated in this heat."

"Let us hope so." He gave her a quick grin.

She raised the antenna of her hand-held, then tried to contact the Navajo police. "I've got bad news. The radio extender won't transmit from here, or else they've shut off the base unit in my car. This means we won't get help anytime soon."

"Then we will have to rely on ourselves," he answered simply.

Julia took a deep breath. "The odds aren't good."

"Do you believe your radio would have made that much of a difference? The tide of battle can turn in seconds, and nobody even knows exactly where we are. Even if you had been able to talk to someone, do you think the others would have arrived by now?"

"No, undoubtedly not. The distances out here are too great for immediate response times," she admitted. "But what bothers me most is that I suspect whoever set up this trap counted on my not being able to use my radio where we were ambushed. That's why they're taking their time coming after us. They know we can't call out. I don't know if they're motivated by revenge or are just trying to stop the investigation in its tracks."

Benjamin nodded. "We are most dangerous to them. They know that."

She watched Benjamin as they hurried along, and she wondered how any civilian could take what was happening so fearlessly. His knife was in his hand, ready for instant, deadly applications should the need arise.

As they made their way into the brush and tall grasses of the *bosque* that bordered the river, she wondered about him. He had that hard-edged look, one she'd seen in seasoned cops who'd been through too much action, or in fugitives who'd lived with death on their shoulders for a long time. Fear was absent, but there was an awareness—an instinctive response to the crisis—that kept his senses acute. There was a terrifying grace in the way he held the deadly blade, too. She had no doubt the weapon was an old friend and a comforting companion.

"Stay in my tracks. We'll make them believe they have lost one of our trails. It'll confuse them even more and force them to backtrack."

When he looked back at her, she saw the calm assuredness in his eyes. His confidence bolstered her courage, though it also made her wary. "You're very comfortable handling your weapon. Have you had much practice with it?"

His eyes grew as hard as the sandstone boulders that surrounded them. "Say what you really mean, woman."

Her tongue seemed to suddenly become tangled in her mouth, and for a moment, she couldn't quite speak. "Have you ever killed a man?" Julia asked a beat later.

He just looked at her, that's all. But with that one glance, she'd received her answer. At that instant, she knew his experience with the blade had come from the need to survive. Life-and-death struggles had left their unmistakable imprint on him. Yet he had no military record.

"You speculate, yet you're not afraid," Benjamin commented, his voice as gentle as the breeze.

"Neither are you."

He gave her a puzzled look. "What is it that you think I should fear? The men pursuing us? You?"

"Both?"

He shook his head. "I have no fear of you. Not because you're a woman," he added quickly, seeing the narrowing of her eyes, "but because honor is more than just a word to you. There's violence in the work you've chosen, but that violence doesn't reach your heart."

He'd hit on the one fear that every cop harbored deep within their souls. To enter the world of crime and violence, yet re-

main uncorrupted by it, was a challenge that demanded everything from her at times. He might have said many things, but
that one observation meant more to her than he'd ever know.

"As for my fearing the men who pursue us—" he shrugged
"—there's no reason. My skill exceeds theirs. They move fast
and require immediate results. Out here—" he gestured around
him "—time is his own master."

"Are you saying that to maintain the advantage, a person
has to be in tune with the land?"

"You have to know the desert, that's true, but you must also
know the people who live within it. Few have been able to
understand the *Dineh*. Colonel Kit Carson did, and he had the
endurance to wait us out. That's why he was so successful
fighting us, though others always failed."

Benjamin signaled for her to stop, and then moved toward
the tall grass alongside the San Juan River. While he lay another false trail, she slipped the shotgun off her shoulder and
adjusted the web sling.

Benjamin soon returned to where she stood, walking backward slowly, stepping in his own tracks. "It might help us if
you allowed me to carry that weapon. Two people who each
have a firearm can defend their position better than one holding
two guns."

"Have you ever used a pump-action shotgun?"

"No. But I have fired guns many times before. Show me
how this one works."

She started to pull the slide back to demonstrate how to feed
and eject shells, only the mechanism wouldn't budge. "Great.
The slide is bent. I must have smashed it against a rock when
we slid down that incline."

"It is useless?"

"At least for now, but I'll have to keep it with me," she
said with a scowl. "I don't want to advertise our reduced firepower."

"Let me carry it. It might still give us some advantage if
they think that two of us can shoot back."

"No. If I give you a useless weapon, I'll be marking you as

a definite threat to them. They won't hesitate to shoot you. You may have more of a chance if they perceive you as unarmed." She saw him glance down at the knife. "A gunman won't consider that a serious threat."

"Then perhaps they will have a few lessons to learn before we are through." His tone was cold and matter-of-fact.

It took effort *not* to look away from his gaze. "We all might."

Benjamin turned north and headed diagonally toward the riverbank. "The ground ahead isn't rocky enough to hide our passing. We should stay in the shallow water as much as we can from this point on. Movement will be harder, but it will be impossible for them to track us."

She kept up with him, slogging through biting-cold, knee-deep water, but her legs soon began to ache from the strain. "If they can't find tracks, they'll figure out what we're doing."

"Yes, but they will still have to search for us, and I have left enough false trails to confuse and slow them down. To follow us, they will have to keep searching the banks, looking for the site where we will be leaving the water. Men softened by riding in cars aren't going to be able to maintain a march like this for very long."

He emerged from the water a second later and walked about twenty yards from the river's edge through some tall grass. Working quickly, he bent back a willow branch, tied it loosely with a strip of bark and positioned a medium-sized rock on top of it. "This will dislodge on its own in a while and send the rock about twenty to thirty feet to their right. If luck is with us, they will hear and go investigate the sound."

"And a trek uphill, particularly after trudging through water or sand, is going to tire them out even more."

He nodded. "We will be leaving the river soon. There is plenty of gravel on the ground ahead. Our tracks won't be as easily followed there. Then I believe we should split up."

Her eyes narrowed with suspicion. "Why? What do you plan to do?"

"Force *them* to divide up, and then lead them around in

circles. If I can manage to get a few of them lost, that is even better.''

"It might work," Julia agreed with a nod. "And it's about time we turned the tables on these guys. So far we're evading them, but I'd prefer to take the offensive."

"By eluding them we *are* fighting."

"Yeah, but I'd rather take a more direct approach." She smiled grimly. "I was suckered back on the highway, and that really bothers me."

"You don't like losing," Benjamin observed wryly. "Well, neither do I." He gestured toward the mouth of a narrow canyon about a mile ahead, above the river. "At sundown, we will meet there. That is a good defensive position. The entrance is narrow enough to discourage anyone from entering once we are inside."

"I wish I knew how much of a lead we have on them now."

Benjamin glanced back. "They are nowhere close. I am certain of it."

"Good. That'll give me a chance to try leaving a few false trails of my own."

"Remember. We will meet at sundown." With that, he left the riverbank and disappeared through a thicket.

It was as if the land itself had swallowed him up. She heard no footsteps, nor rattling through the brush, or anything that might indicate where he'd gone. His moccasins were soaked, yet despite that, only the barest imprints remained in the sand, and the breeze was doing its best to obscure them.

She moved forward, left the river several minutes later and doubled back a short distance. Her body ached from exertion, but the thought of outsmarting the men pursuing them gave her the extra energy she needed to keep going. She took great pleasure in laying false trails that led into the roughest terrain.

As daylight began to fade, Julia picked up her speed and began the uphill climb toward the narrow canyon. She was careful not to outline herself against the ridges she topped along the route, and she glanced back frequently, hoping to spot some signs of the gang. Yet nothing seemed to move behind her.

Maybe they'd given up. There were very few good trackers still around—not counting those who wore dog collars.

Pushing herself to keep a lively pace, she concentrated on finding Benjamin. When she reached the mouth of the canyon, it was sundown, but he was nowhere in sight. A bolt of fear slammed into her. There'd been no shots fired, but it was possible that they'd taken him captive. She'd give him a few more minutes, but unless he appeared soon, she'd go find him. She tried to tell herself it was simply her duty. He was a civilian under her protection, and she couldn't abandon him. Yet deep down, she knew her motives went way beyond that.

As the last rays of daylight turned the horizon a light shade of orange, she stared intently down the hill. There was still no sign of Benjamin. Unwilling to wait any longer, she worked her way back to the mouth of the canyon. Suddenly, she saw him coming around a rock, ten feet away.

"Where are you going?" he whispered, puzzled.

"To rescue you, if you must know," she answered acidly. "What the heck took you so long?"

"You were going to rescue *me?*" There was no smile on his lips, but his eyes gleamed with amusement. "Why? I was not in any danger."

"What *were* you doing? You said we should meet at sundown. You made a special point of it, in fact. Then you failed to show up. What did you expect me to think?"

"That I was occupied trying to learn how many are pursuing us."

"You returned to take a count?" She cringed, thinking of everything that might have gone wrong.

"I found a hidden place where I could observe them. There are four men down there. They followed the river, then split into groups of two as they picked up our separate trails. All are tired, though, and slowing down. Once it is nighttime, I don't think they will continue the search. They would be taking too great a risk, considering their lack of stamina and skills."

Julia walked with Benjamin back into the shadows of the canyon and selected a vantage point where they'd be able to watch the entrance. If they had to make a fast getaway, they could climb straight up the hillside. If not, the canyon would still serve to protect their backs.

Her stomach growled furiously, and she smiled sheepishly. She unsnapped her shirt pocket and pulled out one tiny piece of foil-wrapped chocolate candy. "Want half a kiss?" She chuckled softly, seeing the thoughts that flickered in his eyes. "That's what they're called." At least some basic things didn't change, despite cultural differences. "Let me borrow your knife, and I'll split it into two."

"No, you eat it. I'm not hungry."

"Of course you are."

"No."

She shot him an icy look. "Fine. I'll eat it myself. You want to act superhuman, that's your problem." She took a bite of the melted mess, then saw him watching her. "Oh, forget it. I can't stand the guilt. You *are* hungry—neither one of us had lunch." She glanced down at the candy, then up at him. "I already took a bite out of it, but if you don't mind that, you can have the rest."

"The taste of your mouth can only improve it," he murmured. He took her hand and brought her fingertips up to his lips.

He ran the tip of his tongue over the area she'd tasted first and felt her shudder as he sucked the tiny morsel into his mouth. "Very sweet," he said, licking clean the chocolate traces that remained on her fingers.

It was just one tiny piece of candy, but the sensuality of that moment practically stopped her breath. Her heart was hammering so loudly, she was sure he could hear it.

Need—vibrant and powerful—sparked the air between them, making her feel light-headed. Everything seemed to fade into the background until the only reality was the man before her.

With effort, she tore her gaze away from his, breaking the spell. "I knew you were hungry."

"Yes, perhaps even more than I realized," he said in a raw whisper.

His words made her ache in a very disturbing place. "Don't be so stubborn next time," she said brusquely, trying to hide how much he'd affected her. "You don't have to impress me with how tough you are."

"If I wanted to impress you, I would use other ways that would assure me of success," he answered.

Her eyes widened. "A little overconfident, aren't we?" she teased, trying to break the tension.

"No, not at all," he whispered, then walked away.

The intense warmth that filled her seemed even more pronounced in the cold of the desert night. She shifted her thoughts to the entrance of the canyon, determined to stay focused on the business at hand.

Silence stretched out between them. Benjamin shifted, searching for another vantage point in the dim light of the moon. "We have to know where they are," he said at last.

"Yeah, but I don't see any safe way of finding out," she answered, joining him near the outcropping of boulders. "I know you've got certain skills, but even the wind isn't cooperating. It's died down completely."

"For now." He gazed up at the sky as the moon disappeared behind a cloud, and began chanting softly. The whisper-soft sounds mingled with the air that seemed to stir and grow stronger with each syllable he uttered. She couldn't make out any of the words, but the rhythmic cadence drew her in, holding her attention.

As the wind grew in strength, he glanced at her for the span of a heartbeat, never disrupting the chant.

Julia heard the rustling of branches, and leaves blew across the ground. As she struggled to keep her hair out of her eyes, a tremor of fear shot through her. Who was Benjamin Two Eagle, and how real was a *hataalii*'s power?

Suddenly, he stopped chanting. "They are several hundred yards away. They seem to be stationary for now."

Julia swallowed, alleviating the dryness in her throat. She searched for a way to logically explain what had just happened, but every answer she could come up with was too preposterous to contemplate. ''Maybe they've decided to wait until the moon comes out again. It's really pitch-black out here at the moment.''

''Could be.'' He paused, then continued. ''One good thing has come of this. You're finally accepting what I tell you, instead of questioning it.''

''I have no way of verifying or disputing it,'' she whispered back.

''You don't believe in magic, do you?''

As he shifted to face her, his thigh brushed against hers. The sensation left her tingling everywhere. ''I believe there's magic in a lot of things, but it's not smart to trust in something you're not sure you can control.''

He smiled, understanding the other meaning she'd laced in her words. ''There are times you have the courage of a thousand warriors, but then I find you're like a wild bird, a creature no one can catch or tame.''

''Maybe I don't want either of those choices.''

''Not every surrender is bitter,'' he whispered.

She felt his breath searing her lips. If she didn't move, he would kiss her, but she didn't want to pull away. Somewhere in the back of her mind, she became aware that the wind had died back down to a breeze. It swirled around her, caressing her skin with the gentleness of a lover's touch.

He angled his mouth downward and captured her lips in an exquisitely tender kiss. She responded instinctively, opening her mouth to draw him in and encouraging him to take more.

He groaned softly, wanting all that she offered. Her softness filled him with a hunger he could barely contain. He locked his arms around her and thrust his tongue deep inside her mouth, drinking in the sweetness he needed. He felt her shiver and press herself into him. Desire clawed at his gut, urging him to conquer the woman who seemed made for him alone. As a river of fire swept through him, he sat down and placed her on his lap, his arms tight around her.

Pleasure sizzled down Julia's body. She could feel his manhood rock hard, pulsing beneath her, making her melt with needs as primitive as the desert itself. When she shifted on his lap, she felt the long shudder that traveled over him. His response electrified every fiber of her being. Passions too powerful to resist raced through her with an intensity she had never experienced before. The need to know life, to know love, cried out from the depths of her soul. Isn't that what she'd asked for back in the arroyo?

With a groan of frustration, Benjamin reluctantly drew away from her. He could not take anymore. She didn't know enough about him to realize the risk she would be taking with her heart. He would not steal or use false pretenses to claim what could not be his.

"I want you. You can feel me," he murmured in a tortured voice. "But be careful who you surrender to. Make sure it is to a man worthy of what you will give him." A shudder ripped through him, as he set her down beside him and moved away.

For one shocked moment, all she could do was stare. Then suddenly surprise turned to anger. Her body shook, and she could barely breathe from the intensity of that one emotion. "You big jerk!" Julia whispered harshly. "Are you telling me that I don't know what I want? Or do you think I'm too dumb to make my own choices?"

He turned to face her, a stunned expression on his face. "It would have been easy to forget everything but my own needs. I wanted that, and still do. If you prefer I didn't spare a thought for you, then by all means let us continue." His eyes blazed like coals.

"Not if you were the last man on the planet!"

He started to reply, then snapped his mouth shut. "Listen."

"To you? I'd rather not. You're a pompous—"

He held up one hand, interrupting her. "They're closer than I thought. *Listen.*"

She stayed very still, straining to hear. For several long seconds, she could make nothing out. Then, through the wind, she heard the sound of muted footsteps. "So, looks like you're not infallible."

"Infallible no, but usually right, yes," he answered smoothly.

She wanted to punch him. Hard. But there was a threat nearby, and this was not the time. She concentrated, trying to come up with a plan. "We'll stand our ground here. They can't see us any better than we can them," she said, unholstering her pistol. "That should help balance things out."

She scarcely breathed as she strained to hear bits and pieces of an argument going on at least one hundred yards away. Although some of the words were lost in the breeze, others came through clearly. "They're not going to give up," she whispered, her nerves taut. "Whoever's leading them won't allow it, and they're more afraid of him than of us."

Suddenly there was a loud crash and a deep rumble somewhere to their right. He grinned at her. "I may have underestimated them, but I am seldom unprepared."

"What was that?"

"A little surprise I planned in case they got too close."

"It sounded like a rock slide just beyond the mouth of the canyon."

"Accurate guess. Now they will search that area and find footprints. Hopefully, they will follow the trail north, thinking they are chasing us."

As they settled back behind a circle of rocks and listened, she watched him speculatively. She just didn't understand how one man could fill her with so many opposing emotions. Half the time she didn't know whether she wanted to kiss Benjamin or hit him.

"If you like," he offered quietly, "we could take turns keeping watch. I will stand guard, then you can. Or the other way around."

"Could you really sleep knowing they're out there?"

"Yes. I trust you to keep us both safe. You have been trained well," he answered softly.

At least he had confidence in her instincts and training as a professional. That mollified her somewhat. "Okay. I'll take the first watch. I'm too keyed up to get any rest."

"It can be difficult under circumstances like these. Knowing how to embrace sleep wherever you can takes practice." He lay down on his back and closed his eyes.

As the minutes passed, she heard his breathing become rhythmic. Her gaze drifted over him in pensive study. Benjamin had the long black hair and body of a warrior—lean, muscled and hard. His self-discipline astonished her. Even in the dim moonlight, she could see that the worry lines around his eyes and forehead had faded. For the first time since she'd met him, he looked at peace.

"Who are you?" she whispered, but the breeze carried the sound off into the night.

JULIA KEPT A CAREFUL watch, listening and watching for movement despite the gloom that hid everything in a mantle of shadows. Time slipped by slowly. Insects lifted their song in tribute to the night, as the minutes turned to hours.

Benjamin stirred a long while later. "It is your turn to rest now," he said.

She watched him sit up and become wide-awake in a matter of seconds. "I doubt I'll be able to sleep, but I suppose I can try."

"Would you let me help you?"

She gave him a wary look. "How?"

He exhaled softly. "I was planning to club you over the head with a rock, of course."

"Sarcasm," she chuckled. "I didn't think you had it in you."

He shook his head. "You bring forth all kinds of things in me, woman. Now, do you want me to help you or not?"

"Tell me what you have in mind."

He moved closer to her as she curled up in a comfortable position. "Now, keep your eyes closed," he said, and began rubbing her temples. "My father used to do this for my mother when she couldn't sleep."

Julia started to ask him more, but he placed one finger over her lips. "No, no questions," he whispered. Then he began to chant softly.

His song was like a warm, silver cloud that enveloped her in a soothing cocoon. Each note danced around her, drawing her away from the worries that had weighed her spirit down. Soon, she felt herself drifting into the welcoming darkness.

It didn't seem like she'd slept for very long, but as her eyes fluttered open, she saw the glow in the east that heralded the new day. She sat up quickly. "You should have woken me up before now! We were supposed to take turns resting."

"We did, and I had all I needed. You deserved the same."

"There's something you've got to understand." She brushed strands of hair away from her eyes. "I took an oath to protect the public, and I take that duty very seriously. I have a job to do out here, and I'm perfectly capable of pulling my own weight."

He nodded slowly. "I am certain of that. It was not my intention to injure your pride."

"Pride has little to do with this. This case is my responsibility, and at the moment we're in big trouble."

"Precisely why we shouldn't spend time arguing," he answered. "We have to get out of this canyon now. The men have seen through my ruse and are heading back in this direction."

"Then let's return to the highway, to the spot where we were ambushed. They won't be expecting that, and the element of surprise will work for us. With a bit of luck, we'll either find my car or be able to steal one of theirs."

"They are certain to have left a guard with their vehicles. Or maybe they have driven them all to another location," he cautioned.

"I figure my car's long gone—they wouldn't want to leave it around for the police to find. But I don't think they'll relocate the other cars far from where they were. They were too intent on pursuing us, and they didn't have much time to make plans without giving us an insurmountable lead."

"All right. We will go take a look."

As they left the mouth of the canyon, she glanced over at him. His body was coiled with tension, and his eyes held the edge of violence that never quite seemed to leave him for long. She was glad they were both fighting on the same side. She had no doubt that he could be a deadly enemy.

Careful to remain hidden, they made their way back across the rugged desert terrain as quickly as they could. The pace Benjamin had set taxed her endurance, but she pushed herself relentlessly. It was imperative they stay well ahead of those pursuing them.

The morning seemed to drag as the desert temperature climbed steadily. "Let's start moving toward the highway," she said, recognizing the terrain.

As they approached high ground, Benjamin motioned for caution. Making sure not to expose themselves against the skyline, they dropped down to their hands and knees and viewed the highway from behind a thick juniper.

"You were right. They moved all the cars," Julia mumbled, then caught a glimpse of color at the base of the embankment a hundred yards farther down the road. "No, wait a sec. Look over there," she whispered. A sedan and a pickup were hidden within a shallow, rocky arroyo. A haphazard attempt had been made to cover them with brush.

"Only one guard," he said, then glanced down at her pistol. "But the weapon won't do us much good. If you fire, the others will hear."

She nodded. "Any ideas? He's sitting in the shade of a solitary tree, with an assault rifle across his legs. The closest cover is fifty feet away, and you'd have to walk up a gravel wash without making any noise to get close. Sneaking up on him is almost impossible."

"I must approach from behind the tree and get as close as I can. If I throw my knife a certain way, I can knock him out with the handle. But my aim must strike true. If I fail, he will know we are here and start shooting. Once the others hear that, they will be on us like bees after honey."

"We can't stay out here indefinitely without food, hoping

the tribal police will come searching for us. This is our chance to turn this around. If things work out right, we can grab the guard and set a trap for the others when they return.''

''It's risky.''

''True, but it's all we've got. The guard has probably been here alone all night. My guess is he didn't get any sleep and, with any luck, will be slow to react. I'm going to use that to help me turn the odds in our favor.''

''You have a plan?''

She nodded. ''I'll wait until you're in position. Then I'll make a noise and draw his attention. When he comes for me, you can make your move.''

''The brush in front of that arroyo is thin, and there are few places to hide. Once he locates you, there will be nothing to stop him from shooting.''

''Only you.'' She managed a thin smile. ''So work fast.''

# Chapter Seven

Benjamin crept through the brush silently. Matters would have been far simpler if the woman hadn't possessed so much courage. As it was, she was taxing his own to the limit. His gut clenched, knowing that the accuracy of his throwing arm might spell the difference between her life and death. He had enough innocent blood on his hands. Though he had no desire to kill anyone who might lead him to the amulets, he wouldn't risk her life. If the guard spotted her, when the time came to throw the knife, Benjamin *would*.

As he thought of Julia, a fierce possessiveness gripped him. She was in many ways a stranger, but in others much more than a friend. He had lost everyone else he had ever cared about. He wouldn't allow her to die, too, even at the risk of the amulets. But without those, he would fail others who had counted on him and, also, destroy himself. A battle raged within his heart, as he stalked the guard and waited for Julia to make her move.

She did seconds later. As twigs snapped off to the right, his adversary sat upright and rose to his feet. Not giving him time to find Julia, Benjamin brought his knife back and flung the weapon. His aim was steady, and the handle of the knife smashed against the base of the man's skull with a sharp thud. The guard collapsed to the ground like a sack of grain.

Benjamin ran toward him, needing to make sure it wasn't a ruse before Julia came out into the open. Moving quickly, he picked the rifle up from the ground, but the gunman never stirred.

Julia emerged from a cluster of stunted junipers, then held her hand out, thumb up. "Well done!"

Benjamin started to smile back, then stopped, hearing the faint sound of men's voices. "The others have discovered our trail." His features twisted, giving his expression a hard edge. "They're advancing quickly."

"Then help me tie this guy up. I'd like to prop him against the front bumper of the car, like he's fallen asleep and is resting his head against the metal. With his assault rifle and my pistol, we now have two working weapons. We can hide behind the car and wait until the others come out into the open. With luck, we'll have them in custody before they even realize what's going on."

Julia searched the unconscious man's pockets and found a spare ammunition clip and a set of car keys. Within seconds, she'd verified which of the two vehicles the keys fit. "This car's our way out if we have to make a quick exit."

Benjamin glanced in the bed of the pickup and pulled out a length of rope. "We'll use this to tie the guard up." He ran the rope in one sleeve and out the other so the unconscious man's arms rested on the bumper in a more natural-looking position. The rope looping through the bumper kept him upright. She put the shotgun across his lap so that it would appear he was still armed.

Once finished, Julia and Benjamin went behind the car, staying out of sight. She handed him the assault rifle and showed him how to eject a spent clip, reload and operate it. "Once they're in the open, their only reasonable choice will be to surrender. They're not suicidal, so I don't expect much of a problem."

"Never be too certain of another's actions," he whispered. "Just a lesson I learned a long time ago." He took a position crouched down by the rear of the car.

Julia gave Benjamin one last look as she heard approaching

footsteps. Keeping her head beside the front windshield post, she brought her pistol up.

"Ace of Diamonds!" one shouted from behind cover on the facing slope of the hill.

Julia cursed softly, shaking her head in disgust. "They've worked out a signal. We're in trouble," she whispered to Benjamin, who nodded back silently.

"Ace of Diamonds, dammit!" the man repeated, anger hardening his tone.

Suddenly bullets whined overhead, slapping against the embankment behind them. "The prisoner!" Julia said.

Instantly Benjamin was beside her, rifle in one hand, razor-sharp knife in the other. Without a word, he cut the rope and pulled the inert man and the shotgun around to cover. "Keep him alive, right?" Benjamin smiled grimly.

Julia nodded, then grimaced as bullets kicked up dust right where the man had been only three seconds earlier. Summoning the strength only fear can bring, they tossed the man into the back seat of the car through the open window, along with the useless shotgun.

"Good job! Now let's see if we can do the same for ourselves." Julia fired over the car into the hillside twice, aiming for spots offering the best cover. She ducked back down as a return volley crashed against a side window, sending cubes of glass showering over them. "But first I've got to disable the pickup. Start firing back and give me some cover."

She was gone before he could argue. The woman would drive him to insanity. He cursed whatever perverse fate had brought them together. Lying flat beneath the car, he started firing from behind the rear tire. Julia had told him there were thirty rounds in each clip, but he wanted to expend them wisely. He squeezed off each shot, taking careful aim, and forcing the gang to keep down.

After fifteen shots, he glanced over toward the pickup. Julia was by the front, underneath, pulling out some wires. He turned back to his grim work, increasing his rate of fire. No one would harm her—he'd see to it. As he noticed she was ready to cross back again, he reloaded fast. He blanketed the places where cover was the densest with a steady barrage. He heard the men yelling and cursing and knew that his instincts had served him well. He had guessed their positions, though he was mostly shooting blind.

"Good shooting!" Julia appeared by the front of the car, crouched low. Allowing a spent magazine to drop from her pistol, she quickly slipped another into place. "Are you a hunter?"

"When it is required," he answered, examining her quickly. She was trembling with excitement, but unharmed. "*Now* are you finally ready to go?"

"Hate loud noises, do we?" she teased.

"Not long ago, you told me to stop acting so tough. Aren't you *ever* satisfied?"

With a curt laugh, Julia opened the front door, just enough to slip into the driver's seat, keeping her head below window level.

Benjamin simultaneously slipped into the back of the vehicle. The prisoner was mumbling something, but was still groggy. Benjamin pushed the man off the seat onto the floor, but refrained from sticking his head up to look outside.

"Okay, hold on! We're going."

She switched on the ignition, but the engine quickly died. "Start, you…" she cursed just as the vehicle roared to life.

Julia slammed down on the accelerator, spewing gravel, sand and dust in a thick cloud that all but obscured the path behind them. Barely peeking over the wheel, she managed to keep the car heading toward the highway above. A bullet thumped against the top of the car, and then another struck the metal post just to the left of her head.

Looking in the rearview mirror, still in place despite the damage surrounding it, she saw Benjamin pointing the assault rifle out through a hole in the back window. "We'll get all the help we need at the first roadblock we come to," she said. "Then we'll return and finish what we started."

"If they're still around."

"They're not going anywhere in the pickup. I made sure of that."

"What you break, they can fix."

"Eventually, yes, but repairs take time. Breaking things doesn't."

Julia drove quickly. There was supposed to be a roadblock about ten miles down the highway. It wouldn't take long to reach it.

Benjamin's heart sank as the miles stretched out between them and the gang. "The amulets have slipped out of our grasp again," he said quietly.

"We'll go back and get them. Don't worry. Then they'll be taken in as evidence and, eventually, you'll be given a chance through the courts to establish ownership."

He glanced at her face reflected in the rearview mirror. "The burden of proof shouldn't be on me, since these amulets are clearly mine."

"That's the problem. The issue isn't as simple as you seem to think. The fact that they were yours once doesn't mean that legally they still are."

Even if things worked out the way Julia hoped and the gang was captured, Benjamin knew that wouldn't be the end of it for him. He still had to get the amulets, and he had no desire to trust the white man's laws.

Julia slowed the car quickly as she approached the roadblock ahead. Identifying herself and Benjamin, she hurriedly related the situation to the three officers present. The bullet-riddled car, Benjamin's assault rifle and their captive added urgency to her story.

After transferring their groggy prisoner to the back seat of a squad car, she set back out to the ambush site, leading the two remaining units. One of the Navajo officers had agreed to use his radio to call for additional support as they raced down the highway. They were less than two miles away when she spotted a growing column of dark smoke ahead. Julia realized the gang must have set fire to the disabled pickup. She just couldn't figure out why they would have risked pinpointing their location to everyone in the region. The thought that perhaps they were hoping for a civilian hostage chilled her.

The pickup was an inferno by the time they arrived at the site. Jumping out of their cars, they searched for the armed men, but the only thing below the roadbed was burning brush.

"They couldn't move the pickup, so they set fire to it to destroy evidence. Not even a fingerprint will survive that blaze," Julia shouted. The Navajo officer, poised by the road with his shotgun, nodded in agreement.

"Or maybe it was meant to divert your attention while they set up another ambush or, more likely, escaped," Benjamin countered.

"It's a possibility," she conceded. "Stay alert," she called out loudly to the others, "and search all around." She jogged over to the officer with the shotgun and handed him the assault rifle. "Take this. And if you see anyone else besides us armed, take care of it."

Benjamin remained beside Julia when she joined the others searching. "They didn't come back here," he said.

"But they couldn't have escaped on foot already," she said under her breath. "No way. Not unless there was another player in this we didn't know about."

"If they had two vehicles, why not three?"

"I suppose that's possible, but let's not assume that just yet. I don't want any of us to walk into another trap."

After concluding a futile search, Benjamin walked down the highway, checking the shoulder of the road. Before long, he waved to Julia, calling her over. "Another vehicle was here recently." Benjamin pointed out the tracks to Julia and the round faced tribal sergeant who'd accompanied her.

The sergeant studied the tracks. "It was a Jeep, I think, judging from the tire size and imprint."

"Put out an APB," she said quickly. "They either had another vehicle patrolling back and forth down the highway or they hijacked somebody's Jeep. I hope they don't have a hostage now."

"We'll check both sides of the road, just in case they

dumped the driver,'' the sergeant answered, "but I doubt we'll find anything.'' He used his hand-held to call it in, then stared into the distance pensively. "Let me make a suggestion. So far they've eluded our roadblocks. That means they may be traveling cross-country, which would explain their use of the Jeep. I think our people should search for tracks leading off the road between here and the roadblocks.''

Julia nodded. "Good idea.'' She watched the officer return to his car. "The gang's outplayed me twice,'' she muttered to Benjamin. "It won't happen again.''

"Setbacks are natural. Learn how your enemies operate from what has happened so far, and it won't taste so much like a defeat. Once you can think like them, the victory will be yours.''

She met his gaze. "You talk like someone who has lots of combat experience.'' She paused, then continued. "Or maybe one who knows about being on the run.''

"I know both,'' he admitted somberly. "And I also know the cost of making mistakes.''

His remark hit too close for comfort. The Bureau and the tribe were counting on her to put an end to the violence outsiders had brought into the reservation. So far, she had little to show for her efforts. Frustration tore into her confidence.

As an additional squad car pulled up, she turned around, her attention shifting. She watched the Navajo officer emerge and come toward her, a manila envelope in his hand.

"Deputy Chief Pete Bowman asked me to deliver this to you as soon as possible and to tell you the other FBI agent is doing well at the San Juan County Hospital.''

Julia thanked the officer for delivering the news, then opened the envelope and found the response to her fax inside. She scanned the papers casually at first, then almost dropped everything, stunned by what she was reading. Her mind reeled as she struggled to accept the information before her, and she reached out to steady herself on the car fender. The pillars that made up her entire sense of reality had suddenly come crashing down.

She stared at the report. Despite an extensive search, only one set of documents mentioned a *hataalii* by the name of Benjamin Two Eagle: a Library of Congress account of New Mexico's early military history. She read the sentence again for the third time, then skipped down to the next paragraph, re-reading it as well. The name Benjamin Two Eagle appeared often in regard to army campaigns against the Navajos. Two Eagle was recorded as a renegade who'd continued to resist the soldiers even after Manuelito, the great Navajo Chief, had turned himself in.

The information left her feeling as if she'd been pulled into a crazy dimension where time and space were only myths. Yet she might have managed to accept it with more grace, if the packet hadn't also included a copy of an old photograph. She held it in her trembling hand as she stared at Benjamin, her heart drumming and her head pounding. "Who *are* you?" she whispered.

"I have already told you."

"No," she answered, shaking her head, refusing to look back down at the papers or photograph she could not believe. "The only record of a Singer named Two Eagle shows he died…over one hundred years ago. His body was found in a peach orchard inside Canyon de Chelly. That was all recorded by a Union cavalry officer."

"No, the soldier made a mistake." His gaze drifted down to the fax photo she held in her hand. "I'm here. You can see me with your own eyes." He remembered the occasion that had been taken. During the time of peace, a traveling photographer had asked for permission, to capture the image of Manuelito, their great chief, and the tribe's *hataalii* counseling together.

Benjamin felt Julia's struggle not to believe what she already knew in her heart. But what hurt him most was seeing her recoil from him as if she had suddenly come face-to-face with a dead man—or worse. "The peach trees in Canyon de Chelly were chopped down and burned by Colonel Kit Carson's troops. Some of the *Dineh* were also killed, but I was not there when it happened.''

She handed him the photo. "You can't really expect me to believe this is *you!*''

He shrugged. "I *am* here and doing my best to help you. Why isn't that enough for you? Why should my likeness on that paper be so important?''

"I can't just ignore this!'' She fought to cling to the logic that had always centered her world, but it was a losing struggle. "Are you real? I mean, are you—''

"I am *not* a spirit.'' He captured her eyes with an intensity that seared a path to her soul. "Remember my lips against yours—and the way you felt when I held you in my arms,'' he said in a heady voice. "I am flesh and blood, like you.''

"If what you're telling me is true, then how did you get here? Some kind of suspended animation or Navajo magic? And why did you come? And when?'' Her voice betrayed her, breaking twice as she tried to hold on to her sanity. "I need to know.''

"Why question what already is? Neither of us can do anything to change this. Accept it, as I have.''

She'd learned to believe many things she couldn't even begin to understand, like Einstein's physics and genetic engineering. But those were concepts that explained and ordered life. What Benjamin was suggesting undermined the essence of everything she'd ever held as true. "We can't pursue this right now. We have other more immediate problems. But I intend to find out a lot more. Get used to that idea, because I won't accept evasions or take no for an answer.'' She paused, then added, "And I never give up.''

"That is something we both have in common,'' he answered, then walked down to join others searching an area far from the highway for clues.

HOURS LATER, Julia and Benjamin sat inside one of the offices at the Shiprock police department, sipping cups of coffee. She had just called and spoken to Bobby Sanchez, who wouldn't be back to work for a month or more. That had prompted a call to her boss in Albuquerque. She had asked that a Navajo agent named Justin Nakai be assigned to join her on the case, but she'd been told she'd have to wait. Nakai was running another investigation in North Dakota and would not be available for two weeks or more.

It was only after promising to work hand in hand with the Navajo police that she was able to get permission to work without a partner until Nakai was available.

Even though she'd managed that small victory, her mood at the moment was undeniably grim. The events and revelations of the past twenty-four hours had shaken her. To make matters even worse, the progress they'd made on the investigation had suddenly come to a screeching halt. "I don't understand it. Burns has spent half his life in prison and barely escaped before going back again. Plea bargaining should have appealed to him."

"Bargaining for time in jail is not the right approach. You need to question him in a way that will convince him to answer you," Benjamin emphasized. "I don't believe in brutality, but Burns needs to be given an opportunity to make the right choice."

"We have rules about things like that." The more Julia was around him, the more logical it seemed to accept that he'd come from the past, where different customs prevailed. One thing was for certain—he wasn't like anyone she'd ever known. How many men in the twentieth century could reverse the wind with a prayer, or find criminals after seeing them only in their mind?

"Let me have some time with him," Benjamin suggested. "Perhaps I can get this criminal to volunteer some information."

"Not a chance." She set her coffee down and looked him in the eyes. "There's one thing you're going to have to accept. Law enforcement is *my* world, not yours. You can't possibly understand it as well as I do. Things are done a certain way or not at all."

"The way of dealing with a criminal may have changed, but the man inside has remained the same."

"You're right about that, but I'm trained to work with a justice system geared to uphold the rights of every individual. It's not enough to trap a criminal. Unless it's done in a certain way, the courts throw out the case, and the prisoner walks free."

"Then that is another thing that has remained the same. The guilty often escape justice, and the innocent still suffer."

"I'm a member of the best law-enforcement agency in this country. Most of the criminals we apprehend are convicted because we know how to gather evidence without violating the rules."

"Perhaps not following the rules now and then would give you more success."

"You're wrong about that, but it's not necessary that you agree with me. Let's just stick to what we each do best. My work is focused on getting criminals behind bars where they belong. You're a *hataalii*. You're trained to teach and heal."

"And survive," he added. "Let me guide you on this search. If you permit me to help, you will capture the men and recover the amulets."

"Your abilities would be a big help to me, but only if you accept that I'm the one who's in charge. Since I'm responsible for all decisions made, that's the way it's got to be. This isn't negotiable. Either you agree to follow my lead, or we can't work together."

He walked to the window and stared out across the mesa. Heat shimmered in waves, distorting the earth into curtainlike walls. "I've always found it difficult not to take charge. I obeyed our chief Manuelito, but in the end, when we had to make tough choices, I did not follow him into captivity. I went my own way." He turned and faced her. "But you and I need each other to finish the tasks we have been burdened with. I have no choice except to do what you ask."

"I know you're reluctant to tell me how you got here, but there is one thing I have to know now. Why do you want the amulets so badly? Do you need them to go back to your own time?"

"Yes," he admitted.

The possibility of him going back and leaving her as abruptly as he'd entered her life made her feel so empty inside, it hurt. She needed to talk to him and ask him more, but was forced to wait as one of the tribal officers came into the room. Julia shifted her thoughts to business and immediately asked him the question foremost in her mind. "Did you have any more luck with Burns than I did?"

The officer shook his head. "We kept working on him, but so far we've got nothing. Burns just won't talk. The other guy you brought in is still in the hospital, and the doctors won't let us question him yet."

"Has either man asked for a lawyer?"

"Burns has, and we've provided him with a public defender. But he's not cooperating with the attorney, either." He placed a folder on the table in front of her. "This arrived a few minutes ago. It's the background report you requested on Burns and Eddie Conway."

"Good. Maybe this'll give us a new lead."

As the officer left, Pete Bowman came in. With a respectful nod to Benjamin, he sat down across the table from them. "We've scoured the area around the ambush site and recovered quite a few shells. This gang carries pretty heavy firepower."

"Yes, even with the assault rifle we captured, we were still outgunned. I believe their leader has some specialized training. He used textbook tactics when he planned that highway trap. We should check out suspects with military or police experience, particularly anyone who has law-enforcement connections. This gang must have found a source who's working against us. Otherwise, it's hard to explain how they knew exactly where we were going."

"Let me get this right," he said, his voice as cold as steel. "You think we might have dirty cops in our department?"

"Or in somebody else's who's involved in the case. It's

worth looking into," she answered, knowing she'd just alienated herself even further from the tribe.

He stood up. "I'll go down my roster, but it's a waste of time to look here. Our department is clean. Respect for duty is ingrained into everything we are and everything we do as Navajos. A bad cop would have been discovered right away, and our people would have handled the matter quickly."

After Bowman left, Julia glanced at Benjamin, wondering if she'd insulted him, too. His gaze was speculative, but there seemed to be no trace of anger there. "The question had to be asked," she explained.

"Yes, but some things should be suggested without such directness."

"I'm no diplomat," she conceded with a shrug.

A few minutes later, a stout officer with a barrel chest came into the room. "We've identified the prisoner who was transported to the hospital. His name is Neil Stillwell. He has a long record that includes armed robbery. The doctors say he can be questioned now."

She sensed disapproval in the officer's tone. Word that she was looking for a possible suspect within their ranks must have started making the rounds. Bad news always traveled fast. "I'm on my way over there, then." She wondered how much cooperation she'd get from the Navajo police department now.

As she entered the outer office, Bowman tossed her the keys to one of their unmarked units. "You'll need transportation until your people in Albuquerque can deliver another car," he said curtly.

"Thanks." She stepped toward him and lowered her voice. "For the record, I'm not out to hurt your department or anybody else's. I'm just doing my job."

"I know," he answered. "But I don't have to like it." Bowman glanced at Benjamin, then walked away.

As Julia walked out to the car, her thoughts were racing. "He hasn't mentioned it directly, but I think he resents your presence on the case."

"What he certainly resents," Benjamin countered, "is outsiders taking over what he views as his business."

"That definition applies to both of us."

"Yes, but more to you than to me. You are not Navajo."

"I guess we'll have to wait and see how much that fact matters," she conceded softly.

The drive to the hospital didn't take long. The highway was nearly empty as heat pounded the asphalt, working its way inside the car despite the air-conditioning. Though she was struggling to stay alert, lack of sleep and long hours were taking their toll.

"You can't maintain this pace," he warned.

The statement had come so quickly after her own thoughts that it took her by surprise. She shifted uncomfortably, then glanced at him. He looked as exhausted as she felt. "Neither one of us got enough rest last night," she answered, stifling a yawn. "I've still got a few more things to do, but I'll be glad to drop you off, if there's someplace you'd like to go."

He shook his head. "Do not concern yourself about me."

With no place in the twentieth century he could call home, she had the uneasy feeling he'd end up camping outside her motel room. But she wouldn't be able to stand the guilt if he had to rough it while she enjoyed a quiet air-conditioned room and clean sheets.

She'd have to rent him his own room out of her pocket. There was no way she could explain him away on her expense account. Of course, there was another alternative. The possibility of sharing a room with him was tempting, but out of the question.

She glanced at him furtively, then sighed. "You're really making me crazy, you know that?" she muttered, then realized she'd spoken out loud.

He grinned. "It is a feeling we share."

Minutes later, they went through the hospital's entrance doors and stopped at the desk for directions. As they passed the glassed-in work space, she noticed her reflection. She'd never seen herself look worse. She ran her hand through her hair in a futile attempt to comb it. As she did, she realized that Benjamin was watching her.

Feeling self-conscious, she shot him an icy look. "Just because I'm a tough cop, doesn't mean I enjoy looking like a slob."

"I am not sure what that is, but you have no need to worry about your appearance. You are a beautiful woman. No weariness or hardship can alter that."

She wondered if he'd succumbed to an attack of gentlemanly manners, or had simply gone blind. As her gaze swept over him, she made an irritating discovery. His appearance hadn't deteriorated as much as hers. He looked pleasantly rumpled, rather than slovenly. No five-o'clock shadow marred his tanned, coppery skin. His eyes looked like twin coals that sparked with life, instead of the red-lined maps she was certain hers had become. She muttered several uncomplimentary remarks under her breath.

"Did you say something to me?" Ben asked.

"No," she said in a clipped tone.

Glancing down the hall, trying to focus her thoughts elsewhere, she saw a tribal officer standing by a closed door. The room number matched the directions she'd been given. Julia flashed her ID, opened the door and went inside the small single room. The prisoner was lying very still beneath a thin blanket, asleep. A Navajo nurse stood by the bed, taking notes with a pen and clipboard.

"We were told he was ready to be questioned," Julia said quietly to the nurse, as Benjamin joined her inside.

"That's fine. We can wake him up," the nurse said, smiling at Benjamin. Looking at the guard, she added, "Would you close the door?"

The officer nodded and shut the door, remaining out in the hall.

The nurse bent over the bed to awake her patient. "Mr. Stillwell, you have…"

Before she could finish, Stillwell bolted upright and pulled the startled woman down in front of him. His arm locked around her throat, the point of her metal ballpoint pen pressed against the jugular vein on her neck. "Back off!" he snapped, using his hostage like a shield. He slipped out of bed, holding the nurse tightly against him. By then, Julia had her pistol ready, pointed at Stillwell's head.

"Your plan won't work," Julia answered, noting he had slipped on his pants under the hospital gown. "You're not going anywhere."

# Chapter Eight

Julia remained between Stillwell and the door, shifting to the side to block his way. The nurse was in danger, but at that range she knew if Stillwell moved to stab the woman, she could use lethal force. Julia hoped he wouldn't force the issue. Although her gaze was locked on the man before her, she could sense Benjamin moving up to help seal off the man's escape completely.

Keeping his hostage in the way, Stillwell spun around to face Benjamin. "You want her dead? Keep it up!"

When Benjamin took only half a step back, Stillwell kicked out, aiming for the groin.

With lightning-fast reflexes, Benjamin grasped Stillwell's leg and pulled his opponent away from the nurse. Collapsing backward, he brought the man down onto the floor with him. Stillwell recovered quickly, rolling away and against the wall. Scrambling to his feet, he dove toward Benjamin, and they both collided against the opposite wall.

Unable to get at Stillwell, Julia swung the terrified nurse off the floor and into the arms of the guard, who had opened the door to investigate the noise. "Get her out of here!" she yelled.

When Julia turned back to the two men, Stillwell was flat on his back. Benjamin had dropped to one knee and was resting the edge of his knife on the man's throat.

"Okay, let him up." Julia reached around her waistband to bring out the handcuffs she kept there in a holder. The Navajo policeman appeared at the door, nightstick in hand, and she nodded for him to enter.

"He and I still have to bargain," Benjamin answered, his voice calm and expressionless. "I will agree not to stain the floor with his blood, if he will give us the names of the others in the gang."

"I know my rights," Stillwell spat out. "Cops can't threaten me this way." He looked for confirmation to the Navajo policeman, who turned to look out the window.

"I am not a police officer, and I am not inclined to follow the white man's laws," Benjamin growled. "Answer me."

*"Let him up,"* Julia repeated, her heart pounding. She gestured with her handgun so Benjamin could see she meant her words. Was she going to have to shoot the man who'd saved her life to protect the lowlife who'd tried to kill her? The Navajo officer, thinking it was all part of a plan, continued his interest in something outside the window.

"Are you willing to lose your life like this to protect your den of thieves? I'm running out of patience, white man," Benjamin growled.

"You'd let him kill me, wouldn't you?" Stillwell stared at Julia, his face deathly pale. He didn't wait for an answer. "Just five of us are left. You captured Burns, and Walt Karns killed Eddie Conway. So it's just Walt, Norm Foster, Bobby Serna, Benny Martinez and me."

"Who gives the orders?" Benjamin tilted the blade slightly, so that only the point was touching Stillwell.

"No one. It's a democracy," he sneered, apparently starting to believe he'd been conned.

"Benjamin, move away from him *now!*" Julia clipped, reaching down and taking hold of his shoulder. Her tone startled Stillwell and the Navajo policeman, who turned around in surprise.

She breathed a silent sigh of relief when Benjamin rose and stepped away, allowing the policeman to turn the man around and cuff him.

"The doctor said he wants him out of here since there's

nothing wrong with him. That means he'll have to go to jail. Do you want me to take custody right now, ma'am?'' the officer asked Julia.

"Yeah, that's a good idea."

The moment the officer led Stillwell away, she turned and gave Benjamin an icy glare. "Let's go outside to the car," she snapped. Walking out the door, she rapidly wrote on a notepad the names Benjamin had forced from the prisoner.

Anger curled and smoked inside her, threatening to erupt any minute like an out-of-control volcano. They were barely out of the building when she turned on Benjamin in a fury. "You broke your word. You said you'd abide by my rules."

"You were the one who refused to let him leave with his hostage," Benjamin answered, his expression one of surprise and confusion. "The moment you did that, you issued a challenge. I joined you and used the circumstances to our advantage."

"What you did was violate the hell out of his civil rights! Nothing he told us would ever stand up in court. I could even bring charges against *you* for what happened after you subdued him." Hearing footsteps rushing up from behind them, Julia turned around.

The nurse they'd rescued was scowling ferociously at Julia. "You're going to have a very tough time if you try to arrest this man." She smiled at Benjamin, then abruptly refocused her anger on Julia. "He saved my life, and maybe yours, too. You couldn't shoot, and Stillwell knew it. He could have stabbed me and escaped, or I might have been accidentally shot by some well-meaning officer, like you." She turned to Benjamin. "Your courage stopped him. Too bad the *bilagáana* woman's pride is getting in the way of the facts."

Julia stared at the nurse. "I know what you've been through and how you feel, but if Stillwell happens to get a greedy lawyer, he can still—"

"No one will believe him. Or they'll figure that Stillwell is just trying to get himself off the hook. Either way, who will corroborate his story? Not Jimmy Begay, who's been guarding him. He's already told several people that this man's courage helped save your life and mine. That only leaves you.''

Julia knew the woman was right. If she said or did anything against Benjamin, all she'd earn was more animosity from the tribe. Besides, Stillwell knew they wouldn't be able to use the information he'd given them—at least, not in court. He would be more likely to want to keep secret the fact that he'd ratted.

To make matters worse, to say anything against Benjamin would mean she'd be repaying her only ally by having him jailed. She cringed, thinking how he'd answer a simple question like "Who are you?'' or "What is your birth date?''

"Don't worry about Mr. Two Eagle, nurse. As usual, he's leading a charmed life.'' She forced herself to sound stern. She would *not* let anyone know that—deserved or not—it would have torn her apart to do anything against Benjamin.

Benjamin gave the nurse a wide grin. "Thank you for your honesty,'' he said.

The woman beamed. "Anytime.''

Benjamin's eyes lingered on the nurse as she walked back inside. Julia felt a stab of jealousy, told herself to ignore it, but couldn't quite manage to do so. "What exactly were you prepared to do back in there?'' she challenged angrily. "Would you have actually cut his throat?''

"Only if he had not stayed still. But he didn't know that.'' His eyes flashed with hurt, then turned hard and as cold as a stormy desert night. "It disappoints me that you thought it necessary to ask. I had hoped you understood me better than that.''

She took a deep breath, then let it out again. "You scared me. I despise vigilante tactics no matter who uses them. What happened in there must *never* happen again. Do you understand me? No excuses, no exceptions.''

"But the man wasn't hurt, and you now have names that may result in good descriptions and drawings of your suspects. Isn't that what you wanted?''

She said nothing, but her gaze could have easily frozen a lake.

Benjamin sighed. "As you wish. But I don't know how you ever manage to conclude an investigation. A man will not tell you what he is hiding unless you apply considerable pressure on him."

"We use legal pressure only. If we need answers, we don't resort to the same kind of violence we're trying to fight. That's not what law enforcement is about."

Benjamin lapsed into silence as he followed her to the car.

"I'm sorry you see that as a weakness, Benjamin."

"I don't," he said. "In some ways that is your greatest strength. A warrior without compassion loses himself or herself in the battle. You're one woman in a thousand. I wouldn't change anything about you, even if I could."

Her stomach tightened as she heard the sadness that ribboned through his words. "Then why do you sound like someone who's just lost a friend?" she asked softly.

"I've reached out for many dreams throughout my life, yet they have always eluded me. Endless circles of hope and loss can defeat even the strongest man."

She started to ask him more, but her radio came to life and she was forced to answer. Julia tried to hide her disappointment. That moment when she might have glimpsed a very private part of his soul had been shattered. Fate had conspired against her.

She forced herself to concentrate on what Chief Roanhorse was saying. His voice came through loud and clear. "The sheriff's department agreed to discuss stepping up the roadblocks just outside the reservation borders, but now we've got to get together and coordinate our efforts." He paused for a moment. "The news that outsiders are creating trouble here on our land is stirring up the tribe. We have to settle this fast."

She racked the mike a moment later, her expression somber. "I don't like this. In my experience, when too many state and government agencies get heavily involved in the same case, people start tripping over each other. It usually creates more trouble than it solves."

"Since you don't have another choice, you must find a way to prevent that from happening."

They were back in Shiprock at police headquarters a short while later. Distrust was mirrored in the faces glancing at her, but what most took her by surprise was the interest focused on Benjamin. Respect and open admiration shone in their eyes as he walked by. She had a feeling news of what had happened at the hospital was already a major topic of discussion here.

As she went down the hall, a San Juan County deputy came to greet her. He was a tall Anglo man with light brown hair and a lean, muscular build. "I'm Capt. Willy McKibben, ma'am. I'm the liaison between the tribe and the county."

Julia shook his hand. "Pleasure to meet you, Captain," she said, and followed him to the chief's office.

Pete Bowman gave her a nod as she came in and pulled up a chair for her. Neskahi, the Navajo police lieutenant already there, stood, and out of deference to Anglo customs, offered to shake hands.

After the chief came in and the men were seated, she stood and gave them all an encouraging smile. "Our progress has been slow, gentlemen, but we are moving in the right direction."

"Not fast enough," Chief Roanhorse interjected. "The People are starting to worry about this *bilagáana* gang. They're questioning our ability to protect them."

"I'm keeping an open mind to any suggestions or comments," Julia answered, "but as we all know—"

"Wait a second," McKibben said, interrupting her. "Who are *you?*" His eyes locked with Benjamin's.

"He's with me, Captain," Julia continued. "He's a…an interpreter and guide."

McKibben glanced at Roanhorse. "One of yours?"

"Yeah, very much one of us," Roanhorse answered. "He stays. Now let's get on with it."

She knew then that something was definitely up, and it was much more than news of the hospital incident. She made a mental note to look into it, even if Roanhorse objected.

"Will your department be able to man extra roadblocks outside the reservation?" Julia asked McKibben.

"We've stepped up our patrols, but we're against the roadblocks," McKibben answered. "I think they're a waste of time. The gang's still inside the reservation and seems to want to stay here for some damn-fool reason. We don't have jurisdiction to come in and get them, so why should we sit around and tie up our force?"

"Things could spill out all over the county if your roadblocks aren't there," Roanhorse said. "Our department is stretched to the limit."

"Your sheriff probably doesn't realize how serious the situation is here on the reservation, Captain McKibben," Julia said, a hard edge to her voice. "I think I should call and point this out. Perhaps he'll decide to send someone to help you with your analysis of the situation." Julia noticed McKibben flinch as she looked around the room, as if searching for a phone.

"No need to delay our meeting. I'm sure we can come up with a plan we all agree on. But I still think you're going about this wrong. The answer is to increase patrols, not just add roadblocks. All that's doing is tying up officers."

"Roadblocks, in locations that lead from the reservation, have to remain in place for now. Your people have to take care of that so the tribal police will have more manpower available to increase patrols. Chief Roanhorse and I are already working closely on this. What I want to do next is meet with the county deputies who'll be manning the roadblocks. How soon can you arrange that?"

"You might be a federal cop, lady, but I won't let you start dictating to the members of my department. You deal through *me*. You got that? I'll get your roadblocks set up. But if you've got something to say to my men, you say it through me." McKibben glowered at her. "I don't like your attitude. You Feds think that you're the only ones who know how to get the job done. Well, I, for one, think you're wrong, and I intend to file a complaint with your superior."

She watched him storm out and shook her head. "Is he always that hard to work with?"

"He is when anyone challenges his authority," Roanhorse answered. "I'm told it started a year and a half ago, when they promoted him out of the field to what's basically a desk job. Since then, he's been acting like a man who's afraid he's being pushed aside. He's fighting back the only way he knows how."

Lieutenant Neskahi glanced at Benjamin, who had continued to stand at the back of the room. "Join us, Uncle," he invited, gesturing to the now empty chair. "Sit."

She watched the other Navajos as Benjamin drew near. Their attitudes clearly indicated his presence was welcomed, openly acknowledging him as one of them. They seemed to relax and close ranks. Suddenly, she felt more like an outsider than ever. "McKibben made one good point. For some inexplicable reason, the gang has chosen to remain on the reservation. Even Conway, who had every reason to hightail it out of here as fast as possible, chose to hide rather than make a run for it."

"There must be something of value here they still covet." Although Benjamin's voice was quiet, it reverberated with authority and power.

"Whatever it is has probably become inaccessible to them for the time being," Roanhorse added thoughtfully. "But until we know more, all we can do is guess."

Bowman looked over at a wall map of the Navajo Nation. "There's a limit to how patient our people are willing to be. We've got to improve our results."

"We'll keep digging," Julia assured, "and following up on what we already know. That's solid police work. But until we uncover a lead, our options are pretty much defined."

An officer knocked lightly, then came in and placed a folder on the table before Julia. He gave the gathering a brief report. "The car you took from the gang turned out to be stolen. The owner, Maria Yazzie, thought her sister had borrowed it. That's why she hadn't reported it. We searched it thoroughly, but besides dozens of smudged prints, there wasn't anything of interest."

Julia tried not to show her disappointment. "I'm going to go down the main highway, making stops along the way and asking around. Maybe I can find out where the gang's been buying food, gas and whatever else they need. Chief, if your officers on patrol would do the same in their sectors, I'd appreciate it. I know it's a long shot, but for now I can't think of anything better."

"Our officers normally visit the businesses on their patrols. It's our way of keeping our ears to the ground. We'll continue it," Roanhorse replied.

When Bowman was called to the telephone, the meeting broke up. Neskahi walked outside with Benjamin. The two men seemed engrossed in their conversation.

Taking advantage of a moment alone with Roanhorse, Julia approached him. "Chief, I need a private word with you." She hesitated, uncertain of how to proceed. If she phrased the question wrong, she'd get nowhere. "At first, no one around seemed to know a thing about Benjamin Two Eagle. Now I'm getting the impression that everyone knows more about him than I do. How about letting me in on what's going on?"

The chief stared pensively at the watercolor painting of Shiprock that stood on the far wall. Silence stretched out between them. "To accept my answer, you would need to understand some of our ways. Maybe even believe them."

"You'd be surprised how much I'm learning, Chief," she answered honestly. "And as far as what I believe, well, let's just say I've become much more receptive to new ideas since my arrival."

He rubbed the back of his neck with one hand. "What I'm going to tell you is strictly off the record. Agreed?"

"Agreed."

"Daniel Brownhat is one of our most respected Singers. Those of us who know him, have learned we can count on his intuition and accept whatever he says as the truth. He assures us that the man with you is a *hataalii* and can be trusted. Brownhat believes he'll restore much of the knowledge that has been lost to our tribe. None of us here need more confirmation that.''

''Thanks for your candor, Chief. I appreciate it.''

''Now tell me, how do *you* feel about the man you've chosen to help you, particularly after what happened at the hospital?''

''I *thought* that news had reached you,'' Julia commented, pausing to consider her reply. ''The man is very unorthodox, Chief, but he's given me the best leads I've had. I won't turn away his help willingly. To be honest, though, I didn't choose him, he chose me.''

''We're in agreement about that,'' the chief answered with a smile.

She started toward the door, then stopped. ''I've got some names I'd like to run a check on.'' She wrote them down and handed him the list. ''I believe these are members of the gang.''

The chief nodded. ''An anonymous tip?''

''You could call it that,'' she answered cautiously. His expression told her he knew who her source had been and was giving her a simple way out. ''We'll probably want the tribal officers and county roadblocks to have copies of any photos available.''

''Consider it done.''

Several minutes later, she met Benjamin outside by the car. An idea had been forming in the back of her mind for the last few hours, and it was time to bring it out into the open.

''I'm out of leads,'' she admitted, slipping behind the wheel, ''but you might be able to come up with something. If you really can, would you try to see through the eyes of the agate amulet?''

''*If?* I thought we had progressed beyond that.''

She said nothing for a moment as she pulled out onto the highway. ''We have,'' she conceded. ''It's just that it's still difficult for me to accept this…you. I've been on my own since I turned eighteen. Life has taught me that I'm far better off when I stay in control of my life and myself. But since I arrived on the reservation, it seems I haven't been in control of either.''

"If you wanted to stay in control of everything that affects you, why did you pick law enforcement?"

"Crime is something that makes people feel helpless—it resists coming under control. I thought I could do the most good in that field. And I have. I'm very good at what I do because I stick to hard facts and let those guide me. Yet here on the reservation, things operate on a different level. I'm being forced to rely more on intuition than on police procedure. Everything I encounter raises questions that make me feel off balance somehow. I haven't been quite sure of anything since the day you suddenly appeared above me at that arroyo."

"Trust your feelings. The things we accept as facts change as new information comes to light. If intuition guides you, then you will be in harmony with yourself and all else will follow."

"My instincts tell me to use your help—to ask you for what I need."

"Whatever is within my power to give you is yours."

Her pulse raced as his words drifted over her. But what she wanted most from him was not something a woman could gain by asking. She forced her thoughts back on business. "I want you to look through the eyes of the agate amulet. Will you do it?"

"We may lose more than we gain if I say yes," he warned.

"I need you," she said, knowing that was true in more ways than she'd ever admit to him. "We're all running out of time. The people are demanding answers from us that we don't have. Will you help me?"

"I will do what I can." He stared at the long stretch of road before him for several moments, then leaned back and closed his eyes.

Julia watched the small prairie dogs near the shoulder of the road as they froze motionless, then scurried quickly away as the car sped by. When seconds turned into an endless expanse of minutes, she glanced over at Benjamin. He looked asleep, his eyes darting around beneath his lids as if he were dreaming.

Suddenly he bolted upright, and she jumped, startled. "What? Is something wrong?" she asked.

"I don't know." He wiped the perspiration that had formed on his brow. "I saw a sign. It said, *art*. They were red letters painted on white. I couldn't see the rest. Something was blocking me. Then I felt…overwhelmed. I sensed hatred. And rage. Then all I could see was blackness and within that the glow of two bright green lights like stars, or cat's eyes."

She saw the tension that lined his face. "Are you all right?"

"Yes. But the men will be coming after us now. I felt it."

"They don't know where we are."

"They will. If you want to catch them before they find us, we must hurry."

"Where do I go?"

"Remember the sign."

"Art?" He'd told her he'd only seen part of the word. Slowly an answer came to her. "There's a Mini Mart about five miles ahead. We'll look there first—and hope I'm right."

# Chapter Nine

As she raced down the highway, she glanced at Benjamin. "Have the amulets ever worked against you?"

"No, but I suppose it is possible someone else has asked the spirits that reside within them for protection."

"So what you're saying is that anyone, good or bad, could ask the amulets to work for them?"

"No, not without ritual knowledge. In our religion we don't plead with our gods in hopes they will intercede. We use chants and other means to compel them." He hesitated, considering the implications of what he'd just said. Surely not many outsiders could know a *hataalii*'s chant. "Whatever the explanation, I know I have just encountered a powerful and deadly enemy."

Before they were in plain view of the Mini Mart, she pulled off to the side of the road and parked behind the cover of a small hill. Leaving the car, they approached carefully and studied the building for a moment. "It's closed," she said, keeping her weapon in her hand.

"The side door just opened." Benjamin pointed to two men hauling boxes to a van.

"I'm going for a closer look," she said.

"They know we are here."

She shook her head. "No way. They're loading supplies as calmly as if they were on a weekend shopping trip."

"The man with the amulets can sense us as clearly as I do

him and his companions. Whether he will credit his intuition
or the amulets is not important. The outcome is the same.''

"Okay. That means they could react at any second. I'll call
for backup and then move in. You can cover the rear with the
shotgun until another unit arrives. I'll go around the front, work
my way to the van and catch them next time they come out.''

They both hurried back to the car. He retrieved the shotgun
while she called for backup. Then silently they moved off, each
heading in a different direction. Benjamin crept toward the rear
of the small wooden building. He was searching for the right
vantage point, when he felt a prickly sensation between his
shoulders. Every instinct he possessed warned him of danger.
A certainty far more chilling than any he had ever known filled
him. A carefully laid trap had just been sprung.

He moved cautiously toward the exit doors, then stopped as
a muscular, light-skinned male appeared. He held an elderly
Navajo man before him in a choke hold.

"I know you're out there," the man taunted, although Benjamin knew he couldn't see him. "Come closer. Let's play.''

Benjamin watched the Anglo man carefully, trying to antic-
ipate his next move.

"I'm getting impatient," he goaded. "Don't tempt me. I
might decide to crush the old man's windpipe.''

"Don't harm him. He has done nothing to you." Benjamin
remained where he was, searching quickly to discern any weakness that would help him counter the outlaw.

The man smiled. "Finally. I figured that was the only way
I'd get a response. Now come out, and let's you and I talk.''

"Let the old man go first. He is of no use to you.''

"I don't want him—it's you I'm after. My partner will get
the woman. We know she's around the front. Come out and
join me, and I'll let this guy go. No sense in letting an innocent
man pay for what you started, is there?''

The words cut through Benjamin as he remembered others
who'd died because of him. He unfastened his knife and
slipped it inside his boot. Taking some of the powder from his
medicine pouch, he stepped out from behind the piñon tree

where he'd been hiding. "I am here." He clasped the shotgun loosely in his left hand.

"Leave the shotgun there on the ground and come closer."

Benjamin set it down and walked toward him, stopping right in front of the pair. "Release him."

The Anglo man's smile was a cold, mirthless gesture that signaled his intent. Seeing him tighten his grip on the old man's throat, Benjamin threw the powder into the air. A gust of wind caught the white cloud and hurled it forward directly into their faces.

The Anglo man began to choke and staggered back, releasing his hold on the Navajo. As a coughing spasm shook the white man's body, Benjamin suddenly caught a glimpse of the agate amulet he was wearing from a leather cord around his neck. He wanted to hurl himself against the outlaw and take back what was his. But to yield would leave the Navajo without protection. Moving quickly, he grabbed the elderly man and threw him over his shoulder. The Navajo's cough was less pronounced, but enough to temporarily incapacitate him.

Benjamin ran toward cover, hoping to retrieve the shotgun. He had just placed the elderly man on the ground behind a rock, when a volley of gunfire erupted from the door leading outside. A man bolted out the back, turning to fire several shots that splintered the wood frame around the door. Helping his disabled partner stand up, they ran around the corner of the store toward the van.

Benjamin stared at the back door, waiting for Julia to appear. Fear knifed through him. His brain screamed that she must have been shot, or worse. He ran toward the store, shotgun in hand.

"Benjamin!" Julia yelled from inside, then kicked hard at something blocking her way out. The door flew open and a wooden box shot out. "Stop them!"

Benjamin breathed with relief as she emerged. She was angry—and very much alive. The heart-stopping fear that had held him vanished. As they hurried to the side of the building, the roar of the van's engine filled the air.

Frustration gnawed through him as he scrambled to bring the weapon to his shoulder. He fired, but the shot went wide, kicking up a cloud of dust beside the van. He racked in another shell, but they were already streaking down the highway, out of shotgun range.

Julia raised her pistol, but an approaching car was in the line of fire. She had glanced at the van's license plate, but she had only seen the last three letters. She repeated the letters out loud, then fished out a small notebook from her pocket and wrote them down. She then turned her attention to the man Benjamin had rescued and walked over to his side. "Sir, do you know those men?"

The dusty, frightened man shook his head and slowly stood up. "I did nothing wrong," he said.

"Relax and catch your breath, sir. It's okay now. You're safe."

Spotting two tribal units pulling up from the opposite direction, Julia hurried to meet them. She filled them in quickly, giving them the partial license-plate number she'd managed to get and general descriptions of the men. The patrol cars were soon rocketing down the highway, sirens screaming.

In a few minutes, other police vehicles would join the pursuit. As soon as a unit arrived to process the crime scene at the Mini Mart, she would decide if she wanted to join the chase. In the meantime, there was work for her to do here. She returned to where Benjamin and the elderly man stood.

"Can you tell us what happened, sir?" she asked him gently.

"I walked here like I always do on Fridays. The owner, Shirley Pete, closes early, but she leaves a box of groceries for me by the back door. When I came today, those men were here. They laughed and threw my food all over the ground. I tried to pick the cans back up so I could leave, but they kept knocking them out of my hands."

"How long have you been here?"

The man shrugged. "Not long. I just wanted to get my groceries, then go back to my trailer." Together they gathered the cans of vegetables and fruit that lay on the ground near the back door, then placed them back in the box. "I'm going now," the man announced when he had everything.

"Please stay a bit longer. I'd like to ask you a few more questions. Can you tell me anything else about the men? For instance, did they mention where they came from, or where they were going?"

The man ambled away slowly, talking as he walked. "No, but one said they had a long drive ahead of them. He wanted to leave." He stopped and glanced back at Benjamin. "I just remembered. The man wearing the amulet around his neck was acting very strange. He warned his friend that you'd be coming. He kept staring down the highway waiting, though you were nowhere in sight." He started walking away. "If you need me, just come to my trailer. Everyone knows where Charlie Begay lives."

As she walked inside the store, she saw the case of sodas one of the men had started to load. He'd dropped it after spotting her through the side window. Some cans had burst open, saturating everything around. With a bit of luck, they'd still be able to lift some fingerprints and verify at least one of the names Stillwell had given them.

As the other officers arrived at the scene, she tried to force her mind to stay alert and focused. Exhaustion worked against her, clouding her thinking.

Pete Bowman appeared at the entrance and walked across the room to join her. "Our men lost track of the van in Shiprock, but we have an idea what area they're in, and we're concentrating our search there."

"Good. Keep me posted on their progress, please."

"We've also found some bullets imbedded in the refrigeration unit. Maybe that'll give us something we can use."

"If they're not from my own pistol," she answered wearily.

Bowman studied her speculatively. "When's the last time you had any sleep?"

"A lifetime ago." Julia smiled ruefully. "But that's what I'll be doing as soon as I finish here. I've got a room in a motel this side of Shiprock, and I'm going to hole up for the next few hours."

"Seems to me, you'll need more than that. Won't do anyone any good if you're so tired you start getting sloppy."

She started to protest, mostly out of habit. She didn't like anyone telling her what the extent of her capabilities were, but then she relented. "You've got a point," she conceded. Julia started walking to her car with Benjamin, then stopped and turned her head. "Call me if anything important comes up."

"If that's what you want."

As they drove to the motel, she glanced at Benjamin furtively. "You'll need a room, too. When was the last time *you* had a good rest?"

A haunted expression appeared in his eyes at first, but then he managed a weak smile. "Let us say it seems like forever. But don't concern yourself about me. I am used to sleeping under the stars."

"It'll be under the sun right now. I bet it's ninety-five degrees, and there's very little shade outside the motel," she reminded him.

"I can look after myself," he answered.

Ten minutes later, they pulled into the dusty parking lot that surrounded a simple, L-shaped, one-story stucco building. As far as motels went, this was definitely the generic model. Yet at the moment, a soft bed and clean sheets were as tempting to her as a glass of water would be to a man dying of thirst.

SHE GLANCED AT BENJAMIN. Reaching into her purse, she pulled out several bills. "Here. Get yourself a room."

"No. Keep your greenbacks."

She blinked. "Why?"

"We made an agreement to work together. I have done nothing that requires payment from you."

"Don't worry about the money. You need a place of your own to stay. We'll square it later."

"No. I will remain outside and keep watch while you sleep. Later, after I have done this, I will accept your money."

"You helped me back at the Mini Mart and saved that poor man," she protested. "You were willing to trade for clothing after the incident with the truck and the bear. How's this any different?"

"At that time, I was still trying to demonstrate that we could work together. We hadn't formed a partnership yet. Now that we have, I may only ask for payment when I do something that goes beyond what it is your right to expect."

Julia yawned, not bothering to try and hide the action. "I'm so tired, all I want is some sleep. Don't be difficult, okay?"

"Go. I will be nearby. You don't have to sacrifice your modesty or your privacy."

She started to get out, then stopped. She had considered letting him bake in the car, but it would have been like sitting in a hot oven. She wouldn't be able to stand the guilt. "Look, come inside the room with me. It's air-conditioned and much more pleasant than the heat out here. You can take the easy chair—the bed's mine."

Minutes later, she was inside the tiny room, glad for the arctic temperature. It felt good, almost perfect. The curtains were only open a crack, and the near darkness reminded her of how tired she was.

He shuddered. "It's like a January morning in here! Shall I open the window and turn that machine off?"

"If you do, I'll break your fingers," she murmured sweetly, then lay back, fully clothed, on the bed. Julia pulled both pillows out from under the bedspread and tossed one toward Benjamin. "If you want to sleep, go ahead. No one's coming after us here." She unsnapped her holster and handgun from her belt and placed both under her pillow.

Curling up comfortably, she closed her eyes. Sensing him in the darkened room with her made it impossible for her to relax. She was exhausted, yet her body tingled with awareness, refusing to let her sleep. She pushed back the thought, chiding herself for acting like a hormone-driven teenager.

With great effort, she forced him from her mind. The whir of the air conditioner was the only sound in the room, and its rhythm served to help her unwind. She drifted into a pleasant void, but then, before she could surrender completely to the dark, a vague uneasiness began to creep through her. She fought against it, frustrated and annoyed, wanting desperately to sleep. Yet it persisted.

Feeling the air stir against her skin, she opened her eyes. She could see Benjamin's outline on the chair near the window. She rolled over to her left side, assuring herself that all was well. As she repositioned the pillow beneath her head, she caught a glimpse of a strange, humpbacked figure approaching her bed.

Julia swept the pistol out from under her pillow and jack-knifed to a sitting position. "Don't move!" she ordered. She switched on the nightstand light and saw Benjamin standing in front of her, holding a blanket in his hands.

"Woman, you make it very difficult for anyone to take care of you. Why aren't you asleep?"

She glanced over at the chair near the window. Two blankets and the other pillow lay in a bundle there. "What the heck do you think you're doing?"

"I was bringing a blanket to you. You may like freezing temperatures, but I am certain your body will not." He placed the blanket next to her on the bed. "I made no sound. How did you hear me?"

She wasn't going to admit that having him near had made her incredibly restless. She opted for a good offensive instead. "Are you trying to get me to shoot you? When I'm on a case I sleep very lightly. If you try to sneak up on me, you're going to get hurt."

"You would not harm me," he answered confidently.

"Not on purpose."

"I have watched you as a warrior. You never shoot offhand. You always make certain the enemy is your target."

She sighed. "Do you truly want to do a service for me?" She placed the pistol back inside the holster, then underneath the pillow again.

"Yes, of course. Whatever you need."

"Fine," she picked up the telephone. "I'm getting you a room. And if you have any survival instincts at all, you won't argue with me."

Benjamin opened his mouth as if to protest, then snapped it shut again. He took a deep breath, then slowly let it out again. "Woman, the gods must have been furious with me the day they created you!"

TWENTY MINUTES LATER, Julia lay in her bed listening to Benjamin move about in the room next to hers. Only one thin wall separated them. She stared at the shadows that dappled the ceiling, wondering if he was undressed. The cool sheets brushing against her naked skin fueled her wildly misbehaving imagination.

Frustrated, Julia got up and drew the curtains even tighter, until absolutely no light filtered through. She then returned to bed, closed her eyes, and pulled the covers over her. Minutes ticked by. Still, sleep eluded her.

Ten minutes later, muttering an oath, she tossed the covers aside, picked up her jeans from the floor and got dressed. She'd fill out a report, a boring task that needed to be done, then get some sleep. It was probably better to do that now, anyway, while everything was still fresh in her mind. In fact, that was probably what was bothering her. She hated to leave things undone. Her restlessness had nothing whatsoever to do with Benjamin.

Picking up her hand-held radio, she went out to her vehicle to retrieve the proper forms. As she started to unlock the trunk, she heard an emergency broadcast going out.

The all-points bulletin stated that a tribal patrolman had just been stabbed. After he'd reported his position, the wounded officer's radio had gone dead. As she heard the location, a burst of adrenaline revitalized her. He was just down the road!

Without hesitation, she slammed the trunk and ran to the driver's seat. "My ETA is less than two minutes," she transmitted as she started the engine. "I'm on my way!"

Her tires spun in the gravel, then squealed as she struck hard pavement. Julia sped down the straight stretch of asphalt away from the motel, then slowed, seeing the road sign landmark the dispatcher had mentioned. There was no police car or any other vehicle visible now, but from the tire tracks on the road, it was clear someone had left in a hurry. She drove slowly along the shoulder. Seconds later, she spotted a prone figure partially hidden in the brush near the side of the road.

She grabbed the microphone and made a quick report as she parked. Then, feeling the butt of her handgun for assurance, she approached slowly. The uniformed officer lay still, but his chest, stained red, was moving. At least he was alive.

As she crouched next to him, his lips moved. Trying to hear what he was saying, she bent over him.

Without warning something crashed down against her skull. Stars exploded in front of her eyes, and then the brightness gave way to an inky blackness that sucked her in.

## Chapter Ten

Benjamin moved around restlessly. He didn't understand how she could stand the frigid temperature inside her room. He had pressed all the buttons on his machine, until he found a way to make it stop. Then he'd opened the window, much more at home with the heat. But it was a different kind of heat that made him pace continuously. His hunger for the woman was like a steady, never ending fire coursing through his veins.

He walked naked around the room, his body taut as he thought of her. She was so close. He pressed his palm against the wall that separated them. "You are safe from me," he whispered. "I *will not* take what can never be mine." He tried to force himself to accept it, but desire clawed at him with an intensity he could barely suppress. His fingers coiled into a tight fist.

He moved to the bed and lay down. Then, suddenly, he heard her door squeak open. Quickly, he dressed and raced outside, but he was too late. He could see her car clearly, speeding away from him in the hot afternoon sun. Then, before she had even traveled out of sight, she unexpectedly slowed down and came to a halt. Something was wrong.

He was already running toward her when he saw her step away from her car and crouch near the side of the road. Suddenly, a man appeared from behind a boulder, creeping toward her. Fear seized him. He was too far away to even shout an effective warning.

A breath later, he saw her topple to the ground. Hatred for the man who had hurt her gave him energy he hadn't known he possessed. He raced as if Wind itself carried him.

Someone else came out from behind cover, and together the men carried her off into the brush, out of sight. Fear gripped him as he struggled to see ahead. Then a pickup appeared, tumbleweeds falling off as it moved out of an arroyo onto the road. Leaving a thick cloud of dust behind, it disappeared down the highway.

A rage as black as a moonless night gripped him. "No. I will *not* allow her to be taken from me, too!" he yelled, railing against the gods he had honored.

Hearing a vehicle approaching from behind him on the highway, he ran to the middle of the road and waved until it stopped. The elderly man motioned toward the other door. "I'll give you a ride, Nephew. Where do you need to go in such a hurry?"

"There is trouble, Uncle. I need to catch the men in that pickup ahead."

"You want me to follow that car?" When Benjamin nodded, he let out a whoop. "I've always wanted someone to say that to me." As Benjamin slammed the door shut, the man stomped down hard on the accelerator.

The small car shot forward. Benjamin gripped the sides of his seat as the desert became nothing more than a blur going past his window. He'd never traveled at this speed, quicker than a hawk. But this was exactly what he wanted. The pickup was a long way ahead, barely visible now. The moments passed, but the gap between them narrowed only slightly.

"Sorry my car can't go any faster," the elderly man warned, glancing over at him.

Before he could answer, the distant truck slowed and turned down a dirt trail. Benjamin could see it led to a small house. Beyond that was the river. "Leave me by that road, but out of sight from the building. Then go back and find the tribal police. Tell them Benjamin Two Eagle said the FBI woman agent has been kidnapped, and I am going to get her back."

"I heard about you, Uncle," the man said, no longer willing to call him Nephew. "My brother is Daniel Brownhat, the Singer. He said you and I would meet. He told me to warn you to choose well. Every decision you make will have consequences."

Benjamin left the vehicle, closing the door quietly. "I will remember. Tell your brother I count him as a friend."

As the car turned back in the direction they'd come from, Benjamin ran toward the small house and the river. He was certain Julia lived—he could feel it. But with that knowledge also came the certainty that she was in mortal danger. He stayed in the cover offered by brush as he approached the dwelling. Then, getting as close as he could, he remained still to listen near a window.

"The boss told us to bring her here, tie her up, and then leave. Now let's go," said a voice from inside the house.

"What the hell's your rush? It's better if we stay low for a while. Let's wait until she comes out of it. Maybe we can find out what she knows."

"You think she'll tell you anything you can use, or even the truth? Get serious! Let's stick to the plan. We'll use her as a hostage to keep the police occupied."

"That's fine with me, but I don't see why we couldn't have a little bit of fun, too. Did you get a real good look at her? I've got plans for when she wakes up."

Benjamin gripped his knife tightly. He would kill the man for what he intended to do. As he crept forward, he remembered Brownhat's warning. The death of the white man would serve no purpose now unless it enabled him to rescue Julia.

Swallowing back his anger, Benjamin reached into his deer-skin medicine pouch. As his fingers touched the powder, he chanted softly. Slowly, the mixture became dense and warm to the touch. Satisfied, he advanced noiselessly, knife in one hand, powder in the other. He knew he might not leave the cabin uninjured. But he also knew that he could and would protect the woman. It was a good trade.

Purpose—his life had been defined by it. His best course

was to be so bold it would take the men inside completely by surprise. He braced himself for action, his body poised in anticipation of violence. It was time. If he'd guessed right, he'd live to see the next sunrise.

He came quickly around the building's corner and silently walked through the cabin's open front door. The two men inside did not look up until he was already in the center of the room.

"What the—" One of the men stepped forward to block his path, and the other tall Anglo spun, reaching for his pistol.

Before either could complete his move, Benjamin tossed the powder into the air, crying out loudly. For a moment, light flared hot and bright, as if the sun had found its way into the darkened cabin. Benjamin slashed out with his knife, and the man in his path drew back with a scream. Then the brightness receded, leaving only a gray darkness.

He heard a curse to his right. "I can't see!"

"You don't want to!" came the reply from the opposite side of the room. "There's something in here. It's some kind of animal, and it's cut me real bad. I can't make it out—it keeps moving." Then the man screamed again.

"What the hell *are* those things?" the other snapped back, then howled in pain.

Benjamin went to the door across from him. He sensed Julia's presence in there as clearly as if he'd seen her. Discovering the door was locked, he kicked it off its hinges.

Julia lay on the floor, unconscious, her hands and feet tied. Choking back his rage, he stooped and gathered her into his arms. There wasn't much time left—the illusions were fading. They'd realize what was happening and come after him soon.

As he reached the door, Benjamin saw the tall Anglo blocking his escape route. The gun in the man's hand was wavering, and the glaze in his eyes confirmed that he was still blinded. But if he fired now, Julia would be the first to be struck.

Julia moaned as she slowly regained consciousness. Hearing her, their enemy turned toward them. With her in his arms, Benjamin knew he had only one option. Spinning around so

# GET FREE BOOKS and a FREE GIFT
## WHEN YOU PLAY THE...

## SLOT MACHINE GAME!

*Just scratch off the silver box with a coin. Then check below to see the gifts you get!*

# YES! I have scratched off the silver box. Please send me the 2 free Silhouette Intimate Moments® books and gift for which I qualify. I understand I am under no obligation to purchase any books, as explained on the back of this card.

**DETACH AND MAIL CARD TODAY!**

**345 SDL DU3X**          **245 SDL DU3Y**

FIRST NAME                     LAST NAME

ADDRESS

APT.#          CITY

STATE / PROV.          ZIP / POSTAL CODE

| 7 | 7 | 7 | **Worth TWO FREE BOOKS plus a BONUS Mystery Gift!** |
| 🍒 | 🍒 | 🍒 | **Worth TWO FREE BOOKS!** |
| ♣ | ♣ | ♣ | **Worth ONE FREE BOOK!** |
| 🔔 | 🔔 | 🍒 | **TRY AGAIN!** |

*Visit us online at www.eHarlequin.com*

(S-IMB-06/03)

## The Silhouette Reader Service™ — Here's how it works:

Accepting your 2 free books and gift places you under no obligation to buy anything. You may keep the books and gift and return the shipping statement marked "cancel." If you do not cancel, about a month later we'll send you 6 additional books and bill you just $3.99 each in the U.S., or $4.74 each in Canada, plus 25¢ shipping & handling per book and applicable taxes if any.* That's the complete price and — compared to cover prices of $4.75 each in the U.S. and $5.75 each in Canada — it's quite a bargain! You may cancel at any time, but if you choose to continue, every month we'll send you 6 more books, which you may either purchase at the discount price or return to us and cancel your subscription. *Terms and prices subject to change without notice. Sales tax applicable in N.Y. Canadian residents will be charged applicable provincial taxes and GST. Credit or debit balances in a customer's account(s) may be offset by any other outstanding balance owed by or to the customer.

he could shield her with his own body, he kicked out behind him. The blast rang out a second before the weapon clattered to the floor.

He felt the bullet slam into his back, and then heat flared through him. Before pain could fill his mind, he turned and ran directly at the blinded man, knocking him to the ground.

Julia opened her eyes as he stumbled out of the house into the sunlight. The second man was to one side of the door, down on his knees, desperately trying to bandage a mangled hand with his shirt. He never even glanced up as they ran past.

"You've been hit!" Julia felt the warmth of his blood soaking through her blouse. "Put me down. I'm not hurt," she managed in a choked voice.

"For once, don't argue with me!" He forced himself to run slowly away from the house, despite the cold, numbing sensation passing down his arm. He'd head toward the river and seek cover there among the tall reeds.

"Put me down," she ordered gently, "or we'll never make it."

He did as she asked, staring at the ground. He was leaving a trail of blood and dragging footprints a blind man could follow. "We have one advantage left. They will need more time before they regain their senses. The power of the medicine will continue to work on them for just a bit longer, and the man outside will have to bind his wound."

Benjamin's own shirt was soaked with blood. Her heart constricted as she realized what he'd done. "You stopped the bullet that was meant for me."

He tried to continue running, but fell to his knees. Blood dripped off his elbow to the sand. "But now I am only slowing you down. Run away from here as fast as you can and make for the river."

"If you weren't injured already, I'd kick you in the shin," she snapped. "I don't sell out my partners. Now do us both a favor and be quiet." She pulled her shirt out of her jeans, took his knife and cut a long strip from the bottom. She loosened his shirt and exposed the wound. It took all her willpower to

suppress a gasp. His flesh had been ripped and burned, expos-
ing muscle and a mass of bloody tissue. Since the bullet hadn't
gone through him, she could only surmise it had shattered bone
and that had slowed it down. Gingerly, she placed the makeshift bandage over the wound below his shoulder.

"You can't stay...."

"Quiet," she ordered briskly. Pulling his good arm around
her shoulder, she helped him to his feet. "Now let's get moving."

He weighed more than she'd expected, but she was determined not to let him know that. Forced to maintain a slow
pace, she chose their path carefully, moving through the tall
brush toward the sound of the river. Salt cedar grew in thick
clusters that made it difficult to see more than twenty feet
ahead.

She stopped five minutes later to check his wound. The cloth
she'd placed over it had soaked through, turning a deep crimson. "How's your breathing?"

"It didn't pierce the lung. I know gunshot wounds—this
isn't mortal, just painful. But the bleeding must be stopped."
He reached into his medicine pouch with his good arm and
pulled out a handful of dried leaves. "Bind these over the
wound."

As she took them, the leaves all but crumbled in her hand.
"What is this?" She carefully held on to the brittle pieces,
placing them directly over the wound and holding them in
place with a new strip of cloth from her shirt.

"It's a remedy I've used from time to time to slow the flow
of blood. The leaves also protect against fever."

"An astringent plant of some sort?"

"It is a plant and it works. That is all I can tell you." He
struggled to stand without her help. "Keep going. I will be
right behind you."

"Nice try," she countered.

He made an exasperated noise. "Look at the trail we're leaving! Whenever a branch touches my bandage, I mark the way
for them in blood."

"I'm still not leaving you behind. Let's go into the shallow water. That'll wash away our footprints and you won't be walking directly through the brush."

"I'm beginning to see why you never married," he grumbled.

"What's that supposed to mean?"

"You're so stubborn. You would drive any man looking after you into an asylum."

"At the moment you're the one who needs care. Will you try to be more cooperative?"

They reached the river minutes later. They could hear the men behind them shouting back and forth while continuing to narrow the gap between them. She tried to hurry and steady Benjamin at the same time, but the river bottom was slippery because of mud-coated rocks along the shoreline. "They're getting too close. We're going to have to change our tactics."

"What do you have in mind?"

"I'm going to keep holding on to you, but we're going straight out into the deeper water. We can float downstream with the current and let the river carry us away from them. Can you manage it?"

"Yes, probably better than what we are doing now."

"Good, then let's go."

She held on to his hand and stepped off the sandbar they were on, into the main channel. The current was gentle and they floated easily. Worried, she kept a constant eye on Benjamin. "You okay?" she called out softly. "I forgot to make sure you could swim."

"I am fine, or will be," he said in a taut voice. "I have been through worse."

She believed that, without question. The minutes seemed endless, but she soon realized they were outdistancing the men. Then, from somewhere ahead, she began to hear voices and the sounds of car doors slamming. Through a clearing in the thicket of brush that bordered the river, she spotted a large building ahead. Cars were in the parking lot of what she assumed was either a community center or church.

She swam toward the wide, sandy bank, pulling Benjamin along with her. He was pale and weak, and the lines around his mouth and eyes had deepened, but, otherwise, he seemed to be holding up. She supported his weight as they hiked the short distance to safety.

A few minutes later they staggered to the entrance of the building. A Navajo man standing near the door came toward them quickly. "What happened, Uncle?" he asked, moving to Benjamin's side and helping support him.

"Just a little accident," he muttered vaguely as the man brought them into the meeting hall.

Julia led Benjamin to a chair, then asked the man to call an ambulance. As she glanced up and looked at the people that had gathered around, she saw Chief Roanhorse. His presence took her by surprise. She'd come for help, but she'd never expected to be so lucky as to find him here.

People left their folding chairs and brought jackets and shawls to warm her, but then left her alone. They quickly moved to Benjamin's side, doing their best to take care of him.

Roanhorse took her aside. "What in the heck happened?"

Shivering and dripping wet in the air-conditioned room, she filled him in, detailing the emergency that had started the incident.

"No such call went out," the chief answered flatly. "There was a question about a response you sent in, but we were unable to raise you on the radio."

"That means they have a police-band radio and know what frequency to use to get hold of me."

"And they had a tribal uniform," he added.

"Yes, but dozens of explanations could account for that." Before she could say more, the man who'd met them at the door joined them.

"Help is on its way." As he glanced at her, his eyes filled with distrust and open hostility.

His reaction took her aback. She'd done nothing to deserve it. As she looked at the others, she realized they were blaming her for not protecting Benjamin.

As the man moved back to check on Benjamin, the chief prodded her. "Can you ID them?"

"The one pretending to be the wounded cop was Hispanic, about five foot seven and one hundred and seventy pounds. The other one was Anglo, brown hair, tall and thin. I'd like all the photographs you gathered on that list of suspected members I gave you. Maybe I'll be able to pick them out from that."

"Fine. I'll also send a team over to check out the place you mentioned."

Out of the corner of her eye, she saw the circle of people moving away from Benjamin. Afraid, Julia crossed the room quickly, but before she could reach his side, an elderly woman stepped in her path.

"Do not disturb him now," she said, giving Julia a disapproving look.

Benjamin's eyes were closed, and his breathing barely audible beneath the collection of jackets and sweaters he'd been wrapped in. Fear shot through her and her heart began to hammer, thinking he might be going into shock, or dying.

Julia started to walk around the woman, but another came up, preventing her from getting any closer. "He needs help," Julia said, trying to edge past them.

"He *is* getting help—from himself and our ways. Let him finish what he started. He has stopped the bleeding. Now he has to heal inside."

"He took a round…he was shot," she explained. Before she could find a way of saying that only medical help could make a difference now, the paramedics arrived.

Everyone stepped aside, giving them room, but the two elderly women refused to give ground, even though two of the paramedics were Navajos. "He needs one of our Singers, not this," the smallest of the two maintained.

"He can have both, if he chooses it," Chief Roanhorse said, opening the way for the medical team.

The Anglo medic reached Benjamin first. Working fast, he cut the shirt off Benjamin's back. "What's this stuff?" he asked, removing the makeshift bandage and gently brushing what remained of the leaf fragments away.

"He asked me to place those herbs on the wound," Julia answered.

The medic cleaned the area carefully. "You're a lucky man," he told Benjamin, whose eyes had remained closed. "The wound isn't very deep. I can see the slug you took."

Julia's eyebrows knitted together in confusion. "Not very deep?" she repeated dully, trying to angle around. Was he trying to reassure the patient? She couldn't get a clear look, however, with the medical team blocking her.

"It's not bad at all," one of the Navajo medics insisted, as he prepared a fresh dressing. "I think half of the mess on his clothes came from the blood mixing with water. The stain spread."

She knew better. She'd seen the wound and the blood. Maybe the herb was more powerful than she'd suspected. "He seems so still," she said. Benjamin's breathing was calm, but shallow.

"I could shake him awake, but I think it best not to. He's withdrawn—meditating, to use a simpler term. That'll help him control any pain. He'll be fine," the Anglo medic assured.

Julia watched, lost in thought, as they placed Benjamin on a stretcher and took him away. The mind was a powerful tool, she knew that. Holy men in Eastern cultures could walk on burning coals without any injuries. Other mystics were able to significantly alter body temperature, blood pressure and respiration.

What Benjamin had done shouldn't have surprised her. Yet it did, because his extraordinary gifts came in a package that was so thoroughly human. She remembered when he'd held her in his arms. The memory of his kiss still made her burn and tingle with need. A woman wanted a man whose loyalty and strength she could depend on. Benjamin could be as tough as tempered steel, and then turn around and be as gentle as a soft breeze, if that's what the woman in her needed from him.

He had awakened a side of her she'd never even known existed. He was everything she'd ever wanted in a man, and more.

"You want to ride with me?" Roanhorse asked, interrupting her thoughts.

"I'd appreciate that," she answered.

As they got underway, she felt a vague sense of uneasiness. "What kind of meeting hall was that back there?"

He hesitated. "It's a chapter house. Local government and public concerns are aired there. It's closed to outsiders." He took a deep breath. "You might find it interesting to know that the gang of robbers roaming the reservation was the scheduled topic tonight."

"And my arrival interrupted it?" Seeing him nod, she continued. "Well, your next meeting should be interesting," she commented pensively. "At least I kept things on topic."

"I want to ask you something," Roanhorse said after a moment. "You've spent a lot of time around Two Eagle. What do you make of him? Does he seem like an ordinary person to you?"

"No," she answered softly. "*Ordinary* isn't a word I'd ever use to describe him." She paused, struggling to find the right words. "I'd say he's an extraordinary man caught in a gigantic tug-of-war between his responsibilities and his own personal dreams."

"That's very close to what Daniel Brownhat said," Chief Roanhorse answered thoughtfully.

Julia sat up abruptly. "There's my car! It's still where I left it."

Roanhorse pulled off the highway. Weapon in hand, he walked toward the vehicle. He moved slowly, his eyes darting everywhere. Julia, unarmed, stayed with him, approaching from the passenger's side until she could get a clear look inside.

"Nothing's been touched," she said, studying the papers on the floor and the keys that still dangled from the ignition. Taking the keys, she retrieved a spare pistol and holster she had hidden in the trunk in case of emergencies.

Moments later, a patrol car came speeding down the road. The officer pulled up beside the chief's car and got out.

"Thought you might be down this way, Chief. I heard from John Brownhat that there was trouble at Ernest Yazzie's old house. Henderson Blueeyes and I got over there as fast as we could, then we heard your call over the radio. Henderson's still checking the scene now."

"What did you find, Rudy?"

"At least four people had been there. One set of tracks was small, probably a woman's. There were signs of a fight in the house, and a lot of blood inside and out. A big vehicle with oversized tires, most likely a pickup, had been there. From the way the rear end fishtailed around the road, they must have taken off in quite a hurry."

"Like they'd realized we'd received help and would soon come after them," she mused, new questions forming in her mind. The chief's presence at a meeting so near where Benjamin and she had almost met their death made her uneasy. And how convenient that the men had made such an immediate and successful escape. Nagging suspicions crowded at the edges of her mind.

"Why don't you leave your car here for now," Roanhorse suggested. "My men can deliver it to you later. You can continue on to the hospital with me. I'll be glad to drop you off at the motel after you check on Two Eagle. You really look too tired to drive."

"You won't be going to the house to oversee the search for more evidence?" asked Julia.

"Not necessary. My men know what they're doing. I trust them," he said, adding pointedly, "and they trust me."

"I'm sure," she replied in a toneless voice.

The chief studied her in silence for a long moment. "You don't have to worry about being left without transportation. My men will have the car waiting by the time we reach the motel."

His offer to drive would have been tempting, if she could have been sure of him. As it was, she'd be making it too easy for him to plant a listening device or homing beacon in her car. And if he was involved, that would be precisely what he'd do.

"Thanks, but no. I'll take my car. I'm still keyed up and there's no chance I'll doze off at the wheel."

He looked at her, unconvinced, but agreed with a shrug. "Follow me, then."

As they set out, the chief decided to use his siren. She wasn't sure whether it was out of deference to her, or to make sure she stayed awake.

It was almost sunset by the time they reached the hospital near the north end of Shiprock. The moment she walked inside, people turned to stare. She didn't blame them. Bits of algae and mud were tangled in her hair, or had fallen off onto her shoulders as it dried. Her blouse was torn and stained and had begun to ravel into a million tiny threads.

Trying not to imagine how she must look to others, she went directly to the information desk. Before she could ask the nurse any questions, Benjamin came out. The green hospital shirt he wore hung open, revealing a bandage that went around his chest and over his shoulder. Yet, despite that, he looked fit and spectacularly masculine. His smooth copper-colored skin, the hard muscles on his chest and his warriorlike strength of spirit sent separate impacts reverberating all through her body.

It was then, she realized, that no matter what this handsome man went through, the worst he would look was appreciably rumpled. She, on the other hand, usually ended up resembling something out of a horror movie. "They're releasing you?" she managed at last.

"There is no need to keep me."

"He's right." A Navajo woman in her late fifties, wearing a white lab coat, came out of the examining room. The tag over the breast pocket read Dr. Bernadette Kodaseet. "His wound was mostly a scratch. The slug practically fell out on its own."

Roanhorse glanced at Julia, letting her know with that one look that *he* knew differently, too. Julia remained silent. There seemed little need to point it out to the doctor.

"Make sure the bandage over the wound stays clean," Kodaseet told Benjamin. "Other than that, you're in good shape."

"You're not serious!" Julia blurted. "He was *shot* with a large-caliber pistol." She stared at the doctor.

"I've given him a shot of antibiotics. There's no need for concern. I figure that either the shot lost all its energy by ricocheting off something before it struck him, or the gunman was very far away."

She started to assure the doctor it had been neither, then changed her mind. What good would it do?

"Looks like you've got a more immediate problem," the doctor said, looking down at Julia's wrists. "Those small cuts are getting infected."

She stifled a groan. This was like adding insult to injury. He'd been shot and there was "no need for concern." She'd suffered nothing more than chafed wrists, and *she* was the one with the problem! Sometimes fate had a very black sense of humor. At least no one from the Bureau was around. If they'd heard the doctor, the teasing would never have stopped.

Julia emerged from an examination room several minutes later. Her cuts, which had been cleaned and disinfected, stung more than ever.

"You'll be going back to the motel to get some sleep now?" Roanhorse asked.

It had been more than a hint, but less than an order. She smiled. "Yeah, I'm going off duty for a while."

He nodded in approval. "Good."

She glanced at Benjamin. "Jeez, you're tough on clothes! Those were practically new," she teased with a smile. "Guess it's time to negotiate again."

Just then a young orderly came up and held out a shirt and a new pair of jeans. "We figured you'd need these, Uncle. Please accept this token from the staff for fighting the gang of *bilagáana* thieves."

Benjamin took them with a grateful smile. "My contribution has been small, but thanks to you and the others."

Julia walked outside with Benjamin. So much for a little fun negotiating. Word about him was sure spreading fast. She found herself a bit envious of the respect everyone accorded him. She didn't begrudge it, but it would have been nice if people on the reservation weren't quite so negative about federal agents.

"You make friends everywhere you go," she observed with a thin smile.

"And you feel all you make are enemies?" he asked, completing her unspoken thought.

She shrugged. "Face it. My inability to solve this case fast isn't endearing me to anyone," she answered.

"You will find answers soon. I feel it."

Julia drove directly to the motel, but it was almost dark by the time they arrived.

"I'm not sure I should let you out of my sight," he said slowly. "Last time we separated, it didn't benefit either of us." He walked Julia to her door.

She knew there was probably an answer that would counter his argument, but at the moment she was too tired to think of one. "You're in no shape to sleep in a chair, and I sure as heck am not about to try it."

"We can share the bed."

She choked. "No way. Go to your own room."

"Give me your word that you won't try to leave without me if there's another problem."

She forced herself to meet his eyes. His gaze burned with an intensity that made her blood turn to fire. She suddenly became acutely and achingly aware of everything about him, from his hard, masculine body to the warmth of his skin. She fought the impulse to step into his arms, though she desperately wanted to be held by him, to feel his heart pounding against her. With a great burst of willpower, she looked away. "I won't leave without telling you."

"No. Don't leave without me at all. Remember what happened before. You could have used my help then. I needed to be there for you, too," he admitted.

She felt his desire and his vulnerability weaving itself around her heart. A jolt of naked longing ran through her. She yearned to invite him inside her room, but the words wouldn't come.

He brushed his palm against her cheek. "We need each other, *be'at'ééd*."

"What does that mean?"

He smiled. "My sweetheart or darling."

His whisper was like silk against her skin. If she didn't go inside the room now, she'd never find the strength to send him away. "I have to get some rest," she said with a sigh.

"We both do," he agreed quietly. "Sleep well."

She entered her empty room and closed the door. Her thoughts were all obscured, as if they'd become engulfed by a thick fog. But no amount of exhaustion could shield her from the sudden ache of loneliness that enveloped her. A shiver of desire cascaded down her body as she thought of him alone, in the room next to hers.

She stripped slowly, allowing her clothes to fall to the floor in a tangled heap. She imagined him looking at her, wanting her as much as she did him. She closed her eyes, all her senses attuned to the muted sounds Benjamin made as he moved around his room.

She'd gone crazy—there was no doubt about it. She exhaled softly and crawled between the cool sheets. She was exhausted, and her head ached from where she'd been struck only a few hours earlier. Yet instead of wanting sleep, all she felt was an acute longing to seduce Benjamin or be seduced by him.

She twisted and turned restlessly. Then she heard the soft song that seemed to flow through the walls, touching and soothing her. She could almost feel Benjamin's arms wrapped tightly around her.

She surrendered to the golden circle of warmth the soft melody spun out of the darkness that surrounded her, and the throbbing in her head faded away. Then she greeted the yawning void, and knew nothing more.

# Chapter Eleven

Julia emerged from her room after sunrise. She felt fully rested and eager to tackle the case. Even the headache and muscle soreness she'd expected to experience after yesterday's ordeal were absent. As she stepped out onto the porch, she saw Benjamin standing in the sun. He mouthed some words she couldn't hear, then released something in his hand.

As he turned around and saw her, a smile, bright and dazzling, lit up his face. The simple gesture stole her breath away and made her pulse race. She felt as silly as a teenager, but knew it was useless to chide herself for the response.

She waited for him to join her. "What were you doing?"

"It's a prayer to the new day," he explained. "Pollen is life, and we scatter it as a blessing."

She was about to ask more when two tribal police vehicles pulled up in a hurry, sliding to a stop in the gravel. Bowman emerged from the lead unit, excitement gleaming in his eyes.

"We're on our way south. There's some trouble at the Shiprock airstrip that may or may not be connected to the gang," he said, striding up to her.

"What's going on?"

"One of our tribal council members has a small airplane he flies around the rez. He called a local gas station that keeps a supply of aviation fuel on hand, and spoke a few words in Navajo to the attendant. He said he was being held at gunpoint by a *bilagáana*. The attendant called us. He wasn't sure whether to deliver the fuel or not."

"Hijacking an airplane. That's certainly one way to avoid the roadblocks. I'll bet this *is* connected to the gang," Julia said. "That's why you stopped here, isn't it?"

"The thought occurred to me." He smiled.

"Then let's get things rolling." She motioned Benjamin and a tribal sergeant over, then continued. "Have the station attendant meet us at eight o'clock someplace away from the airstrip. You can pick a suitable spot," she told Bowman. "We'll make the final arrangements then."

"West side of the bridge," Bowman said, giving the tribal sergeant a nod. The man went to his car and picked up the mike. As he relayed instructions, Bowman glanced at Julia. "Now what?"

"I'll give you the rest of my plan when we meet that fuel truck. I need to work out a few things in my head."

Julia hurried to her car with Benjamin. Minutes later they were following Bowman down the road. As they approached the San Juan River Bridge, they turned off the highway onto a dirt field and parked there. She and Benjamin got out of the car minutes before the red fuel truck pulled up to where they were waiting. Everyone gathered beside it.

"I'm going to drive the truck in myself," Julia informed the group.

"That would be unwise," Benjamin answered. "If the gang is involved, you will be recognized, even if you wear a disguise."

"He's right," Bowman agreed. "I'll drive the truck."

She considered it. "We're going to need two people in that truck. One to hold the hijacker's attention and protect the hostage, while the other takes the kidnapper out. I'm small. I'll ride on the floor of the truck," she said, looking at Bowman. "While you distract the hijacker by pretending to have problems with the refueling, I'll slip inside the cockpit and deal with him. We should be able to take him by surprise."

Bowman took a deep breath, then let it out again. "I don't

know about this. It's risky. If he catches on to what we're doing, he's going to force a take off with whatever fuel he has in the tank already. At that point, he'll have to take the pilot as hostage. Then we've lost both of them.''

A short, thick-shouldered tribal officer who'd met them there joined the discussion. ''That leaves only one other alternative. Someone has to disable the plane.''

''There's a limit to how many of us can get close without being detected,'' Julia objected. ''And anyone firing a rifle or pistol at that airplane could easily hit the hostage.''

The officer glanced toward the back seat of his car. ''I've got an old-style bow and a quiver of arrows I bought for my son. I thought we'd learn together—a father-son project. Is there anyone here who can use one of these things accurately? It's a silent weapon that could puncture a tire fast if someone could get close. There's a drainage ditch on the far side of the runway. Crawling up that would get the marksman within range.''

''May I see the bow?'' Benjamin asked.

''Yeah, sure,'' the officer answered, turning to retrieve it.

''Well, this plan leaves me out for sure,'' the sergeant grumbled. ''The only way I'd ever hit the tire with an arrow is if I walked over and stabbed it.''

The officer returned with the handmade hickory bow and held it out so Benjamin could see it. ''It's not one of those fancy big-game ones. It's an old straight bow a hobbyist I know in Farmington makes.''

''May I try it out?'' Benjamin asked.

The officer handed it to him. ''Be my guest.''

Benjamin examined it carefully, then pulled back the string. ''It's well made, and balanced. You have arrows, too?''

The officer offered him his choice from the soft leather quiver. Benjamin withdrew an arrow, examining the flights and tip. ''These will work,'' he announced to Julia.

''Good. Let's try a practice shot. See that small cardboard box in the field about fifty feet to your right?'' Julia asked, pointing.

"The green-and-red box?" Benjamin clarified.

"Yeah. Aim for that."

The sergeant scoffed. "Lady, that's impossible. I'd need a rifle to hit that six-pack box myself."

"In the red circle," Benjamin said quietly.

"Get serious," she chuckled. "Just aim for the carton."

"The red circle," he repeated. Positioning the arrow, he drew back the string, aimed quickly, then released it. The arrow whisked through the air, finding its mark with the accuracy of a laser-guided missile.

The sergeant gave out a low whistle. "You're better with that thing than I am with my rifle." The box was transfixed through the middle of the red, pinned to the ground.

"Looks like you've got the job," Julia said, glancing at Benjamin. "We'll give you time to get in position. Then Bowman and I will arrive in the truck. When he starts swearing loudly, that'll be your cue to puncture the tire. We'll take it from there." She glanced at the sergeant. "Go through that ditch with Two Eagle and protect him if the hijacker comes that way or starts shooting."

"No problem. We'll drive in a little closer, then crawl down the ditch until he finds a spot that suits him."

As the sergeant motioned for Benjamin to accompany him, Julia caught a glimpse of Benjamin's expression. Her blood turned to ice. "What's wrong?"

His body was tense and the skin across his cheekbones was drawn taut. "At least one of the amulets is here," he said loud enough for only her to hear. Before she could ask anything more, he joined the sergeant in the patrol car.

Julia watched them drive away, then waited impatiently for the minutes to tick by. After giving them time to get into place, she followed Bowman to the fuel truck and crouched down on the floorboard on the passenger's side. Bowman, clad in workers' overalls, slipped behind the wheel and switched on the ignition. "Here we go," he said.

Tension gripped her as they drove toward the airstrip. She felt the vehicle approaching the highway, then a bump as they pulled out onto the asphalt. The thin layer of perspiration that covered her body chilled like ice. Pistol cocked and ready, she waited.

A gravel road led to the airstrip, which was about two miles from where they'd assembled. The dust thrown up swirled around the interior of the truck, making Julia want to sneeze. After another bump, the going was much smoother, and she realized they were on the runway even before Bowman whispered their location.

"I'm going to park so that you'll be on the far side. The truck will shield you when you slip out," Bowman said softly. "From what I can see, the gunman's still inside the plane. Both aircraft doors are open, probably because of the heat coming off the runway. Fred Benally is standing half-in, half-out of the left-side cockpit door, and I can just make out the shadow of someone behind him." He slowed the truck down and parked. "It's time."

As Bowman enacted his planned problems with the fuel pump, Julia crept away noiselessly. She moved in cautiously, hoping that Bowman had the kidnapper's undivided attention. Julia edged toward the plane, working her way to the door on the far side. As she reached the cockpit window, she raised up just enough to peer inside. She had her first clear look then. The man holding Benally captive was no one she recognized.

For a moment, she wondered if this would turn out to be a separate incident that had nothing to do with her case. But then she remembered Benjamin's warning. If the amulets were nearby, she was on the right track.

Pete Bowman continued the show of refueling. A few seconds later, she heard him start muttering that the pump wasn't working.

Benally was shoved sideways as the gunman tried to get a better look. Bowman, catching movement out of the corner of his eye, glanced up just as the gunman came into view. Feigning surprise, he stepped back quickly. "Whoa, what's going on here?" he demanded. "Look, buddy, I don't want any trouble. You want this bird fueled, it's not a problem for me. But this pump keeps giving me fits.''

"Just get it working," the gunman growled, "or I'll take this guy's head off. Now move it.''

Bowman kicked the truck tire and started a long, loud string of curses. Julia waited just below the aircraft's single engine, out of sight of the cockpit.

During Bowman's evocative tirade, Julia saw an arrow appear as if by magic and imbed itself in the right aircraft tire. Bowman continued a string of loud obscenities, but Julia could see he'd noticed the arrow, too. As the tire deflated, the airplane began sagging on that side.

The gunman, alert and nervous, whirled the hostage around to face Bowman. "Shut up, or I'll blow his head off right now!''

In one silent, fluid motion, Julia jumped inside the plane. Coming up from behind, she pressed the muzzle of her pistol against the gunman's neck. "Don't even breathe." She grabbed the gun from his hand as Bowman came in front, reached for Benally and pulled him safely out of the way.

"Okay. Now step out slowly." Julia prodded her prisoner with the barrel of the pistol.

The man stepped down into the hands of Bowman, who had produced his own weapon from the pocket of his overalls. Benjamin and the police sergeant ran across the narrow runway to join them.

After the man had been cuffed and read his rights, Julia was ready to question him. "What did you want to transport from the reservation in such a hurry?" she asked.

"I don't know what you're talking about," he answered smoothly.

"What's your name?"

He hesitated. "Bobby Serna.''

"Were you hoping to go meet the other gang members and then fly off the rez?''

"What gang?" he sneered. "I was just looking for a little joyride around the state.''

Benjamin took a look inside the plane. "It's here," he said, and started to reach behind the pilot's seat.

"No, don't touch anything!" She relinquished custody of the prisoner to Bowman and the sergeant, who had additional questions.

Turning her attention to the plane, Julia poked her head inside. The turquoise amulet lay in a clear plastic box, the type used to display inexpensive jewelry. Relief and satisfaction swept through her. The amulet that had been in her family for so long was finally back in her possession! The victory tasted sweet, filling her with newfound confidence. She picked up the container by the edges and slipped it inside a small envelope she'd extracted from her pocket.

Benjamin's expression was controlled, but his attention was riveted on the envelope. "And now?"

"I'll tag the envelope, then sign and seal it. It's considered evidence, and I have to maintain custody until I sign it over to another officer. But because of its special significance to me, I intend to keep it in my possession for now."

"One more question before we leave," Benjamin mumbled, looking over the airplane with amazement.

"It flies—higher and faster than an eagle," Julia answered with a smile, knowing what was on his mind. "But not as beautifully as one."

"Maybe I could go up into the sky once, before I..." Benjamin began, then his voice faded away. After an awkward silence, he spoke clearly again. "Let's get back to the prisoner."

Julia nodded sadly, unable to look him in the eye.

Together they walked over to where Bowman was questioning Serna. Julia held up the envelope in front of the Hispanic man. "And shall I wager that this plastic jewelry box will have your prints?"

"So what? I may have handled it inside the plane." He paused for a second, then continued. "It's the Indian guy's. Belongs to the pilot."

"No, I don't think so. Try again?"

"Where's the agate amulet?" Benjamin asked softly.

"The what? I don't know what you're talking about."

"If you cooperate, things will be easier on you," Julia reminded Serna. "So far we've got conspiracy, murder, kidnapping and a dozen other charges on the list."

Serna shook his head slowly. "Lady, you don't know who you're up against on this. If I talk to you, I'm a dead man," he muttered.

"If you don't, you'll be eligible for social security by the time you leave prison. Who's behind the operation?" she insisted.

"Forget it. I tried to get away because I wanted to live. That hasn't changed."

"What were you doing with the amulet?"

"I came across the carving and it looked valuable, just like the agate one Eddie stole from a trading post a few years ago. So I brought it along."

"You sure you don't want to tell us about your boss? From what I hear, life in prison isn't pleasant," she added smoothly.

"But I'll be breathing. You can't protect me from this guy. If I tell you anything at all, he'll come after me, no matter where you hide me."

"Not if we get to him first."

"In your dreams. This guy will keep you running around in circles for years if it suits him. Admit it. That's what he's been doing to you all along."

She found his tone and the observation incredibly annoying, but she was determined not to let him know that. "Why have you guys stayed on the reservation instead of skipping the state? What's here that's holding you?"

"You don't know anything at all, do you?" Serna observed. "All the answers are right there under your nose. If you aren't smart enough to figure them out, don't ask me. I've got enough problems of my own."

She nodded to the sergeant, who led him away. Serna had a point, and that's what rankled her the most.

"Well, that's another one down. We're capturing the gang

one man at a time, but we're getting them,'' Bowman commented.

"Yeah, but at what cost?" she asked pensively. "Benally could have been hurt or killed in this latest attempt. And how do you think the tribe would have reacted if a tribal council member had been the victim?"

"There would have been repercussions, and heads would have rolled," he admitted somberly. "But no sense in worrying about what never happened. For now I've got to go and make a full report to Chief Roanhorse. At least this incident represents a success. Anything you want me to tell him?"

"No, I'll talk to him myself later."

After Bowman drove off in his patrol car with councilman Benally, she and Benjamin were left alone at the small airstrip.

"I will need the amulet you have," he said softly.

"You haven't told me the whole story, and that makes me uneasy. I know you'll act according to your sense of right. But I'm bound by oaths of my own and the laws of twentieth-century America. This amulet is now evidence, and I'm sworn to protect it."

"I could give you assurances, telling you what I think you want to hear, but you deserve better than that," he said. "I've grown to admire your courage, woman, and to admire you. If I could... If my life were different than it is..." He paused, reluctant to say anything else. Then he met her eyes as they gazed into his. The softness he saw reflected there made a fire start in his loins. He fought the desire to pull her against him, knowing it would only make his leaving all the more unbearable for both of them.

"If things were different, you would what?" she asked. "Finish it."

"Do you need to hear me say what you already know?" He took a step closer to Julia, wondering how one woman could have so much power over him. "I would take you as a man takes a woman, and make you completely mine," he said, his voice a raw whisper.

The words wrapped themselves around her, squeezing the

air from her lungs. She touched his arm with her fingertips, assuring herself he was real, then drew her hand back. That was the problem. He was all too real, and her heart had awakened to yearnings too powerful to ignore. "But what you want the most from me right now is the amulet, so you can go back to the past," she said tonelessly.

"It is what I must do, not what I desire."

She avoided his gaze, not wanting him to see the pain he was causing her. "Then tell me the rest of the story. Convince me that I should help you do this."

"The twin amulets have been part of the medicine bundle carried by the *hataaliis* in our family for generations," he said, his voice gentle and sorrowful. "I benefited from the knowledge of those who came before, so I was able to do things with them that none of my predecessors ever could. Soon that made me the *Dineh*'s most powerful Singer. Yet my knowledge and magic were not sufficient to protect those under my care. I had sworn that I would not allow any who stood with me to fall into the hands of our enemies. We had all seen what they had done to the others, breaking our people's spirit through starvation and captivity. To me, and my small band of warriors, death was preferable. But then our group grew to include women and children who had also refused to surrender. My goal was to lead them to a new home where we could remain free."

"You did your best. No one could have expected more. You were their leader, but a man after all."

"No. I was their *hataalii*, the one they looked to for guidance and assurance. I was also overly confident. I was certain I knew exactly what was needed to succeed. My plan was to search for someone who sympathized with our cause and would be in a position to help us. I thought I found him."

"But he betrayed you?"

"Yes. I failed to take one very important thing into account. What is honor to one is dishonor to another, depending on whom they serve." Though pain laced his admission, Benjamin's dignity commanded her respect. "I chose to trust a cavalry officer we called Green Eyes. He had captured many of our people, but he had also made sure that no one under his protection was ever mistreated or starved. He would often take from his soldiers rations, and share them with the *Dineh*.''

''What made you think he would go against orders to help you?''

''He had been reduced in rank twice because he hadn't pursued the remaining bands vigorously enough to suit his superiors. He had even complained to the leaders in Washington that they couldn't adequately feed the six thousand they held at Bosque Redondo. It was foolish for them to bring in more prisoners of war. Then, when he captured a band of warriors but allowed their women and children to escape, his commander threatened him with a dishonorable discharge. Green Eyes became very bitter against those he served.''

''How did you approach him?''

''I stalked him for a week, until I could catch him by himself. He was unarmed, shaving. I could have ended his life and he knew it. Instead, I asked for safe passage south into Mexico for my band. I promised that during his lifetime, none of us would return. He told me which routes to take so we would not run into his patrols. In payment, he asked for one of my amulets. I had no choice. I gave him the turquoise Twin.''

''What happened?''

''He set a trap for us instead of keeping his word, and we walked into an ambush. We had to retreat into a canyon, but the soldiers knew we were boxed in. They burned our supplies and killed our animals. Rifle fire slowly claimed more of us. I saw my brother's family perish, one by one. All went down except for me.

''I swore then I would avenge their deaths, but to do that, I had to survive without being taken captive. I called on the agate amulet to help me. In my chant, I compelled the spirit of the amulet to protect me, its owner. I demanded to be one with its power. As I finished the song, I felt myself being drawn into the agate Twin. Something went wrong just as it happened, but I could no longer reverse the spell.''

"Once the soldiers left, why didn't you come back out?"

"My magic wasn't strong enough to command the powers from inside. My spirit and body essence were held within the stone, in a world only the *hataalii* understand. I had trapped myself in a prison stronger than any the white men could have devised."

His story rang with the raw emotions that can only come from the truth. Everything in her assured Julia she could trust his words. "But now you're free. The past is gone."

"No, not gone. It remains there, still waiting. And now I need the amulet to return to my own time. Green Eyes must pay for what he did to the *Dineh*."

"But what's to keep the amulet from trapping you again? Maybe it's not meant to be used for revenge, and that's why it failed you before," Julia suggested, though she knew she was far from comprehending the metaphysical world Benjamin fought to control.

"No. For over a hundred years my Wind Breath, my soul, has been one with the spirit of the agate Twin. I've learned much about patience and the ancient ways. Old debts must be paid. That's the only way to restore harmony."

"Even if you make it back to your own time safely, what can one man do against so many? It would be the same as committing suicide. You've been freed in a new time. You have a great deal to offer your people here. Share your knowledge with them and enrich them that way. You can do more good by staying than by going back."

"I have to return. It is my duty. Without honoring that, I would have no harmony, and my words would be as empty as I would be."

"I've also taken oaths that are part of what I stand for." The thought of losing Benjamin was knifing through her. She stared at the envelope that contained the turquoise Twin. "You're asking me to turn my back on one loyalty, so I can honor my debt to you."

"What I did for you, I did freely. If there is a debt, then I release you from it. I want you to do as I ask because you respect the right we all have to make our own choices. But even more than that, I want you to comply because I've earned your trust.''

Julia swallowed the lump in her throat. Unsure of her voice, she remained silent.

''But I also understand that the amulet is linked to the job you must do here,'' he continued. ''When I return to my own time, I will leave the amulet in a place where you can reclaim it.'' He started back to her car. ''Take me to the hills above the trading post. On the tallest mesa there, near the arroyo where we first met, is a flat stone with other stones placed upon it, one on the other. It is a shrine that existed before I was born and is still there. I will bury the amulet beneath the flat rock after it has served its usefulness to me.''

She drove him to the area where he wanted to go, her heart breaking. She wanted to beg him to stay, but no woman could hold a man by begging. Sadness poured over her, but she was determined to hide it from him.

Julia took her vehicle as close to the hillside as possible, and they walked the rest of the way to the summit. Benjamin led her to the shrine, and Julia found it was just as he'd described.

''I will leave it here for you,'' he said, pointing to the base of the largest rock.

She'd learned a long time ago that to care deeply for another person was to invite pain and heartbreak. That was why she'd chosen to center her life around her work. Her job fulfilled her and gave her purpose, and the success she'd found reflected everything she'd ever wanted to be. The Bureau had become her home and her family. But now it seemed like an empty shell, a promise without substance.

She opened the envelope and stared at the small amulet nestled inside. The only treasure she'd ever possessed would end up costing her dreams that had never been given a chance, a wealth of might-have-beens that would haunt her as long as she lived.

''You've earned more than my trust.'' Julia saw the flicker

in his eyes and knew he understood. She handed him the en-velope. "I'll hold you to your promise to return the amulet."

Benjamin started to speak, but she turned and walked away. She couldn't say goodbye. She had lost him; there was nothing more to be said. Her eyes blurred with tears as she went down to the car. Each step filled her with an acute longing for the man whose touch had awakened her soul. But she'd known this time would come, and she had to let him go.

She'd almost reached her car, when she suddenly stopped in midstride. Her thoughts sharpened, forming with a clarity they hadn't possessed minutes before. Revenge was never noble, no matter how many grand words and motives it hid behind. Benjamin was acting out of a misguided sense of justice, and for her to do nothing while he threw his life away was just as wrong.

When a man was too foolish to see his mistakes, it was a woman's duty to point them out—repeatedly, if necessary. She'd tie him up and throw him in the back of her car until he listened to reason, if that's what it took.

She started back, increasing her pace to a run as she heard his chant fill the air.

# Chapter Twelve

Julia spotted Benjamin sitting in the shade of a piñon tree, looking tired. Before he could stand, she dove headlong, knocking him sideways to the ground. In a lightning move, she twisted his arm back, forced him facedown on the ground and cuffed him. Overwhelmed, he offered no resistance.

"Woman! What are you—"

"Quiet," she muttered, grabbing the amulet, which was lying on top of the envelope by the tree. "I changed my mind about letting you go back. It's a dumb idea. You need me to explain a few things to you." Julia was excited to see him and relieved she'd caught him in time. Though she was determined to sound authoritative and brusque, she couldn't deny the thrill coursing through her. He was here—with her!

"Will you take these handcuffs off me," he demanded irately.

"No, not yet. First you're going to walk back to the car with me. And we're both going to try and relax."

Benjamin stood and fell into step beside her, a tiny grin digging at the corners of his mouth. "Were you *that* upset at the thought of losing me?" he asked quietly.

"Yes. I mean no." She cleared her throat and prodded him forward. "I realized you needed my guidance very badly, and I didn't want to deprive you," she added, enjoying the bewildered look he gave her.

"I'm here and going along with you peaceably. You don't

have to keep my hands bound. That is, unless you enjoy seeing me helpless.''

"Enjoy it? No, but I think it's good for your…Wind Breath.'' She had to find a way to convince him that he was wrong to return to the past. But now that she had her chance, the words were getting all tangled up in her mind. "Listen to me,'' she said, concluding she'd have to use logic to reach him. "When you tried to impose your will on the amulet before, it trapped you. You were about to do the same thing. You were brought to this time for a reason. You have to figure out why and see that through first.''

"I know.''

"Don't argue. Just be quiet. I'm not going to uncuff you until you give me your word you won't chant or do…'' She stopped speaking. "Wait a second. Did you just agree with me?''

"Yes. Now will you unlock these bracelets?''

"No. That was too easy. How come you're not arguing with me?''

"If I am doing what you wanted, why are you still fighting? You won. Now, what other concessions must I make to get you to release me?''

"You could try appealing to my good nature,'' she said, trying to suppress a smile.

"A task easier accomplished if my hands were free,'' Benjamin said, his voice a dusky murmur.

She felt the blood rush to her face. "I'll tell you what. I'll settle for finding out what made you change your mind. I heard you begin the chant.''

His expression turned somber. "I had every intention of going back,'' he said. "Whether you are in agreement or not, I know it was the right thing to do.''

"So I did stop you in time,'' she concluded.

"No. I failed. The stone blocked my passage,'' he admitted grudgingly. "But I finally understand what happened to me before. To summon the full power of the amulets, both must be brought together, touching. One alone only achieves partial and uncertain results.''

At least this had postponed his return—now he'd have more time to consider his actions.

''We'll probably have to catch the entire gang before we can find the agate Twin.'' Behind her calm words was the heart of a woman undeniably happy to have him back.

''Then we'll have to proceed quickly,'' he warned softly. ''The situation has become very dangerous for me. When I started the ritual, I felt surrounded by an intense and violent hatred. That rage tore through me, though I fought to keep it at bay. The spirit in the amulet holds me responsible for not taking possession of the Twins after they'd been reunited at the trading post.''

''You tried. None of what happened was your fault,'' she protested gently.

''Perhaps, but that doesn't change the way things are. If either amulet is destroyed, the disposition of the gods will be uncertain. It's possible they might abandon me here in your time. But they might also choose to annihilate me. If that happens, I would simply disappear from existence, and all memory of my presence would be lost forever. Not even my Wind Breath would remain to join with universal harmony.''

The thought of losing Benjamin and all memory of their time together made her whole body ache with sorrow. Her soul would be dealt a mortal blow, condemned to spend a lifetime yearning for something she'd never be able to define. ''They would be punishing me, as well as you,'' she said. ''That is, unless they allowed you to remain here.''

He brushed her face with a feather-light caress, but then drew away, his expression hardening once more. ''You don't understand. My hands are stained with the blood of many. I am not the gentle man you believe me to be.''

''You are when you're with me.'' She reached for his hand and brought it back to her face, nuzzling kittenlike against it.

''To you, what I'm saying is nothing more than a few dreary pages of New Mexico history,'' he whispered sadly, stepping away and staring into the distance. "What have you experienced that could compare to the devastating toll my mistake exacted? You're a woman warrior who has known a career filled with success."

"You're wrong. We all face failures—none of us are exempt. But it's how we deal with them that determines what we become," she stated emphatically.

"But you're not responsible for the deaths of everyone you cared about," he answered bluntly. "You can't possibly know what it's like to have to live with that."

"No, but I know what it's like to feel you've failed someone you love." She hesitated, not wanting to bare her soul, yet knowing she had to, if she was to reach him. "When my mother got sick, the state placed me in a foster home. I was eleven, old enough to speak up for myself, but seeing her dying a little bit at a time scared me. I didn't want to be around her. So I went away, willingly, to live with strangers. Those people didn't care about me, and I didn't care about them. Yet I felt safer there because of that." Memories she'd never quite come to terms with knifed through her. "My mother was dying, and when she needed me most, I wasn't there."

"But you were a child. Decisions were made without your consent. Your protests probably wouldn't have done any good. You're not to blame for the way you felt. It was natural."

Julia shook her head. "I should have been there for her." She paused then forced herself to meet his eyes. "But the point I'm making is that what we blame ourselves for, often has little to do with logic. I've spent my life proving I'm not the coward I was then—that I can stand up to anything. But intense emotions still frighten me. Love has never brought me anything but tears. Going from one foster home to another was wrenching and I wouldn't let anyone get close to me. As I grew up, it became a habit I couldn't break. It left an emptiness inside me—a hunger that I desperately wanted to fill. I kept thinking that if I became a big success, that need would vanish. So I loaded myself up with work, gave my job everything, but no matter what I achieved, it was never enough to make it go away.''

"You started off wrong, and your search only led you farther from your goal."

She nodded slowly. "I looked in places that were safe for me because the alternative was too frightening," she admitted, her voice barely audible. Julia took a step closer to him. "Hold me, Benjamin," she whispered.

He forced himself to stay still. "No. I care about you, woman." His voice was dusky with needs he was fighting to suppress. "I could do more harm to you than good. You deserve a man who will stand beside you, who belongs to your time, and who has a life you can share. You need a future, and I can't give you that. All I have is the past."

She wanted to snap back at him, accuse him of being blind to everything good the present held out to him, but to her own surprise, she did something quite different. She wrapped her arms around his neck, straining upward to kiss him.

He tried to hold himself in check, but as she coaxed his lips apart, a long shudder rippled through him. "You don't know what you're doing," he gasped, his arms tightening around her.

"Sure I do," she answered, pulling his mouth back down to hers. "Now, just kiss me. I'm sure you can do a better job if you concentrate."

"Are you criticizing the way I kiss, woman?" he growled.

"Yes. You're not doing a very good job. You talk too much."

His eyes glittered with annoyance and male pride. She held her breath. Maybe she'd gone too far.

Wordlessly, he imprisoned her against his chest. His hand curled behind her head, and he pressed her into his kiss. Her mouth opened to him easily, and hunger shot through him like a lightning bolt. Unable to resist what she offered, he thrust his tongue between her parted lips, slowly savoring the taste of her.

She moaned softly, trembling in his arms. Her response fueled the fire in his blood. He shouldn't have listened to her taunting. The woman made a shambles of his control, something he'd always prided himself on—both as a *hataalii* and as a man.

He groaned as she fit her body instinctively into his. "What did I ever do to deserve you?" he gasped, tasting the column of her neck.

"That didn't sound like a complaint this time," Julia managed as she undid the snaps of his shirt.

Feeling her soft hands against his skin, Benjamin moaned deep and low. "You go too far, woman."

"Not yet, I haven't," she murmured, pushing the folds aside and tasting his warm flesh with tiny flickers of her tongue.

He tangled his hand in her hair, forced her head back and brought his mouth crashing down over hers. His kiss was hard, hungry and as wild as the wind. "You need someone to tame you, woman. You don't know when you should be afraid." He drew back, struggling to keep himself in check.

Driven by needs too basic to deny, she pushed his shirt away from his shoulders. His body was tense—every muscle seemed to stand out and ripple as her gaze took him in.

"Don't. I need you far too much," he cautioned in a raw voice.

"I won't run away," she promised breathlessly. "I've spent too many years running, first from myself and then from my own feelings." She met his eyes. "No more."

"I can offer you nothing—nothing," he repeated.

Responding wordlessly, she trailed a long moist line down the center of his chest with the tip of her tongue. "Tell me you don't feel anything for me and I'll move away," she whispered.

"I can't lie to you." He shuddered, desire coiling around him. "I've wanted you and needed you for a long time. Maybe a lifetime."

He belonged here with her, and the rightness of it took her breath away. "You were sent to me…and for me. Fate brought us together, Benjamin, because this is *our* time. Don't you see?"

"I see only a beautiful woman, who touches me and makes

me feel strong and weak all at once,'' he murmured. ''I see
the face of gentleness and love.'' He drew her to him and
kissed her, hunger driving him. She wanted and needed him,
and he could scarcely deny that this knowledge filled him with
pride and a sense of triumph.

He slipped his hand beneath the cotton top she wore and
caressed her body tenderly. Her skin was as soft as the petals
of a rose. His thumb traced a lazy circle around the tiny bud
that tightened beneath his touch.

She gasped as he cupped her breast, kneading the pliant
flesh. She cried out softly and pressed herself into him.

Her passion fueled his own. Flames raced down to his groin,
but he forced himself to go slow. This was their moment, one
that would live on in their memories and sustain them long
after time and duty separated them forever.

Stripping the garments away from her body, he feasted on
the beauty he uncovered. His eyes drifted over her as she stood
before him. Then slowly, he rained kisses down the center of
her until he knelt on the ground before her.

He teased her, loving her with his mouth and tongue, bringing her to a fever pitch of desire. He kissed her deeply, stilling
her hips between his strong hands. He felt the tiny explosions
that rocked her body and drank in her sweet essence.

She collapsed against him, leaning on his shoulders for support, gasping his name. Tremors shook her like powerful af-
tershocks.

He stood up slowly, his arms steadying her all the way, and
then held her until her breathing evened.

''*Sawe,* my baby,'' he whispered, ''I need to take more.''
His voice shook with passion.

She stepped back and began to unfasten his jeans. But her
fingers wouldn't work. She wanted to see him, to know this
man who made her blood sing, yet her hands were trembling
too much to accomplish even the simplest task. She forced
herself to go slower.

The jeans finally came undone, and with infinite care she
slid them down his body. She felt him shudder as her hands

brushed his skin, but he remained standing, naked and proud in front of her. Her breath came out long and shaky, and the center of her pulsed with need as she memorized everything about him. His body was lean, muscled and touched by battle. Each scar that marred his hard flesh tore at her heart. He'd come from a time of violence and too little compassion. It filled her with the desire to touch him with kindness and love.

She ran her fingertips over a long, jagged welt that gleamed pale against his copper skin.

"Does it disgust you?" he asked, his voice unsteady.

"No. It makes me want to love you until you remember nothing that ever caused you pain."

He gathered her into his arms and kissed her deeply. She pressed herself against him, wanting to join him, yet needing each precious second to last forever.

He turned her around gently until she faced away from him. As she reached back with her arms, winding them around his neck, he caressed her everywhere. His fingers probed inside her, his touch inciting her past reason.

"I can't stand up anymore," she cried as he stroked the tiny bud at the center of her.

"Hush, *sawe,* just surrender." He tightened his grip around her waist and drew her against his member.

She felt electrified, his body piercing hers while his fingers continued to work a different kind of magic. Lights exploded in her head as a host of fiery sensations ripped through her.

She couldn't breathe, she couldn't think. She could feel him deep inside her, moving, taking as he gave. The pleasure was so exquisite she cried out time and time again.

Benjamin's arms encircled her tightly as he thrust into her softness. She was so hot and so wet. His head was sizzling. His heart thundered like a freight train. Every movement drove him a little closer to the edge.

Then thoughts vanished. Passion, raw and elemental, ruled him. Wild as the summer storms that gave the desert life, he spilled his seed into her, and their spirits were joined, taking wing in the blue of the skies overhead.

He lowered her gently to the ground until they lay on the blanket their discarded clothing made. With infinite tenderness, he rested her head upon his shoulder. At that moment, there was only one truth. This was the woman eternity had destined for him. Even if they were not fated to spend their lives together, their hearts would be forever entwined.

She stirred and opened her eyes slowly. She started to speak, but then fell silent, snuggling deeper into his arms.

He waited, his heart troubled. She was part of him now. The bittersweetness of that tore through him. It would take all the strength he possessed to leave her when the time came. "Do you regret what we shared?"

"I regret only the pain we may cause each other, but never the love I found in your arms."

SHE STOOD UP A LONG WHILE later. She had yielded to love, but reality already lay like a shadow over her heart. Perhaps love wasn't meant for people like her. In her hands, love's blossoms were always filled with sorrow. Their beauty was passing and tainted with death from the start.

"No matter what comes, you are a part of me forever," he whispered.

His words caused a lump the size of a baseball to lodge in her throat. But their courses were set. Feelings could no longer play a part in what they had to do. His life was linked to the amulets and his survival depended on them. Nothing could be allowed to interfere with the investigation that would lead them to the agate Twin.

They drove in silence to tribal headquarters. Julia turned her thoughts to the case, reviewing each detail in search of answers. There still had been no word on the van they'd spotted at the Mini Mart. She couldn't understand it. Between the detailed description and the partial license number she'd managed to get, someone should have seen it by now.

She picked up the mike and called in a request for an update. No more progress had been made. "This is very frustrating. I know I'm not seeing something I should be."

"The gang would not keep a car that could be easily recognized. Maybe they hid it someplace on the reservation where people rarely travel."

"That's one possibility. There's another worth checking, too. From what I've learned, people don't always report things like stolen vehicles right away around here. I want to take a look at the most recent printout listing hot cars. We might find it there. If we can establish where the van came from, we'll know where the gang's been. With luck, that'll help us uncover a trail we can follow."

The controlled acceleration as she drove down the highway, along with the sense of purpose that working on the case gave her, helped her fight the sadness that lingered at the edges of her mind. She'd have to find a way to make her career as all-absorbing as it had once been. After Benjamin was gone, it would be all she'd have left.

Thirty minutes later, she sat across the table from Benjamin at the station. The photos corresponding to the names Stillwell had given her had been circulated, and with Benjamin's help she'd been able to identify the two men who'd held her captive. They were Benny Martinez and Norm Foster. Bobby Serna's photo was there, too.

With that finished, they began to tally the reports of stolen vehicles in the Four Corners area, which covered parts of Utah, Colorado, Arizona and New Mexico. The stack was small in comparison to what it would have been in a large metropolitan area, but it was still considerably larger than she'd expected.

Minutes ticked by as they checked license plates against the partial she'd managed to get. The job was a slow one, but she didn't want to miss anything, particularly any plates whose letters might be close—it was easy to mistake a *B* for an *E* when the vehicle was racing away.

The long columns, coupled with the faded ribbon used on the printout, soon began to wear on her. Leaning back, she rubbed her burning eyes. As she opened them again, a young sergeant walked inside the room.

"Here's another vehicle and plate I hadn't entered into the

system, since it was found right away. It had been parked in a different place than it normally was, that's all.'' He handed her a file. ''I'm certain it has nothing to do with your case, but in the interest of being thorough, here's the report.''

She glanced at the sheet, then stood up quickly. ''It's a van, and it fits the partial license plate and color. I'd like to see it right away.'' She just couldn't figure out why no one had noted this before. ''It says here it's in the impound yard. Can you take me there?''

The officer shrugged. ''If that's what you want.''

As he stopped to get some keys from his desk, Julia thought she sensed his disapproval. His attitude baffled her. Maybe the sergeant didn't want to be put through any extra paperwork, and he felt she'd create more work for him. She discarded the thought. That wasn't it. The sergeant was apprehensive about something.

As they all went outside, she looked at Benjamin to gauge his reaction, and caught the look he gave her. At least she wasn't the only one who had felt something wasn't quite right.

''Through there,'' the sergeant said, gesturing with his lips in the manner she'd come to associate with the members of the tribe.

Slipping between a row of closely parked cars, Julia approached the blue van. ''This is the one I've been looking for. Here's my handprint on the chrome. A fingerprint comparison will verify that. I purposely left it there when I went around it.''

Julia started to open the door when she saw the radio equipment and weapons rack inside. She snapped her head around and stared in shock at the sergeant. ''This is an unmarked police vehicle!''

# Chapter Thirteen

The Navajo officer remained stone-faced and silent. "If you'll excuse me now, I have other work to do."

"Wait a second." She peered around the van's interior, careful not to touch anything. "I'll need to have this vehicle checked for prints."

"I'll start the paperwork on your request when I return to my desk. Anything else?"

"I want a complete list of every person who used this van in the last two weeks."

He shrugged. "Right now?"

"As soon as you can," she answered.

"Sheriff's department Captain McKibben and Chief Roanhorse," he said flatly.

She blinked. "They're the only two?"

"Yeah, and you'll have to get the chief's permission before we can do a fingerprint search on this vehicle—only he's not around now."

"If I can't get a hold of the chief, who else is available that can authorize it?" Roanhorse was well liked and respected by his department, so she knew the repercussions of any action she took would be far-reaching. But the longer this was drawn out, the more complicated it would get.

"I believe Deputy Chief Bowman has the authority to okay the dusting," the sergeant suggested with a marked lack of enthusiasm. "Shall I see if he's in his office?"

"Please do."

Seeing that the window was open, Julia flipped up the door handle with one finger. She crawled to the rear cargo compartment of the van and looked around. Something was lodged between two rows of cardboard boxes placed next to the van's side. She glanced back at the sergeant, but he'd already moved away.

She shifted her gaze to Benjamin. "I need some help. Can you crawl in here and push those boxes apart, touching them only on the edges?"

"I can try. What are you after?"

"I think it's a little notebook," she said, pointing.

He knelt by the boxes, placed his wrist against the edges and gave them a labored shove. "Is that enough for you to reach through?"

She strained forward. "Yes! I've got it." She grasped the notebook by the metal spirals and pulled it out, placing it in front of her on the van's floor.

The sergeant appeared a moment later. "The deputy chief is away from his desk, but I left a message for him." He glanced down at the notebook. "Anything useful?"

"I don't know yet." Julia slipped her pen between the pages and started to flip it open, when she suddenly felt something catch. She stopped immediately and uttered a single curse word.

"What's wrong?" The sergeant moved toward her, and Benjamin stared curiously.

"Maybe nothing, but I've got a bad feeling about this," she said. "Get a flashlight, will you?"

"Back in a minute. I've got one in my unit."

As the sergeant jogged away, Benjamin studied her expression. "What is the problem?" he asked, starting to move closer.

"Stay where you are. If you come too close, you might bump into me."

"What have you found?" he insisted.

"I'm not sure. It could be something very dangerous. Experience tells me not to do anything until I can see what I've got here."

"Well, patience is my most tested virtue," Benjamin said, forcing a smile. "Is there anything I can do to help you?"

"No, not really. But I'm afraid you're stuck in this van with me."

"I prefer that to standing out there wondering what is going on." He stared past her at the station's main building. "Your request for fingerprints is going to create some very serious problems for you here," he said, trying to divert her thoughts.

"I don't have a choice. There are some tough questions that this vehicle's involvement raises. For example, why didn't anyone match the description and partial plate I'd given them before now? There's also the matter of when—and how—the vehicle was stolen."

"You think Chief Roanhorse is involved somehow?"

"I don't know if he is or isn't. That's the problem."

"They will remain loyal to him," he said, glancing back at the building. "If you make any accusations against their leader, you will find yourself with more enemies than you could ever imagine."

"Including me." Pete Bowman appeared by the front door of the van. "What's going on?" The deputy chief reached through and handed her a flashlight. "Here. I was told you needed this."

As she bent down and shined the beam between the pages, her heart began thundering in her ears. "I... We've got big problems."

"I can authorize a search for fingerprints, if that's what you're worried about," he said in a clipped voice, "but first—"

"Forget that for now," she snapped. "Do you have an explosives expert?"

"Yeah, I'm him. We all wear more than one hat around here." He glanced down at the notebook. "What've you got?"

"There's some kind of trigger mechanism attached here. I think it might be a thin sheet of plastic explosive. If it's pure, this whole parking lot could go up in a chain reaction.'' She glanced over his shoulder. ''Are those propane tanks over there against the fence?''

He nodded. ''They're used to heat the station in winter and are probably about half-full right now. That would still be enough to send all these cars a half mile straight up.'' Crawling through, he took the flashlight back from her and directed the beam between the pages. ''Don't move your hand any more than you absolutely have to.'' He studied the notebook for what seemed like an eternity. ''Yeah, you're right. We've got trouble.''

''You want to clear the area?''

''That would be best, but we can't wait until everyone evacuates to start working on this.'' He nodded to the sergeant, whom they'd heard approaching, and clipped out several orders fast. ''Get busy.''

As the junior officer moved off, Bowman opened the rear doors and crouched down again.

''Should we ask for flak jackets or something?'' Julia asked.

''Nah. This is C-4, and the blast would be concentrated within the van. You can think of it as being sealed in an oil drum with a stick of dynamite. Jacket or not, they'd still have to sort us out piece by piece.''

She tried not to shudder. ''Okay, so much for that. Tell me this—can you defuse it?''

''Maybe, but it won't be easy,'' Bowman said honestly. He lay on his stomach and studied the simple device. ''From what I can tell, it's a sheet of C-4 plastic explosive with a detonator buried in the middle. There are two wires leading to the terminals of a film-pack-type battery. The contacts are only being held apart by a matchstick. When you started to open the notebook, you moved that matchstick halfway out.''

''And we have to try to make it go back in?''

''How lucky do you feel? We could have you slip the pen back out, letting the notebook close naturally. But the way I figure it, the odds that things will slip back exactly into place aren't very good.''

"Don't rely on my luck," she protested. "Look at the mess I'm in."

"So we'll do it the hard way," he said. "It should improve our chances of walking away from this. This bomb might be crude and small, but it's extremely effective."

"What do we do first? I'm not sure how long I'll be able to keep my hand perfectly still. This is an awkward position to maintain."

"Brace your wrist, then. If that matchstick moves even a fraction, or falls out, we're all history."

Benjamin glanced at her. "That description suits me more than it does you," he said, teasing her gently. "So hold your hand steady, okay?"

Julia smiled and continued to hold her body immobile. Wondering if Bowman had attached any significance to Benjamin's comment, she cast him a furtive glance. Bowman was focused solely on the explosive device. She sobered immediately.

"I have to get at the mechanism," he said over the sound of starting engines and departing vehicles. "And that'll be as risky as it is difficult."

"What can I do to help?" Benjamin asked.

Bowman's glance went to the knife at Benjamin's waist. "How sharp is that?"

"Very," he said, and withdrew it from its sheath. He handed Bowman the weapon, handle first. "You are welcome to use it."

Bowman studied the handcrafted blade for a moment, then shifted until he faced a box he could see was empty. Using only the tip of the weapon, he sliced through the cardboard effortlessly. "You weren't wrong, Uncle," Bowman said respectfully. He held the handle in his palm, feeling it for balance and weight. "This is a magnificent blade."

"May it serve you well now."

Bowman glanced at Julia. "I'm going to cut through the top of the notebook so we can have direct access to the mechanism. But the tricky part will be severing the two wires that lead to the detonator. That has to be done at *precisely* the same instant." He glanced back at Benjamin. "Your help would come in handy."

"You have it."

"Is there anything I can do?" Julia asked.

Bowman looked at her. "Just make very sure you don't move your hand."

She felt her nose itch and willed the sensation away. Then her back itched, and her palm grew sweaty. It was hard to hold still when every nerve in her body was screaming for action!

"I'm going to have to get a few more tools," Bowman said, sliding carefully out of the van. "I'll be right back." He started to go, then stopped. "Is there anything you need? Your religious beliefs might help you…"

She gave him a grateful smile, then shook her head. "I've been praying since I opened the notebook. What I need is for this to be over."

As Bowman left, she glanced at Benjamin. "Anything you can do?"

"No. If I had both amulets, I could have invoked their protection, but if I try now, I may just complicate matters."

Bowman returned before she could reply. "I think this is all we need," he said, holding out a pair of cutting pliers. "Once we cut a hole through the top pages, we'll be able to work from two different directions. Your blade is sharp and flat enough to slip through the opening she's holding for us. These pliers will be more handy for me as I tackle it from the other angle."

Bowman eased forward slightly, studying the portion of the bomb he could see through the tiny gap. "The problem is that once I actually start to cut the opening, I'll be working from the top, and I won't be able to see the wires. I'll have to keep checking back and forth, and that'll increase the chance of a mishap."

He'd phrased it delicately, but getting blown up was not her idea of a "mishap." "Maybe we should come up with another plan."

"I have one," Benjamin said, looking at Bowman. "You can guide me while I cut the opening at the top."

"You'll need a steady hand," Bowman warned. "We won't get another chance if that knife slips."

"My hand will be as steady as you need it to be," Benjamin assured him. "Shall we start?" His voice was quiet, but unmistakable determination reverberated through it.

"Okay, let's do it. If you need to stop and take a breath, tell me. Better that than to have you pushing yourself and making a mistake."

Julia braced her hand. "When you're ready to have me release my hold, just say so."

"You've got to be steady as a rock until we finish. Remember that you're holding the match in its place." Bowman stretched out on the van's floor and aimed a flashlight beam into the small opening. "Okay, let's start." He glanced at Benjamin, who nodded, signaling he was ready. "Insert your blade slowly about a quarter of an inch deep at the center."

Benjamin pushed the sharp edge through the top carefully, moving millimeters at a time.

"Stop."

Benjamin held his knife hand as frozen as a block of ice.

"Be very careful when you continue. It's extremely important that you hold the point straight down. If you're the slightest bit off, you risk touching the wire connection."

Benjamin's heart hammered against his ribs, and he held his breath as he pushed the blade straight down. "Now what?"

"Start cutting a round hole about the same diameter as a lug nut."

"What kind of a nut?"

Julia cleared her throat. "The size of the glass on my watch." She caught his eye and glanced down at her wrist.

He nodded and started cutting.

Bowman's eyebrows knitted together for a fraction of a second, but his attention quickly shifted back to the job at hand. "Slow down as you start to curve around."

Benjamin felt the perspiration that covered his forehead flow down into his eyes. He wished he had worn a headband the way many warriors did in his time, but it was too late for that now. He focused his attention on Bowman and the directions he was calling out.

"Stop. From this point on, you can't push the blade as far in as you have been. I'll direct you."

Benjamin listened to Bowman's precise instructions. Suddenly the notebook slid out from under him, shifting under the pressure of his knife. He froze as he felt the tip of the blade touch something solid.

"Don't even breathe!" Bowman placed one finger on a corner of the notebook, steadying it. "I can't hold it any firmer than this, so be very careful. Pull the blade straight up *slowly.* If you feel it make contact with anything other than paper, stop instantly. Start."

Benjamin pulled the knife upward with infinite care until it was free. "Shall I continue?"

Bowman nodded.

A minute later, Benjamin lifted the small paper circle and exposed the tiny device inside. It was only then that he allowed himself to suck in a long breath. "That's completed." Benjamin leaned back away from the bomb.

Bowman raised to his knees and looked down at what they'd exposed. He pointed to the two wires leading to the flat, foil-clad battery in the center. "Those are the ones we have to cut at the same time. I want you to take the wire that's by the spirals. I'll take the other one. Slip your hand beneath mine and work through the opening she's holding apart."

"Wait a second," she protested. "We're talking exact timing, right? There's no way you can achieve that kind of precision with a knife, even if the wires are thin."

"With *that* knife we can," Bowman assured her. "Look at what it did to the cardboard. That blade could probably cut through stone."

"It will do the job," Benjamin stated calmly. He reached into his medicine pouch and rubbed some of the white powder onto the sharp edge as he chanted. His song stirred the air, as if unseen forces were amassing.

The song seemed to gain strength as its rhythmic cadence reverberated within the confined space inside the van. Bowman unconsciously straightened his shoulders, and his eyes filled with a steady confidence that hadn't been there moments before. Julia watched the change and felt her own courage and strength building.

By the time the last strains of the strange words drifted into silence, their moods had changed dramatically. Fear was no longer the driving force behind their actions—they were suddenly filled with determination and the will to succeed. Julia stared at Benjamin, filled with wonder.

Bowman's gaze reflected respect. "It's time we finish this, Uncle," he said quietly.

Benjamin leaned down, easing his blade through the tiny opening between pages.

Bowman knelt and poised the clippers over the wire. "On the count of three. One...two..."

Julia closed her eyes.

"Three."

Julia didn't even breathe. The click of wires snapping echoed in the dead silence of the van.

Bowman smiled. "We're finished here."

Julia leaned back, letting the pen that had held the pages open drop to the floor. "I think I've aged a hundred years."

"Then I'm just thirty years older than you," Benjamin chuckled, sheathing his knife. "Things *were* simpler in the old days."

Bowman wiped the perspiration from his brow and smiled dutifully at Benjamin's odd joke. "Simpler maybe, but just as dangerous." He looked at Benjamin closely for a moment, then shrugged skeptically.

Benjamin nodded somberly. "Yes, unfortunately, that is also true."

They crawled out of the van and headed for the deserted tribal building. "I suppose you want that van fingerprinted now more than ever,'' Bowman said, turning and holding up ten fingers toward the fence, signaling to the station personnel that it was safe to return in ten minutes. "Chief Roanhorse and Captain McKibben have used that van for about two years. Their fingerprints are bound to be everywhere.''

"I expect that, but if the criminals were counting on the van blowing up, they might have been careless about their own prints. We may yet find some solid evidence that'll help us catch this gang. The names we've managed to obtain need to be linked with physical evidence.''

"Then I'll do the fingerprinting myself before the men get back. News travels fast on the reservation, and I won't have the chief be the focus of any gossip,'' Bowman said, his expression unyielding.

"I'll help you,'' she offered.

"That'll speed things up.''

Bowman went inside the building and returned quickly with two fingerprint kits and some surgical gloves. He handed a pair to Julia. Benjamin stood close by, guarding in case anyone approached unexpectedly.

They searched the van carefully for more hidden explosives. Once they were sure there were no other devices, they began to expose and collect fingerprints. Julia lifted the handprint she'd left on the chrome, then moved to the interior.

She worked on the steering wheel, the ashtray and the glove compartment. After several minutes, she sat back. "Nothing. It's been wiped clean.''

"The prints I found on the door handles and the exterior are so smudged they're useless. What now?''

"Let's go to your office,'' she said.

He led the way inside, then gestured to a couple of empty chairs. As usual, Benjamin remained standing. "Make it quick. My people are bringing the vehicles back and will soon be at their workstations.''

"Whether you like it or not, Chief Roanhorse is a suspect.''

"That's ridiculous. Besides, he certainly had nothing to do

with the heist at the Mini Mart. He's too well-known. He'd be recognized no matter where he went on this reservation."

"Maybe, but he still could have provided the gang with information, instructions and the van. I'm going to need a chance to look into this. But for the time being, this has to remain between us. I don't want the chief to know that we're investigating him."

"*We're* not—you are," Bowman growled. "And you're way off base." He stood by the door, signaling that the meeting, as far as he was concerned, had come to an end.

Julia left Bowman's office, Benjamin by her side, and returned to the car. She was making enemies by the second, and the thought depressed her. She wasn't working against the tribe. Why couldn't the others see that?

As she pulled out of the station's parking lot, she saw the line of cars heading back in. It would be business as usual before long. "Let's interview the Mini Mart owner. That place might have been targeted for a particular reason. Maybe it's close to the gang's permanent hideout. Or perhaps the owner has had some new, repeat customers she can identify for us."

They rode down the highway, each lost in their own thoughts. Benjamin could see Julia was trying hard to appear cool and collected. Their slow progress on the case was beginning to undermine her confidence, though he knew she would rather die than admit it.

As they approached the small store and slowed down to turn, he noted the tension that coiled through her body. She was worried she wouldn't receive the cooperation she needed. "Patience is your best ally," he counseled.

She nodded. "I'll keep it in mind."

As Julia walked into the store, she noticed a middle-aged Navajo woman sweeping by the back door. Her face was smooth and her eyes were bright with life and intelligence. She glanced up as they entered. Her gaze strayed over Julia, then drifted to Benjamin. She gave him a courteous nod, but pointedly ignored Julia.

"Ma'am, if you have a minute," Julia said, "I'd like to ask

you a few questions. I'm with the FBI, and I'm investigating a series of crimes, including the one that took place here.''

The woman gave her a blank stare, then continued sweeping.

"Could you translate what I said into Navajo?" Julia asked Benjamin.

"I speak English," the woman said abruptly. "But I don't like wasting time. Ask your questions, then leave. You bring problems to our people." She glanced at Benjamin. "Don't remain with the white woman much longer. It will only bring you sorrow. That's what I hear, anyway," she said, then swept some broken glass into a dustpan.

Julia schooled her face into polite neutrality, determined not to show how deeply the old woman's words had cut her. "Are you the owner?"

The woman nodded, not bothering to look at Julia. "I am Shirley Pete."

"Has Chief Roanhorse had the opportunity to speak with you?"

"The chief has his concerns. I have mine. The policemen took away the refrigerator where I keep drinks, milk, sandwiches and most of the items customers want during the summer. Not very many people come now."

Julia knew they'd found bullet holes in the unit. They'd probably run into trouble getting the rounds out and decided to take the machine in. "I'll see to it that it's returned as soon as possible. But in the meantime I'm going to need your help. Have you had many Anglo customers lately?"

She placed the broom against the wall and walked to a chair. "We get a few, but no strangers. My customers are mostly from the tribe. I had been getting a few deputies from the sheriff's department. They had been stopping by because I'm the closest place to their roadblock, even though they're positioned outside the rez."

"Do you have any idea why the thieves targeted your store?"

The woman leaned back in the worn armchair and closed her eyes. Minutes passed. Julia thought Shirley Pete had fallen asleep and started to say something, but Benjamin touched her arm lightly and shook his head. She waited for what seemed an eternity, then the woman met her gaze.

"Maybe it's because we're isolated, yet still near the border of the reservation. Or maybe because it's easy to break in through our windows." She shrugged. "But then, the store has always been isolated, and the windows were always there. It's only since the *bilagáana* thieves came into our land that my problem started."

"You must have had other break-ins sometime before this," Julia protested gently. "How long have you owned this store?"

"Thirty years. And yes, once or twice we had some kids come through the back and steal a few cases of pop, but no one has ever put bullet holes in my door or my refrigerator. Maybe times are changing, but not for the better."

"I'll do everything I can to get your refrigerator back quickly. You have my word."

The woman smiled wearily but said nothing.

"I don't make promises easily. When I do, you can count on them," Julia assured.

"I will judge on what I see," the woman said slowly.

She had her chance. If she could come through for Shirley Pete, word would spread that she could be relied on. Maybe then she could begin to bridge the gap that separated her from the people she'd come to help.

Julia left the Mini Mart with Benjamin and returned to the car. "I'm going to do whatever it takes to get that machine back to her. If the rounds haven't been extracted yet, I'll do it myself." She paused. "These people are worthy of my respect. I want to earn theirs, too."

"Pride."

"Yes, but not on a personal level. If I'm going to make progress, I'm going to need to earn the people's confidence. Helping this woman is one way I can go about that."

She picked up the radio and asked to be patched through to the chief. She explained what she wanted to do. "Have the slugs been taken out of it yet?"

"No. We haven't had the manpower to spare. The job's going to be time-consuming because the bullets are lodged deep, and we wanted to do as little damage to Shirley's refrigerator as possible."

"Would you mind if I took care of that? At the moment, it's one lead I'm free to pursue."

"Go to the portable building directly behind the station. All our oversized pieces of evidence are stored there. I'll have an officer meet you with the key."

Twenty minutes later, they joined a tribal lieutenant at the door of the building. He had her sign a form recording the date and time. "Before you leave, stop by the office and sign out," he said. "We have to keep close tabs on anyone who enters this area."

"No problem." She unlocked the door and stepped inside. Merchandise and equipment, stacked almost ceiling-high in a random pattern, practically engulfed the room. "Where's Shirley's refrigerator?"

The officer shrugged. "It's in there somewhere. Just look around. If it seems a little crowded, it's because we have to use part of this building for storage, too."

They started searching after the officer left, Benjamin taking one side and Julia the other. They finally found the glass front unit against the wall, but books and equipment crates blocked their way. Working together, they began moving things aside.

Slowly, Julia became aware that the temperature inside the metal building was soaring. "I'm going to have to prop that door open. It's so hot, I can barely breathe."

"I'm not sure that'll help. There's not much of a breeze today."

"It couldn't get any worse." She propped the door open, then returned to the job at hand. Her back ached as she pushed aside crates that seemed to weigh as much as she did. Perspiration streamed down her body. She was about to suggest that they take a break and go into the air-conditioned main building when she heard footsteps. Wondering if Roanhorse or Bowman had decided to pay them a visit, she walked toward the door.

Suddenly something flew past her. "Get down!" she yelled, diving behind one of the crates.

# Chapter Fourteen

She heard glass shatter and smelled gasoline just as a spot on the floor directly ahead of her exploded into orange flames. Before she could react, the door was slammed shut, trapping them inside. Julia rushed in search of a fire extinguisher, yelling a description of the device to Benjamin so he could help her look.

As the flames spread to boxes on a wall shelf, she heard a loud snapping noise by the metal door. It didn't sound like a rescue attempt, but she couldn't be sure of anything except that the door remained shut. "Keep looking—there's got to be something we can put that fire out with."

"What did they throw in here?"

"A Molotov cocktail—a firebomb. It's a bottle filled with gasoline and a rag that's been set on fire," she said, as cardboard boxes and papers turned into a mass of flames. "We've got to make it out that door. There's no rear exit that I can see."

He found a wool coat on one of the metal shelves against the wall and then moved forward, beating the flames back with it. Julia raced through the path he cleared. As she grasped the knob on the metal door, the heat singed her hand. "It won't budge!"

Benjamin forced his shoulder against the door, and when that failed kicked it hard in hopes of dislodging whatever held them prisoner. Firmly attached to its steel frame, the metal door didn't give. "We're wasting time. We've got to find another way out while we can still breathe."

"There's probably a vent—an opening—in here some-place."

He glanced around. The fire had spread all the way across the front and part of the side of the building. "There is no opening, unless it is behind something." His eyes stung from the smoke.

"There's a gas-heater closet over there," she said, gesturing to her right. "The unit won't be turned on this time of year, but there has to be a vent around it to meet local codes."

As Julia and Benjamin groped their way across the room through acrid smoke, a stack of boxes toppled over, crashing to the ground. The papers inside them caught fire, and the flames spread quickly to a wooden table that had already begun to smolder.

Coughing heavily, she kicked a box out of the way and searched for the closet. Seconds later, she found it, opened the door and poked her head inside. "I found it, but it's going to be a *very* tight fit." Her lungs were burning, and her tear-filled eyes made it hard to see. She held her sleeve in front of her mouth, trying to filter out the smoke. "But we've got to squeeze through. It's our only chance."

She turned to Benjamin. He was tall and lean and probably wouldn't have much trouble making it. Her chances weren't as good, however. Although she was slim, her hips were definitely those of a woman and, unlike her breasts, they wouldn't compress. "You go first."

He stared at her as if she had lost her mind. "No."

"Don't argue with me, Benjamin, just do it!"

"You are afraid you won't make it. If I stay, I can push you out."

"True, but if I get stuck, pulling's going to be more effective, and you can go get help." She suppressed a shudder, thinking of what it would be like to die that way in the fire.

"You will make it through," he said quietly. "Now go."

"We're wasting time." She choked again on the fumes.

"Exactly. Now go."

She muttered under her breath, knowing he wouldn't yield. She'd have to play it his way or risk dying of smoke inhalation while they argued. Julia shoved the vent outward, then looked at the rectangular opening. It was about the size of a small file-cabinet drawer. It wouldn't be an impossible fit; she could make it.

She stooped down and slowly threaded her head and upper body through. The narrow opening hurt her shoulders and breasts, bruising her every inch of the way. She was halfway out when her hips caught against the metal rim of the opening. Pain knifed into her.

As she tried to force her body forward, she felt her slacks tear. Then something hard sliced into her skin. A slippery warmth, which she instantly knew was her own blood, began to trickle down her left side, and her hip began to throb. She bit down hard to stifle a groan.

"You'll be okay," Benjamin said quietly.

She heard him begin to chant and felt his hand next to her wound. As the soft rhythmic cadence drew her in, the pain receded, and her skin began pulsating with the steady beat of his song. Then slowly, the song became all and the pain only a memory.

With an odd sense of detachment, she felt his palm smoothing over her injured hip, then moving down her leg. Somewhere in the back of her mind, she realized he was spreading the blood, using it to help her slide through. Yet each note continued to spiral around her, enfolding her in a safe cocoon. The chant tugged at her consciousness, enticing her to surrender to its power.

"Now. Pull forward, *sawe*. Gently."

She heard his words and felt compelled to obey, but she had to struggle against the fear of renewed pain. Then she felt his hand stroking her hip, and the warmth melted away her concerns. Confidence and the will to survive surged through her. She moved forward, surprised by how easy the task was now.

She tumbled out of the opening just as two officers came

rushing forward. They caught her and eased her to the ground. "No, don't worry about me." She felt light-headed and disoriented, as if she'd just emerged from a very odd dream. "Benjamin's still inside," she added, wondering why her speech was thick.

One of the men held her up as she limped over to a safe spot fifty yards from the burning portable. Julia sat down, vaguely aware of a distant soreness in her hip. She glanced down at her slacks and noted with surprise that there was very little blood staining the fabric. It was certainly a far cry from the amount she'd imagined she'd lost. She cursed an overactive imagination. Benjamin had undoubtedly concluded that she was a weakling who couldn't take a little discomfort without falling apart.

Benjamin appeared moments later. It had only taken him a few seconds to wiggle through. Wiping the soot from his face, he walked over to her side and smiled as she looked up. "See? I was right. You made it through." He held out his hand. "Come on."

A Navajo medic came toward her. "No, don't walk around. We've got to check that cut on your hip."

"It's not much more than a scratch," Benjamin said calmly.

"Uncle, when there's blood, we've got to check it out."

Julia struggled to her feet, astonished to find she didn't feel sore anymore. "Then let's go inside. I'm not about to take my pants off here," she said, cocking her head toward the dozen or so officers manning two fire hoses. They had run lines from a building valve and a yellow hydrant.

Once inside an empty office, the medic checked her out thoroughly, but as Benjamin had promised, there was only a small cut. The blood had clotted over it, and the wound was dry. "You heal quickly."

"With help," she muttered, suddenly remembering the song and the warmth. "I better go back outside," she said, not wanting to try to answer questions she didn't have answers to.

She walked around the burning building, which was being sprayed by steady streams of water. Suddenly her heart lodged in her throat. The door, now broken open, had been bolted and padlocked. No wonder they hadn't been able to get out.

Benjamin watched with her as a fire truck pulled up, adding its trained crew to the police volunteers. "It seems someone went through a great deal of trouble to put an end to us."

Bowman joined them and studied her at a glance. "You okay?"

"Sure."

"In that case, I've suddenly got a lot of extra work to do."

As Bowman walked away, her gaze narrowed. "The gang's been second-guessing us too accurately. There's a leak in this department."

"Maybe not."

"Somebody around here had the gall to set fire to a police department building in broad daylight with officers roaming around. Who else besides another cop would ever have a chance to pull off something like that without being noticed?" She met his gaze in a challenge. "Can you think of any other possible explanation for everything that's happened?"

Benjamin took a deep breath, then nodded. "The power of the amulets. The agate Twin is helping the man who carries it."

She shook her head. "It's true that I understand very little about that power, but I doubt the amulet can give the criminal tactical training. Our answer, when we find it, is going to be simpler and very human."

"I would like to walk around the police station. If the one with the agate amulet is here, I will find him," Benjamin said.

Julia nodded. "Just be careful. If he does control the power…"

"I have my own strength. You know that." Benjamin turned and moved toward a group of officers who stood to one side, watching the action.

Julia took the opportunity to find Bowman. He stood behind the fire hose still manned primarily by police officers. "Deputy Chief, could you find out at what time exactly Chief Roanhorse's van was reported missing? I know it was the day after the robbery.''

Bowman's gaze hardened, and he took her aside. ''I told you, it wasn't his van exclusively. McKibben of the sheriff's department used it, too.''

''When was it reported missing?'' she repeated.

Bowman's jaw clenched, and the vein on his forehead bulged. ''McKibben noticed it was gone the next morning at around eight or nine. The report, as you know, was vague, since the van reappeared shortly thereafter.''

As she stared pensively at the burning building, she remembered the Mini Mart's owner. A knot formed at the pit of her stomach. ''Shirley Pete really needed that commercial refrigerator of hers,'' Julia said, her voice taut. ''Most of her business came from selling cold snacks and sodas.''

''Our insurance will cover the replacement costs. Hers should fill in for the loss of income.''

''But settling a claim can take a long time.''

He shrugged. ''Shirley Pete's family will help her. A Navajo always has family.''

The words made her ache. She envied them that. ''Tell me about McKibben,'' she said, returning her thoughts to the work that defined her. ''Was he ever a field officer?''

''Yes. In fact, he used to be one of the best SWAT instructors in the state. They promoted him out of that position a while back. It was either politics or they wanted someone younger.''

So that meant he had tactical training. ''What about Chief Roanhorse? Does he have any special skills?''

''Not like McKibben's,'' Bowman said shortly.

She knew he was trying to protect him, but she refused to back away from the questions she had to ask. ''How did he become a cop?''

''Joined after a long stint in the marines. He was some kind of lieutenant. That was more years ago than I care to remember. No one has ever complained about his job performance.'' His tone held a warning.

"I want to change the way we've been doing things," Julia said after a brief pause.

"In what way?"

"Ever since the sting at the trading post went sour and my partner was shot, we've been on the defensive. I'm tired of only reacting to events. It's time to lay a trap. I'm going to use standard radio channels to send a couple of phony messages—one to the chief and another to McKibben. You and I will use a special frequency to stay in touch while the operation is underway."

"I'm not sure I can do this." Bowman shook his head. "I answer to the chief, not to you."

"You said you wanted the chief cleared fast. If my plan works, it should do just that. Will you work with me on this?"

His face hardened. "I don't have the authority to act against the chief, and you don't have enough actual evidence to get a court order."

"There's always the tribal council. They could order an investigation of the whole department if I convinced them it was necessary. We know there's a leak. The timing of the fire in the evidence building isn't coincidental."

"It still doesn't point directly to our chief. Anybody here could have done it."

"I'm offering you a chance to clear the man without giving rise to rumors and gossip that could hurt his integrity and ability to command. I thought that was what you wanted," she countered.

"This is on your head if it backfires, you got me?"

"That's the way it's always been, hasn't it?" she replied cynically.

They watched the men working their way into the building, soaking down glowing embers. Finally, a lieutenant in the fire department approached. "We tried to save what we could, sir, but there's not much left inside. It's a mess in there."

"Is your fire investigator on the way?"

The fireman shrugged. "I suppose, but he won't be here

anytime soon. This is his day off, and they're still trying to locate him.''

"We'll need a copy of his report as soon as he's done. We have to know what set this off.''

"A Molotov cocktail,'' Julia said.

Bowman pursed his lips, then glanced at the lieutenant. "See if you can gather up anything that'll help us trace some part of it.''

"Already done. We think it was a ketchup bottle,'' the fireman answered slowly. "I mean, it's the only candidate in the right place. We found bottle fragments that smelled like gasoline in the area near the door where the fire started.''

"Careful how you handle the glass. If we can't lift prints here, the Bureau's labs have technology that might help us,'' Julia said.

"We'll do our best.''

As the fire lieutenant moved back toward the building, Bowman glanced at her. "Meet me in my office in fifteen minutes. We'll discuss your plan there. I want to take a look around in the evidence building and see what, if anything, is salvageable.''

Julia nodded, then started toward the office building when Benjamin joined her. "The amulets are not here.''

"So much for that.''

He gestured toward the fire-damaged building. "You gave your word to the woman at the market. What will you do now?''

"I've been thinking about that, but I wanted to ask you about this first. Bowman was adamant that her family would take care of her, and I don't want Ms. Pete to think I'm interfering. Still, I thought I would give her some money. Maybe she could find a simple refrigerator that could replace the cooler for the time being. That way, she wouldn't have such a long wait.''

"There is a better way,'' he answered slowly. "Ask the officers to join your efforts to help raise the money needed. Then everyone will have the chance to participate. No one will have to carry the full burden and it will be easier for her to accept.''

Benjamin glanced back where the firemen were still working. "They might still need help. I better go see if there is anything I can do."

Julia nodded and went inside. She stopped by the receptionist's desk, then proceeded to Bowman's office. A few minutes later, Bowman entered the room. "Okay. I'm ready to listen to your proposal."

She leaned back in her chair. "I'm going to send a message to the chief telling him I've received a tip and I'm on my way to a stakeout. I'll pick someplace remote where we won't endanger any civilians. Then I'll do the same with McKibben, only I'll give him a different location. If either man is connected to the gang, they'll probably take the opportunity to set up an ambush. And we'll have our answer."

"It's risky," Bowman said, after a long period of silence.

"Yes, it is. You'll need a top notch officer to stake out McKibben. I'll take Chief Roanhorse. If either of us senses trouble and we need backup, we can radio each other using a prearranged signal."

"*I'll* watch McKibben. No need to stir up more trouble than we absolutely have to," Bowman snapped. "I guess you aren't willing to trust me watching the chief, are you?"

"That's not it. I'm trying to leave less margin for error. You're more likely to give the chief the benefit of the doubt, and that might leave you vulnerable. On the other hand, I don't see you doing the same thing around McKibben."

"All right. You're calling it. At least we'll be keeping down the number of people involved—and the gossip it would create."

"Do you have any suggestions for appropriate stakeout sites?"

He studied the map of the reservation tacked up on the wall behind his desk. "There's a potato warehouse at the end of this road, north of Shiprock High School. It's empty this time of year and pretty much by itself. Another place is this old ruin, which is east of here, close to Hogback. It's been isolated by erosion so that it stands in a canyon."

"Sounds okay. Give me a chance to check out the sites." She started to walk out, then stopped. "I'm going to ask the officers if they'd like to chip in so Shirley Pete can replace her cooler right away. I know her relatives will see her through any tough times, but that'll add a burden to other lives, as well."

Bowman fished out his wallet and handed her a twenty. "Okay. Sounds good. Only, make sure to tell her that we'll all get our money back later from the insurance. Shirley's a proud woman. She can use the help, but whether she'll accept it or not, that's another matter." Bowman walked out with Julia and made a general announcement to the officers in the outer offices.

While one of the secretaries kept tab, money was collected. Julia placed fifty dollars into the box, then waited as each of the officers made a contribution. Before long, a substantial amount had been accumulated.

Bowman stood behind her. "I know this was your idea, but she might have an easier time accepting it from her nephew," he said, gesturing to a young Navajo officer who stood in one corner, watching.

"Good thought. Do you want to ask him?"

"If it comes from me, it might sound like an order. From you, it'll be a request."

"Then I'll ask," she said.

Julia approached the young policeman, and in a voice that no one else could hear, explained why she'd done what she had. "I hope you're not offended by my action. Since the item taken was in our care, I thought it would be okay for us to help her out now."

"I find nothing to be offended about," he answered calmly. "Without a place to keep sandwiches, ice cream and cold beverages, her business is going to drop sharply. She can't afford that. Winters are always lean for her since there's not as much traffic going through here." He picked up the box containing the money and, nodding to the others there, walked out of the building.

She'd sensed his pride and was grateful she hadn't wounded it in any way. A moment later, she felt Benjamin approaching. She hadn't turned around, there'd been no need to, but she knew with absolute certainty that it was him. Her skin pulsed and her body thrummed, buffeted by an awareness so strong it stunned her. "Shall we go?" she asked quietly.

"Your senses are good," Benjamin commented when she finally looked back.

"Let's hope they stay razor sharp until this operation is finished," Julia answered, filling him in on the way to the car.

They were underway minutes later. Julia first checked out the place near Hogback, which was some distance from the highway. An abandoned Anasazi village stood in the middle of a wide canyon. It was too open to make an ambush easy, yet closed-in enough to make it tempting. "Bowman selected this place well. Do we use it for McKibben or the chief?"

"The chief wouldn't set up a trap here—he knows this land too well. He'd choose a location where the terrain would be more to his advantage. That is, assuming he's guilty."

"You still don't believe either of these men is the gang's leader?"

"The leak you're searching for isn't a human one," he answered. "The person responsible for the crimes may know the right tactics, but the information comes from the amulets. I am certain of it."

"If you're right, neither of these men will take the bait, and no harm will be done."

She drove down the highway through Shiprock to the second location Bowman had selected. Purple asters were in bloom, dotting the desert in a patchwork of blue and violet. The land seemed ablaze with a radiance of its own, tempting her to forget about their grim mission. But the intermittent calls over the radio drew her thoughts back to the job she had to accomplish.

They arrived at the spot twenty minutes later. The big barn was isolated from the main highway down below a mesa, but a network of dirt roads gave her the choice of several escape routes, if that became necessary.

She went to the top of the mesa and glanced around. Two of the side roads led out to some isolated homes barely visible in the distance along the river.

"If I was going to set up an ambush, this place would be my choice," she said at last. "There are enough cottonwood trees, tall brush and ditches close to the barn to provide hiding places. A lot could happen at this location."

"We should go to the mesa east of here. We need to watch the spots someone would pick to watch the watchers. That position is higher in elevation and will give us a clear view all the way to the highway. But I wish you wouldn't pursue this plan," he said, shaking his head. "It is a mistake. You are risking too much."

"They can't sneak up on us. We're way ahead of them."

"I am not in fear for our lives," he answered. "What concerns me is the damage you will cause the tribal police. Word of what you are doing will eventually get out. You will make many enemies. Then you might find that when you need help, no one will be willing to come."

"That has happened to our agents before," she commented thoughtfully. "It's a chance we take wherever the Bureau sends us. It's impossible to take over a case from local authorities and not make at least a few people angry. So if this does escalate into a situation like the one you mentioned, well, that's my job and what they pay me for. But there's no need for you to be involved in this part," she said in deference to his objections. "Your concern is for the amulets, and this won't further your search."

"My concern is also for you," Benjamin affirmed, his voice soft as the caress of the breeze.

She felt the gentleness behind his words envelop her like an embrace. An aching hunger that started deep within her belly wound its way around her heart. "I'm trying to give you a way out. It's my way of protecting you from dangers you don't have to face."

"But you're wrong. I do have to face them. Since I came here, I've learned many things about myself and about the amulets. There was a time when I thought I knew both. But now I see that you and I and the Twins are connected in ways we haven't even begun to understand."

Julia walked back to the car. "Looks like we're both learning, and that isn't always easy," she admitted slowly. "I've had to accept that I'm not nearly as tough or as smart as I've always thought I was. And that my heart isn't encased in steel, nor is it impregnable. But I can take life as it comes, enjoy the good and take the bad. That's what makes me a survivor," she said, lacing a deeper meaning in her words. She was trying to assure him, or perhaps herself, that she was prepared to face the day when they would finally say goodbye.

Once inside the car, Julia sent the separate radio messages to Captain McKibben and Chief Roanhorse. Her last message, coded and on a special frequency, went out to Bowman. "Now we'll hide and wait to see what surprises the night brings."

HOURS PASSED, AS THEY SAT waiting for the afternoon sun to go down. The car was hidden two hundred yards away in a grove of salt cedars. Benjamin had helped her hide the vehicle tracks and disguise the car with branches. Even when she looked directly at the spot where she knew the car was, it remained invisible.

She shifted restlessly, amazed at how Benjamin could sit perfectly still for endless periods of time. "Once it's dark, we'll have to move closer to the top and keep a sharp eye for headlights or moonlight reflecting off glass and metal," she said. "They'll expect us to be here for hours, since stakeouts are usually long and boring. So I'm certain they won't be making their move until night falls. We're fortunate that there's only one way to approach this location."

"Unless they come from the houses, or on foot along the river."

Julia wiped at the perspiration that covered her brow. She was looking forward to nightfall. Any respite from the intense heat would be welcome. "By now I would have expected to see at least one vehicle or person checking out the place."

He nodded. "If someone were planning an ambush tonight, that is precisely what they would have done. How long do you want to wait?"

"A few more hours, at least. It might take them some time to set up their ambush, especially if they have to travel out of their way to avoid the roadblocks and patrols. If there hasn't been any activity by then, we'll head back." She glanced down at her hand-held radio. "I'm glad Bowman told me he took a partner along on the stakeout. That's one less thing for me to worry about. Lucky for us his brother works for the department. From what Bowman said, he'd trust that man with anything, including his own life."

Benjamin gazed off into the distance, lost in thought. "That's the way it was between *my* brother and I. He was a little older than I was, and we were always close. Even more so after we both became adults. Then he was killed." He paused. "The one friend I had whom I could always count on was gone, and I was alone."

"What happened to the rest of your family?"

"Most were killed fighting the soldiers. Some were taken captive."

"I know what it's like to find yourself alone," she answered. He'd just shown her what she knew was the most vulnerable and wounded piece of his heart. She longed to say something that could soothe his hurt, yet she knew that no words could fill the hole that life had left there.

Time went by slowly, and finally night descended. The full moon bathed the desert ground in a muted silvery glow that pushed back the sharp edges of darkness.

"They won't come," Benjamin said.

"Now who's losing patience?" she retorted with a tiny grin.

"It is not a matter of patience—it is a feeling. Mine are usually correct, as I'm sure you've noticed," he said, injured pride coloring his words.

"It's too early to go," she said, smiling. "And you're not *always* right."

He scowled. "Are you trying to annoy me? Or are you just being temperamental?"

"Neither. I'm teasing you." She gave him a squeeze on the arm.

"I could start teasing you back," he said, moving closer until his breath caressed her face.

Julia swallowed. "No, that would disrupt my concentration."

"I certainly hope so."

She saw the gleam in his eyes and laughed. "Okay. You win."

"No, that's something neither of us will do," he murmured with a touch of sadness, then moved away.

Julia watched him for a moment, then turned and glanced toward the empty warehouse. She wanted Benjamin Two Eagle and needed him in every way a woman could need a man. But the knowledge that he'd eventually leave her, and that she'd have only memories to sustain her, made her draw away. Her survival instincts were too well honed.

They remained watchful for several more hours, then finally she brushed the dirt from her jeans and stood. "It's time for us to leave." She started down the rise. "If you say 'I told you so,' I'll sock you in the nose."

"You mean you'll try."

"No, I mean I'll sock you in the nose."

He continued walking, saying nothing.

She found his self-assurance annoying. "In case you forgot, I'm well trained in hand-to-hand combat. They don't pass out gold badges like mine at the local deli, you know."

"The what?"

She sighed. "Never mind." Discouraged after a wasted evening, she helped Benjamin remove the camouflage from the car. Five minutes later, they were on their way back to the motel. "I might as well call Bowman." She picked up the radio. "There's nothing happening over here," she told him. "My lead didn't pan out. I'll check in with you tomorrow morning and see if there's anything new."

"Yeah, fine," Bowman said over the radio. "I'm calling it a night, too. Over and out."

She racked the mike. "I was so sure something would happen," she muttered softly.

Julia pulled into the motel's parking area a half hour later, then glanced at the all-night diner across the highway. There were very few customers over there, but it was open. "What do you say we walk across the road and get something to eat? It's late, and I'm starving."

"So am I, and I am curious to see what food they serve."

She grabbed her hand-held and locked the car. As they crossed the highway, she saw a pair of headlights pulling out onto the road to her right. The prickling down her spine warned her of danger. Grasping Benjamin's hand, she darted forward. He didn't need any encouragement. His speed told her he'd sensed something was wrong, too.

In a heartbeat, the car rocketed toward them, bullets peppering the ground just ahead. Julia zigzagged toward a large Dumpster. It seemed a million miles away, but it was their best chance.

"We won't make it this way." Benjamin wrapped his arm around her shoulder and dove down by the lip of the pavement. Julia dropped her radio, but before she could retrieve it, a spray of bullets bracketed the area where they'd stood. The car squealed to a stop, spinning around to make another pass.

Julia saw her hand-held lying on the road, riddled with bullets. But that was the least of their problems at the moment. They had to reach cover fast. Jumping up, they sprinted toward the Dumpster again. Julia gripped her pistol hard as their attacker closed in on them.

As the rapid-fire semiautomatic cut loose, a stinging shower of rock fragments and dust covered her ankles. "They're not going to give up!" She snapped off two quick shots, but there was no time to aim. The vehicle had slid into the parking area and was getting so close it would be impossible for the gunman to miss them.

As they plunged headlong into the deepest shadows, she heard Benjamin begin a chant.

# Chapter Fifteen

The song was oddly compelling. It was as if it were lifting her and gently pulling her toward safety.

Somewhere in the back of her mind, she became aware that the shooting had stopped. Then, when it began again a split second later, she realized they were aiming at a spot much farther ahead. She peered out to discover why and saw the shadows of a man and a woman clearly outlined on the ground.

"Civilians!" She aimed her weapon, intending to draw the fire away from the couple, but Benjamin quickly grabbed her arm.

"No! Illusion." He made an odd gesture with his fingers, and the shadows seem to move farther away.

"But how—"

"Is it really important?" he whispered urgently.

The car wheeled around and made one more pass at the shadows, and the ground was peppered with bullets. Then, as the odd ululant cry of a coyote rose in the night, the shadows vanished.

Abruptly the car's brakes jammed on, and the vehicle turned one-hundred-and-eighty degrees and rocketed down the darkened highway.

"It's over," she said, getting to her feet as the red taillights faded.

"It looks like your trap worked after all. It is the timing that came as a surprise.'' He jogged across the street with her, staying at her side.

"I'm calling Bowman." She quickly reached her car and reported the drive-by shooting.

"I was on my way home, so I'm not too far from your location. I'll be there in a few minutes," Bowman said.

She placed the mike back and glanced at Benjamin. "What's your gut feeling about Bowman?"

"I don't believe that he planned this, if that is what you're thinking. If he had, he would have tried to find a way that would clearly implicate the sheriff's man. Misleading you would have served his purpose."

"Misleading me might not have been his priority. He may have hoped to kill us both and get rid of his two biggest problems—at least, temporarily." She shook her head. "I don't know anymore. Being on the reservation puts me at a disadvantage. I can't seem to think the way others do here."

"To adapt to our ways, you must learn to relax. Stop trying to hurry what cannot be forced."

She was thinking of a reply when she saw a tribal vehicle pull up and Bowman emerge.

He glanced at the small group of people standing across the street near the doors of the restaurant, then focused his attention on Julia and Benjamin. After listening to their account of what had happened, he rubbed the back of his neck. "It was a smart move on the gang's part. They deliberately waited, like a smart cop would have before staging a raid. They wanted you tired, sleepy and complacent before they attacked."

"One thing might still work in our favor." Benjamin glanced from Bowman to Julia. "They aren't sure if we are alive or dead."

Bowman stared across the road. "There are three people over there, and I know two of them. I'll ask them to keep the truth quiet. I'll also make sure the department doesn't release any statements about either of you. You can lay low for a few days. Any more than that and the chief is going to demand extensive explanations."

"What do you plan to tell Chief Roanhorse?"

"Just that there was a shooting and that you've asked us to withhold information about you for now. You have a plan you want to pursue."

"Good." She glanced back at the motel. "Of course, we can't stay in there anymore. If they came gunning for us again, we'd be sitting ducks."

"I can try to find a safe house for you, but I need some time to do that. Maybe by tomorrow morning I'll have something."

"So tonight we camp out," she said with a shrug.

"I have some gear in the trunk of my unit which you're welcome to use. I was going to take my son fishing with me this weekend, but I won't need it until then."

"I'd appreciate the loan," she said.

Together they transferred the equipment to her vehicle. "What *are* your plans?" Bowman asked when they were done.

"I haven't really come up with anything firm yet," Julia admitted. Although it was the truth in this case, she was becoming increasingly reluctant to disclose information to anyone except Benjamin. "I need a chance to think. What I'd like to do is go over the evidence confiscated from each of the suspects. Can you bring that to me? Maybe after I take another look, I can come up with a new idea."

"I don't want to let that out of the station," he said flatly. "We're lucky it's been locked in the chief's office instead of the evidence room."

"Okay. I'll have to use my own reports, then. I'll study them and try to come up with a new angle."

"Check in by telephone from time to time. The second I have a safe house, I'll let you know."

Julia and Benjamin waited for his car to disappear down the highway before entering her own. She drove across the street and, while Benjamin kept watch from the car, ran inside for some food. She returned in a few minutes with four sandwiches and two cans of soda in a paper bag.

"Here's our dinner, and breakfast too, probably. We'll eat once we're well hidden."

Benjamin nodded, then looked into the bag. "Why did you buy artillery shells? We have no cannon." He pulled out one of the silver soda cans. "It's cold. The powder is probably wet."

Julia laughed. "Never seen canned food, huh? It's a cold drink."

"Oh." Benjamin nodded and placed the can back into the sack.

Julia drove up to the highway and looked both ways carefully. She pulled out and accelerated to highway speed immediately, glancing in the rearview mirror to see if they were being followed.

"A safe house might be a great idea," she commented as they headed down the road, "but if there's a leak in the department, it won't be very safe at all."

"Depending on where it is, we may be able to improve its defenses. A building by the road is difficult to protect, but I think the police will choose a place with few entrances."

"Limited access could also become a trap."

He nodded, conceding. "We better concentrate on finding a safe place to rest tonight. We'll worry about tomorrow when the time comes. Do you have any suggestions?"

"I thought we'd camp out in the canyon behind the motel. I'm almost sure we'll be able to see my room from there."

"You think they'll try again?"

"Not really, but it's worth keeping an eye on the place just in case."

She slowed and turned off the highway onto a dirt track that was barely passable. The deep furrows swallowed the tires and bounced the vehicle hard. She tried her best to avoid any large rocks, but the ground was covered with them. "I wish I'd been given a four-wheel-drive vehicle. I guess they have more of these highway units than the more expensive all-terrain types."

Reaching the base of the hill, she slowed to a stop. "This is as far as I dare go. Let's take the camping gear from the trunk and hike uphill."

He brought out the two sleeping bags and a large flashlight.

"A blanket and a fire, whenever possible, was all I've ever needed," he muttered.

"Yes, but we'll be more warm and comfortable than you used to be." She thought of how it might have been in his day. The thought of sharing a campfire with him as man and woman filled her with an intense longing. A blanket and their bodies pressed together... Perhaps simpler *was* better. Her skin prickled and desire awakened within her. As she picked up her small accordion file of papers, she caught a glimpse of the look he was giving her. She felt her cheeks burn. He'd guessed her thoughts! She refused to meet his gaze. This was the last thing she needed!

"I have to find a spot where I'll be able to use the flashlight and do some reading without giving our position away," she said in a brusque, businesslike tone.

A tiny smile tugged at the corners of his mouth as he gestured ahead to an outcropping of rocks. "How about in among those large boulders? There's not much room, but the rocks will hide the glow."

Several minutes later, they'd set up camp. Benjamin took a borrowed pair of binoculars and slipped into the darkness, searching for an unobstructed view of her motel room. Julia sat down between the rocks with her flashlight, concentrating on reading the files on her lap.

The gang's buy sheet gave extensive descriptions of the jewelry and artifacts they'd already purchased with their stolen money. It also listed pieces they were still looking for. That was of no immediate use, however. She then looked through the list of personal possessions taken from the crooks. There was nothing of particular interest to her there, either. Even the recovered weapons had been stolen or purchased with phony IDs.

Finally she turned to some bound photocopied pages taken from a book on artifacts, which tribal detectives had learned dated back to 1920. The original volume was now a valuable collector's item. She read through some of the descriptions, but none of the items cross-referenced against the buy sheet. It was interesting reading, but useless to the investigation at this point, as far as she was concerned.

She took a deep breath. Why had she thought she'd find a clue to the gang's whereabouts here? She was just wasting her time. Discouraged, she flipped through the remaining pages of the notebook. Then her gaze fell on the last page, and her heart suddenly lodged in her throat.

Both amulets were listed there, although only her turquoise Twin had been photographed. As she read the brief history beneath the photo, a chill twisted all through her. The turquoise Twin had originally belonged to an unknown Navajo medicine man, but it had come into the possession of Capt. Alger Thayer of the United States Cavalry.

She recognized the last name from the stories her mother had told her. Capt. Alger Thayer was one of *her* ancestors! The world stood still for a moment as Julia absorbed the information.

Benjamin suddenly appeared at the edge of the circle of rocks. "What's wrong?"

Julia jumped and reached for her gun. "Did you see someone?" she asked, quickly scrambling to her feet.

"No," he answered slowly. "I felt something wrong...with you."

She stared down at the papers in her left hand. She wanted to keep this from him. The thought that he might come to hate her as much as he hated the man who'd betrayed him was terrifying to her. She had forced herself to accept that one day he'd return to his own time. But she wasn't sure how she'd deal with it, if fate cheated her of even the closeness they shared now.

"What have you discovered?" he asked gently.

She took a deep breath, then let it out again. "If I could hide what I've just learned from you and still live with myself, I would."

Benjamin gave her a puzzled look. "There is nothing so terrible that you cannot tell me."

"You may wish you'd never known me after you hear what I've got to say."

She sat down on the hill overlooking the motel and gestured for him to join her. Julia explained about Captain Thayer, watching Benjamin's reaction in the dim light of the moon. The skin over his cheekbones seemed to grow taut, and his eyes slowly narrowed. An unbearable ache spread through her chest. "Your Capt. Green Eyes was my great-great grandfather," she said at last.

He stood up and moved away from her. "Are you certain?"

She nodded. "Once I saw his name and read the history of the amulets, I remembered a story my mom told me a long time ago. I've always known that the amulet was our only family heirloom, something treasured and passed down from generation to generation. To me that was what was important, not the details so much. Then, when I was reading the amulets history, I began remembering certain facts. My mom had told me that it was the only possession my great-great grandfather had left his pregnant bride. He simply vanished one day, leaving only his horse and the amulet behind." Now she knew the entire story, but unraveling the mystery only filled her with sadness.

"And over the years, the amulet became a source of pride to you, a treasure you considered rightfully yours," he said bitterly.

"Yes," she answered in a raw whisper, "but I didn't know about you. The amulet and my mother's story were my only links to a family I'd never known. It was all I had to hold on to as I was sent from one foster home to the next. I know now that it was a symbol of dishonor, but I'm glad I didn't know that then," she answered honestly.

His eyes mirrored the struggle going on inside him. "History has brought me full circle. All this time I've vowed to take the life of the man who betrayed my people and led to my years of imprisonment. Now I find that if I do, I may cause terrible harm and alter your life path." His voice shook, but he cleared his throat quickly and turned away. "I need time to think. I'll be back," he said, slipping silently into the darkness.

Julia waited for what seemed an eternity. She kept a close watch on her motel room through the binoculars, but her thoughts remained on Benjamin. He'd channeled a century of hatred into dreams of that one moment when he'd finally take his revenge. Now he had to think all that through again. This newfound knowledge, coupled with the choice he was being forced to make, would rip him to pieces.

As the minutes ticked by and Benjamin failed to return, she prepared herself to face the inevitable. She felt the cold emptiness growing inside her, numbing and shielding her from the pain, and was grateful for it.

At long last, Benjamin came out from behind an outcropping of rocks and approached. "I didn't go far. I wanted some time alone, but you were never abandoned."

She felt the first touch of hope bathe her like the beams of sunlight that heralded a new dawn.

"I would never go back on my word, or my responsibilities."

Her heart sank. He was talking about duty—not love. "Nothing's happened. I can continue watching if you want more time to yourself."

He shook his head. "It's not necessary."

"Have you come up with any answers?"

"At first, all I felt was rage. At myself, at you, at the gods who released me in this time and place. Then I thought of my need to destroy Capt. Green Eyes."

"You were willing to do that once, even at the cost of your own life."

"Yes, but never at your expense." His voice vibrated with emotions too raw to contain. "In many ways my darkest enemy redeemed himself through you and what you have chosen to do with your life. But the scales of justice still need to be balanced. I won't take his life in payment for the ones he took, but I will find Green Eyes and exact revenge. His body will carry the badge of his shame."

His return, particularly now, seemed as inevitable as the rising of the sun. She had only one hope. Maybe after both amulets were together again, and his fate was no longer at their mercy, he'd see that those who'd died were beyond his help. His own life was as precious as the ones he wanted to avenge, and here he would have the chance to do the good he would never be able to accomplish in the past.

"We have to take things as they come," she said, hiding the turmoil in her mind. "For now, we have to concentrate on finding the gang," she said.

"Tomorrow, at first light, you and I should leave here and pay Daniel Brownhat a visit."

"The Singer?"

"Yes. It's possible he knows something about the amulets that can help us find the agate Twin."

"That's a good idea," she said. "I don't know where he lives, but Bowman might. Do you think we ought to risk asking him?"

"He's not our only source of information. Any of the *Dineh* will know where we can find Brownhat."

"You're probably right," she conceded. "But whether they'll tell us is another matter."

"True. Even though I am one of them, they know that I am involved in the troubles here, and they may feel inclined to protect him. There is another problem, as well. The moment we come out of hiding to seek his whereabouts, we are letting people know that we are both alive and uninjured. Word might be passed to the wrong person."

"So we either ask Bowman or take a chance on a stranger."

He considered it for a long moment. "Shirley Pete would help," he said with conviction. "And she will not tell anyone, if I ask her to remain silent."

"All right. Tomorrow morning, early, we'll go see her. But if she hasn't received the money we collected, or if she doesn't know I had something to do with that, she may not be as eager to help as you think."

"She knows everything that matters by now. And she will help," he affirmed.

They took turns watching the hotel with the binoculars, but no one appeared to have any interest in where they were supposed to be staying. By morning, she felt as if she hadn't rested at all, but Benjamin seemed full of energy. She gathered up the camping gear, muttering under her breath.

"I had a restless night. How did you manage to sleep so soundly?"

He picked up the flashlight and a bedroll, and together they carried everything down to her vehicle. "Discipline," he answered with a shrug.

"Are you implying I don't have any?" She shot him a hard look.

"I simply answered you with the truth. Anger is pointless," he said calmly.

His logic was as irritating as it was unassailable. "Forget it. I'm not going to let you bait me into an argument."

"I wasn't trying—"

She held up a hand. "It's a mistake to annoy me too much after I've had a rough night. Trust me."

He clamped his mouth shut, and they rode to Shirley Pete's in silence. Julia was the most complicated, confusing woman he had ever known. She had a way of gnawing at him as if she were deliberately trying to make him lose his patience. A *hataalii* didn't lose control. To achieve harmony and to walk in beauty, one had to find balance. Nothing should be in excess—particularly emotions. But then, his teachers had never met Julia.

He had always been a pleasant man, one not easily provoked or swayed by passion. However, around Julia, everything inside him went crazy. He wanted to claim her and tame her. He wanted to assert himself in the most basic way of all until she surrendered to him, crying out his name. Perhaps if he had done that last night, she would have been less shrewish today.

He felt himself getting hard thinking of what might have been and quickly focused on the small cacti that dotted the desert—beautiful plants with lots of needles. He glanced over at her, then shifted his gaze to the road.

Out of the corner of his eye, he caught her smiling as if she'd guessed his thoughts. Perhaps his body had betrayed him. "Why did you do that?"

"What?"

"You were smiling? Why?"

"Why are you worried about it?" she countered.

"I am *not* worried," he said, his voice rising. Hearing himself, he stared at her, appalled at what he'd done. He'd never shouted at a woman before. "Concentrate on your driving, please. If you must travel this fast, then your attention should be solely on that."

He saw her smile again, but this time he clamped his mouth shut. Determined to focus his thoughts away from her, Benjamin kept his attention on the surrounding desert. That, at least, was something he understood. The thought comforted him.

They arrived at the Mini Mart twenty minutes later. Shirley Pete was sweeping off the porch when they parked. She waved at them as they approached.

Julia smiled at her. "Good morning," she greeted.

"My store is now fully stocked," Shirley said. "Come in." She went over to a shelf and grabbed a box of breakfast bars. She then opened the door of a large, brand-new refrigerator that stood against the wall and brought out two cartons of milk. "Take these. You both look hungry."

Julia hesitated, uncertain whether or not to accept, but before she could say anything, Benjamin tore into one of the bars. "Thank you," he said.

Julia followed his lead almost immediately. "It's very nice of you, and you're right, we hadn't had anything to eat today."

"I heard about the shooting," Shirley commented quietly. "Some people thought you had been killed. Is there anything I can do to help you now?"

"We would be grateful if you do not tell anyone you saw us," Benjamin said.

"Easily done."

"Could you also tell us where Daniel Brownhat lives?" Julia asked.

Shirley nodded and glanced at Benjamin. "It's about time you two met." She reached over to an insurance-company wall calendar and tore off the page for the previous month. "I'll draw you a map. He's in a very remote area, and the only landmarks are the land itself." She gave Julia a speculative look, then shifted her gaze to Benjamin. "I think you'll have to help her."

Julia held her tongue with difficulty. The woman might be right, but that didn't make it any easier to swallow. A moment later, she studied the map Shirley Pete had drawn. "What's this?" she asked, pointing to a series of vertical lines with a birdlike image superimposed on them.

"It's a cliff. On its face are those markings. You must turn left there, and go farther up the canyon until you reach the point where the canyon divides. You then take the right fork. The Singer's place is at the end of the canyon. You can travel by car, but make sure you go very slowly and choose your path wisely. Some of the rocks can tear up your tires, and the sand makes it easy to get stuck."

Julia stared at the map. In its own crazy way, it made sense. Maybe she was finally getting used to things out here. "We'll find it. Thanks," she said, taking the map from the counter.

As they walked to the car, Benjamin glanced at her. "May I take another look at that map?"

"Sure. Here you go." She handed him the paper. "You navigate. I'll drive."

The journey turned out to be quite frustrating. Several times, they had to double back or take a different route when they came upon places where summer rains had washed out the road. The trip took most of the day and led them through a desolate and rugged expanse of desert. By the time they arrived at Daniel Brownhat's small house trailer, the sun had already set and the last rays of light bathed the horizon in a wild blaze of pink, orange and lavender.

"How can anyone stand living in an area this remote?" she mused.

Julia parked and got ready to wait until Brownhat appeared and issued an invitation. She knew that walking to the front door without being asked in would be considered unspeakably rude.

"My guess is he chose it because it is removed from people," Benjamin said. "Being a Singer carries many responsibilities. A man needs time to be alone. When he wants to be with others, it's easy enough for him to go into town." He called her attention to a blue pickup parked next to a tall juniper.

A tall man with a strong, wiry frame emerged from the trailer moments later and waved. He stood with his back erect, like someone accustomed to wearing the mantle of authority. As they walked up, Julia noticed his soft, dark eyes. He wore an easy smile, full of pleasure, but not surprise, at seeing them.

"I'm glad you have both come. It's time." He led them around the trailer to a hogan that stood fifty feet away. "I heard the reports of the shooting, but I knew you were both fine." He held aside the blanket covering the entrance and glanced at Julia. "No, I didn't tell anyone."

The question had been on her mind, and she wondered if her expression had given her away. Unnerved, she took a seat on the ground beside Benjamin. A small kerosene lantern had been placed near the door, and eerie shadows flickered against the walls as the two men watched each other in silence. She sensed no animosity between them, just an easy tranquillity. Time dragged on, and the quiet seemed almost deafening to her. She couldn't shake the feeling, however, that there was plenty of communication going on, though at a level she didn't understand. She waited impatiently, trying hard not to show it.

"Uncle," Brownhat said at last, "I am honored that you have come."

She stared at Brownhat, who was at least forty years older than Benjamin. She couldn't help but wonder how much he knew about Benjamin.

"I am a Stargazer," Brownhat said quietly.

"I am not familiar with the term, Nephew," Benjamin answered.

"It is said that it's an ability the gods didn't give to any of the *Dineh* until after our captivity at Fort Sumner. I use this—" he opened his palm and revealed a small rock crystal "—to see beyond the sight of others. I stand quietly, facing Big Black Star—" he glanced at Julia "—the one your people call Venus. I ask for help, and then a vision appears in the crystal." As he finished the explanation, his gaze came to rest on Benjamin.

"I sense power in you, Nephew." Benjamin's deep voice held a compelling resonance. "Can you help us finish what is started?"

"I know you're searching for the amulets. That's at the center of all you are and all you must do." He paused. "But your task goes beyond that, Uncle," he said sadly. "And the outcome is…uncertain."

"I know," Benjamin answered.

"Have you seen something specific?" Julia asked. The words slipped out before she realized that she might not want to hear the answer.

"I see what could be, but time passes and things change. I will go outside and ask Big Black Star. Then I'll tell you all I can."

He stood just outside the doorway of the hogan. The last of the day had already faded into darkness as he began to chant softly. A breeze seemed to grow, swirling in the piñons around them, then a stillness settled over the desert. It was as if every denizen of that barren land had abruptly stopped going about their business, listening to a higher call.

Julia shifted so she could get a clearer view. The crystal in the Singer's hand began pulsing with light that grew more intense with each passing second. Suddenly, that light flared into a blinding flash. For one long second, it was as if the stone had turned into flame.

Brownhat staggered back, groaning in pain, then his legs buckled. As he dropped to his knees, the crystal rolled out of his hand and fell to the ground.

## Chapter Sixteen

Raw power, like a raging fire that robbed the air of oxygen, swirled around Benjamin, leaving him dizzy. Fighting against it, he struggled to his feet and rushed to Brownhat's side. "Nephew, what went wrong?"

Brownhat stared at his shaking hand. A blackened spot marred the center of his palm where he'd held the crystal. "That has never happened to me before."

Julia saw the man's hand and wondered where he found the strength to keep from screaming out in pain. "You've got a bad burn, sir. That's going to need treatment."

"I have something to put on it. It will heal." He bent over and retrieved the crystal, inspecting it carefully.

"What happened?" Benjamin asked.

"We should take some steps to protect ourselves before I answer your question." Brownhat went inside the hogan and picked up his medicine pouch. "Sit down," he said, gesturing to both of them. "It won't take me long to do what I have to."

Julia watched Brownhat walk next to the doorway of the hogan and retrieve a small pottery bowl. Chanting over it, he began burning a substance that smelled like pine incense. Puzzled, Julia glanced at Benjamin.

"Every *hataalii* has a special mixture used to keep away evil," Benjamin whispered. "He is now insuring our safety while we are here in his place."

Brownhat allowed the preparation to continue burning as he

walked around the hogan, sprinkling powders from his medicine bundle. Finally, he came and joined them. "The powders also contain magic and will strengthen the protection that surrounds us now," he explained to Julia.

"What happened?" Benjamin asked.

"I sensed a presence that goes beyond human evil. It shadows you, my uncle. You must remain alert. And you must protect each other. Your destinies are linked." He met Julia's eyes and held them. "Learn to open your mind without fear, and you must learn to trust, though many times you won't understand. If you fail at this, there is no future for either of you."

"You mean we'll die?" she asked in a whisper-soft voice.

"I don't know. I saw nothing—all I felt was sorrow."

"Our enemies, Nephew—can you tell us where they are?"

"They are not where you are searching for them, but will be where you least expect." Brownhat paused for a long moment. "Whatever happens will be hardest on you," he said, looking at Julia. "Choose well and you'll find the happiness your heart needs. But if you don't, your path will bring you only sadness."

It was his tone, and the genuine concern laced through his words, that made her heart ache. "How will I know which decisions are the right ones?"

"Listen to yourself. Despite everything you've learned, there are times when logic will lead you astray, and intuition will be your best ally."

His answer made her more uncomfortable than ever. "And the agate amulet? How can we find it?"

"It will find you. That much is inevitable."

"Thank you, Nephew." Benjamin reached into his own medicine pouch and retrieved a small white shell bead shaped like the crescent of a waxing moon. "This is for you, with my thanks."

"No payment is required of you, Uncle."

"Then accept it as a gift."

Brownhat took the small bead and placed it inside his own

medicine pouch. "I'll keep it with me for as long as I live."
He walked outside with them. "Do you have a place to spend
the night?"

Julia considered going back to the hillside behind the motel
and keeping watch. Even though they now knew the correct
way out to the main road, and the drive would only take a few
hours, something told her it would be futile. Contacting Bowman didn't seem like a good idea, either. If there was a high-
level leak within the department, she wasn't interested in any
safe house they might provide. Maybe this was a good time to
start using her intuition. "All I know right now is where we
*won't* be going," she admitted honestly.

"Stay in the hogan, then. I'll keep watch and you'll both be
safe. The wards will hold and nothing will disturb your sleep."
He paused, then continued hesitantly. "You will need that rest
in days to come."

Julia glanced at Benjamin, who nodded. "Thank you. We'll
accept your hospitality," he answered.

"I'll bring you some food."

As Brownhat left, Julia looked around. "I'll get the sleeping
bags."

Benjamin shook his head. "He'll be bringing some blankets.
Will you spend the night like a Navajo?"

She nodded in agreement. She would have rather had the
sleeping bag, but figured it would be undiplomatic to admit it.
"Shall we take turns watching?"

He said nothing for a while. Finally, he spoke. "Will you
trust me now?"

She exhaled softly. "How do I know I'm not going to like
this?"

Benjamin smiled. "Intuition. See that? You're listening to
one of ours already." Benjamin walked to the doorway and
stared at the nighttime sky. "There won't be any need for either
of us to keep watch tonight. He will guard us with his life, if
necessary. You and I will never be safer than tonight."

She started to argue that it placed a very big burden on
Daniel Brownhat, but then changed her mind. No one knew

where they were, and out here, it would be impossible for anyone to sneak up on them. Besides, she'd always been a light sleeper, and sleeping on the hard ground would insure that didn't change.

Brownhat returned holding two bowls of mutton stew, some fresh fry bread, and several blankets draped over one arm. "I live alone, so I've learned to be a good cook," he said, setting the bowls down before them. "Eat and enjoy," he added, as he placed the blankets on the ground off to the side.

She'd never cared for mutton stew, but the bowl in front of her smelled delicious. She took a small bite. The food tasted wonderful, and it didn't take long for her to finish it. She glanced up quickly, wondering if she'd made a pig of herself, but Brownhat's pleased smile told her he'd taken it as a compliment. "Would you like some more?"

"I couldn't eat another bite," she said with a smile. "But this was wonderful. Thanks so much for sharing your food with us."

He nodded and took the dishes. "Sleep well, and unconcerned. I will remain just outside, and no one will come near this hogan."

She was staring pensively at the door when Benjamin came up from behind her, holding the blankets. "You'll find them warm. They're wool."

"Good, because the desert gets really cold at night." She listened, but she could hear no footsteps or human sounds anywhere nearby. "How can he be so quiet out there?"

He gave her a puzzled look. "He's not. Can't you hear him moving about in the brush behind this hogan?"

She listened. "No. Can you?"

"Of course! The problem is that you're too used to listening for vehicles that make enough noise to stampede a herd of cattle."

"Traffic sounds can be comforting."

"You're not serious!" He stared at her in astonishment.

"Well, they can be, if that's what you're used to," she replied stubbornly.

He spread out his blanket, then watched her working to find a comfortable spot. "Do you miss your world?"

She hesitated. "I'll go back eventually."

He blew out the lantern. "That doesn't answer my question."

She heard him settle down on the ground less than three feet away. In the darkness she could barely make out his outline. Yet his nearness sparked some primitive awareness that allowed her to feel him without touching and that made every nerve ending in her body tingle.

She suddenly found herself wishing that Brownhat were a million miles away. "Home doesn't seem the same to me anymore," she whispered. "I feel at home with you."

"I understand, better than you can imagine," he answered quietly, then said no more.

Benjamin lay awake long after the rhythmic sound of her breathing filled the hogan. He liked having her close by his side. It felt as if she was his woman. But that wasn't true, and he'd never been good at lying to himself. If things had been different, he would have battled whatever stood in their way, but there were powers no man could fight.

HE STOOD BY THE DOOR of the hogan as the golden rays of the morning sun broke from the east, bathing the desert with its warm glow. The land was beautiful and familiar, though little else seemed to be in this time. Hearing her stir, he turned around. She looked soft and beautiful in the half-light of the hogan. He fought the desire to take her into his arms, push her back onto the sand and love her until she was his.

With effort, he forced the thought from his mind. "You slept well?"

She smiled sleepily and nodded. "You're up early."

"Too many thoughts," he answered absently.

She folded up the blanket and set it aside. "Let's say goodbye to our host. We have business waiting for us back in town."

"The Singer is gone. He stopped by earlier when he saw me

at the door. He was on his way to gather the herbs he needs for his rituals. Some of those require many hours of travel and extensive searches because of the places they grow. That's something that hasn't changed over the decades.''

"In that case, we better get going." She stepped outside, then stopped and glanced back at the hogan one last time. A soft sigh escaped her lips as she longed wistfully for the night that might have been. Taking a deep breath, she tore her gaze away and went toward the car.

Benjamin walked with her quietly, sharing her mood. ''What is your plan for today?''

She nodded. "I want to find Roanhorse."

"Remember the Singer's words. Our enemies aren't where you're searching."

"I need to find out once and for all if he's guilty or innocent. If he's innocent, we can use his help."

It was nearly noon by the time they reached the main highway. Breaking radio silence, she called the dispatcher and asked to be patched through to Chief Roanhorse.

"Where have you been?" the chief growled without amenities. "We're supposed to be working on the same side."

"You'll have a full explanation when I see you."

"I'm at the roadblock in Shiprock at the junction of Highway 64 and 666. Why don't you come straight here?"

"My ETA's forty minutes." She racked the mike and pressed down hard on the accelerator.

"Are you going to tell me what you're going to do?" Benjamin asked.

"Mostly, I'm going to play it by ear." She paused, then smiled. "Or if you prefer, I intend to let my intuition guide me."

A short time later she pulled to a stop several feet from the two patrol vehicles blocking Highway 64 just west of the intersection. She saw Roanhorse wave to the deputies, assuring them all was fine.

Julia strode toward the chief, then took him aside while Benjamin stayed with the officers.

"What's this all about?" Roanhorse demanded.

She detailed the circumstantial evidence against him, from the leaks to the vehicle used in the Mini Mart robbery. "It all points to someone on the inside. Someone with a great deal of authority or access to information."

"I hope you're not implying that I'm responsible," he said, his voice all steel and ice.

"All I have is the evidence I've uncovered so far. I can't prove anything yet."

"But you don't trust me. That's what you're saying." He spat the words out as if they'd left a foul taste in his mouth.

"It might help if you'd allow me to search your vehicle right now. I see you're using your personal car today."

"You have no right to ask me that."

"Nor do I have the right to search without a warrant, if you say no. But if you want me to trust you, then you'll have to give a little and cooperate with me." He glowered at her, but she forced herself to meet his gaze without flinching.

"Search the car," he said, "but I want an official apology after you're finished."

"For doing my job?" She shook her head. "If the circumstances were reversed, would you have done any differently?"

He pressed his lips together until they formed a thin, white line. "No," he admitted at last, then started toward his car. "Come on. Let's get this over with."

Julia knew as she took the keys from his hand that if she found nothing, the two police officers watching would spread the story, and she would get zero cooperation from that moment on. Still, this was better done here than in front of everyone back at his office.

His car was open, keeping the heat from building to an intolerable level inside. She glanced at the nearly empty interior and then pulled the trunk-release lever. She could feel the officers staring at her and, out of the corner of her eye, she saw Benjamin step between them and her. She didn't expect trouble, but if there was, it was good to know she had an ally close by.

She opened the trunk and studied its contents. There was the usual array of police equipment and some personal gear. She leaned over and popped open the tire well, mostly as a formality. She didn't really expect to find anything in such an obvious hiding place.

Julia struggled with the cover briefly, then finally it came free. As she pulled it away, a half dozen plastic sandwich bags stuffed with money tumbled out into the trunk.

"I *never* put those there," the chief said in a shocked whisper.

She noticed he'd paled considerably. He was either giving an Academy Award performance, or he was telling the truth. "I'm going to check the serial numbers against the bills stolen from the banks. Then we'll talk."

She walked to her car and returned holding a clipboard and wearing surgical gloves. Julia opened one of the bags and checked several serial numbers against her list. "They all match."

"Someone's trying to frame me."

"This is more than a try, Chief," she answered. "I'm going to have to place you under arrest."

"You wouldn't dare," he growled. "Are you forgetting where you are?"

"We can do this the easy way or the hard way, Chief. But I *am* placing you under arrest," she said, pulling a pair of cuffs from her rear pocket.

"You can't possibly believe I would have let you search my car if I'd known those were there. Even a rookie would have known to check the tire well!" he roared.

"I'll admit the evidence looks suspicious, but you can't expect me to just ignore it." She read him his rights and, placing a hand on his arm, gently turned him around, ready to handcuff him.

Out of the corner of her eye, she saw one of the policemen start to move toward her. Benjamin quickly blocked his way. "Don't do it, Officer," she called as she finished handcuffing the chief. "It'll just make things worse for everyone."

The tension was so thick she could feel it pressing in against her. She held her breath, hoping this didn't turn into a confrontation no one could win. She had to go past the officers to get to her car. As she stepped forward, the men held their ground, refusing to move aside.

# Chapter Seventeen

Seconds dragged by and the stalemate continued. Finally, the chief took a step forward. Though handcuffed, he stood tall, and his voice was authoritative. "You have your posts and work to do. Remain here. The FBI agent has made a mistake—" he paused "—one she'll undoubtedly regret later."

The officers stepped back.

"I'll be taking in the evidence," Julia said, handing one of the officers a form to sign. "The car will remain here with you until we can have it towed in. It'll need to be fingerprinted, particularly the trunk. What we find then might clear your chief, so be careful not to touch anything. You're responsible for this vehicle."

"We don't take orders from you," the senior officer said shortly.

"But you do from me, Nephew," Roanhorse said. "This car will prove what you and I know is a frame-up. Guard it well."

"You've got it, Chief," the officer answered immediately.

Julia led Roanhorse to her car. "We're going back to your office."

"Don't think you'll find even one person who'll support what you're doing," he warned as she opened the back door and helped him inside.

"It doesn't matter—I've got a job to do," she answered.

Julia returned to the chief's car, took the bags filled with money and placed them in a loose mesh grocery sack she kept for certain kinds of evidence. After storing it in her trunk, they got underway.

"The stolen money shouldn't have been so easy to find," Benjamin said.

"Stashing that loot in there would have taken someone very stupid or extremely clever," Julia said, agreeing with the direction his thoughts had taken.

"Clever how?" the chief protested. "I might as well have put the noose around my own neck."

"Or you might be counting on other evidence you know will clear you. Once it was proven you'd been victimized, I'd never be able to make another move against you. My job would also become increasingly difficult since your department would be very reluctant to cooperate with me."

"Is that what you think I'm doing?" Roanhorse retorted.

Julia found it difficult to treat the Navajo man as a suspect, but she had little choice. "I don't know. But I promise you this much—I'll get to the truth."

"We have something in common. I want the man who framed me."

"Who would want to do such a thing to you?" Benjamin asked.

"I don't know," he answered, after a moment.

"Where do you leave your personal vehicle during the day, Chief?" Julia asked.

"I keep it at home in the driveway. My wife uses it most of the time. I only take it when my unit is in for routine maintenance."

"So when that money was hidden in your trunk, the car could have been parked almost anywhere," Benjamin observed.

"'Fraid so."

Once they arrived at the station, Julia parked, then helped the chief out of the vehicle. "We've complied with regulations about transporting a suspect. I see no further need for these," she said, uncuffing him.

"You're trying to avoid trouble for yourself," Roanhorse commented.

"I don't shy away from trouble, Chief. My profession should prove that. This is a courtesy to you."

Roanhorse nodded. "I accept your answer." He walked inside with her and Benjamin. "What now?"

"I know it's inadmissible, but would you agree to a polygraph test?"

"Yes. Gladly. At least that's one thing that no one can rig against me."

Benjamin looked at Julia, puzzled. Just as she was about to tell him what a lie-detector test did, Deputy Chief Bowman came out of his office and strode toward her. The color of his face had deepened by at least two shades. It was obvious he'd heard the news. "What the hell have you done?" he asked in a deceptively soft tone.

"My job. And the same thing you would have done, I hope, if you'd discovered stolen money hidden in his car. Now, if you'll book him and find someone who's qualified to give him a polygraph test, I would appreciate it. Also, have Chief Roanhorse's car towed in here. We'll need to look it over."

"And what will you be doing? I mean, besides railroading the man?"

She tried not to give way to the anger coiling inside her. "I'll be busy trying to clear him," she snapped. "You might try working toward the same goal, too. You can start by getting a fingerprint kit for me. I'll be back in a minute."

Julia strode back outside, Benjamin half a step behind her.

"What do you want to do now?" he asked as they walked to the parking lot. "Take a look at the money?"

She headed to her car. "First, I have to do a comprehensive fingerprint check on each of those plastic pouches." She pulled the mesh bag out of the trunk. "Someone had to stuff these. Let's see whose fingerprints, if any, show up."

"And if they belong to the chief?"

"Then, I'm sorry, but that'll mean he's implicated, at least in my eyes. It's up to a judge and jury to decide for sure." She carried the cash bags into the station.

Bowman met them by the door and handed Benjamin the large attaché case that contained what she needed. He glowered at Julia. "Don't you dare thank me." He turned on his heels and strode away from her.

Julia went down the hall and glanced inside an empty conference room. "In here. The table is large enough, and it'll be private."

Refusing Benjamin's help, she checked every square inch of the plastic bags, but found nothing. "Things are starting to look more and more in the chief's favor."

"There are no prints you could use?"

"There are none at all, and there should have been some— if not his, then someone else's. These bags have been wiped clean."

"Doesn't that prove he's been framed?"

"Unless he wiped them himself as part of a more devious plan." She considered the possibilities, then shook her head. "But it still doesn't *feel* right. I'm going to work on his vehicle myself when it gets here." She glanced outside the window. "And here it is now."

Julia and Benjamin locked up the evidence inside Bowman's office safe, then went outside. As the chief's car was placed in the impound yard, Bowman joined her in the parking lot. His face mirrored frank contempt. "The man who handles our polygraph tests isn't here at the moment, but he should arrive shortly. You want to be present?"

"Yes." She waited for Roanhorse's vehicle to be freed from the tow truck, then approached the driver. "No one touched the trunk area?"

"No one touched anything except the front bumper. I had to attach the towing apparatus," the Navajo driver said, readjusting his baseball cap. "And this is as far as I go with it. If you need it towed anywhere else, give me a call."

Bowman signed the voucher the driver handed him. "Thanks, Billy."

After the tow truck drove out of the parking area and Bow-man went inside, Julia began her search. Benjamin helped her, using his sharp eyes to spot smudges that might turn out to be prints.

Julia checked around the keyhole and the trunk release, but the only prints there were her own, recognizable from the scar on the pad of her index finger. Wordlessly, they continued working across the entire trunk surface. Though they covered every inch, they found no prints whatsoever. She stood back lost in thought, staring at the trunk.

Benjamin, hearing footsteps, turned around. "Here comes the deputy chief. And he is still in a very bad mood."

Bowman, joining them, saw the one print she had lifted. "Well? Shall I do a matchup on that?"

"No need, it's my own."

"And there're no other ones." Bowman smiled. "Or have you locked them up in your briefcase for safekeeping?"

"No, that's it. And yes," she added before he could say anything else, "that does tend to indicate it was a frame. The chief wouldn't have wiped all the prints off—there was no need. It would have seemed far more natural if we had found his prints and his wife's somewhere on the car. It's very difficult, for instance, to close this trunk without using hands."

"You can see the areas on the car that the criminals wiped clean, if you look closely," Benjamin added. "There's less surface dust there."

Bowman glared at Julia. "You should have believed me when I assured you the chief was innocent. But we're ready to give him a polygraph, if you still think that's necessary."

"Yes, I do. It's a matter of form at this point, but useful to support his innocence."

Ten minutes later they sat in a small room normally used for questioning witnesses. The portable polygraph machine had been placed in the center of a small table, with the technician on one side and Roanhorse on the other. Blood pressure, pulse rate and galvanic skin-response sensors had been attached to the chief.

Sample test questions had been posed to Roanhorse to set up a pattern for comparison, questions to which he had been instructed to deliberately lie. She could tell by the look on the chief's face that he was furious with her for the indignities he'd suffered.

She sat silently as each of the pointed questions she had prepared were asked. The chief maintained his innocence throughout, and the needle recorded no unexpected variations evident to her untrained eye.

Finally, the Navajo technician turned to her. "In my expert opinion, none of the chief's answers suggest any attempt at deception. I believe he told the truth as he believed it to be. Anything else you'd like to ask?" The question, though worded softly, held an undertone of challenge.

"No, that about covers it," she replied.

As the sensors were removed, the chief glowered at her. "Well? By now, you've searched my car from top to bottom. What did you find?"

"No fingerprints, not even on the trunk," she said, then detailed their search.

"I told you it was a frame," he snapped. "Now I'm going to get back to my job and find out who's behind this." Roanhorse rose and walked to the door.

"It would be better if we all worked together," Julia said quietly.

He stopped at the entrance and faced her. "Do you really think that's possible? You thought I was guilty."

"I never personally believed that. I acted on the evidence, that's all. If I hadn't detained you while checking it out, I would have been neglecting my responsibilities." She met his gaze with a direct and candid look. "I hope that won't stand in the way of what we've got to do now."

Chief Roanhorse said nothing. His look was silently assessing, as if he was trying to make up his mind.

"We know whoever framed you is connected to the gang, and possibly this department," she added. "It's a lead we should both follow up on."

"If it's within my department, *I'm* the one who has to pursue it. You wouldn't get far."

"This case has many aspects. We need each other," she maintained.

He nodded once. "All right. Is there anything you need at the moment? If not, I've got work to do."

Benjamin walked over to the chief. "During the day, where do you keep the keys to your trunk?"

"Come with me." Roanhorse led Benjamin and Julia into his office, then shut the door behind him. "I leave them right there." He pointed to an unused ashtray on the corner of his desk.

"Do you keep your door locked when you're not here?" Julia asked.

"No, but you saw that my secretary's desk is right outside. If she's not there, Janet, across the hall, keeps an eye on these offices."

"Someone got hold of your keys," she insisted, then lapsed into a thoughtful silence. "Is there anyone around here who keeps up on the latest gossip? What I'm interested in is internal politics, like the jockeying for positions that normally goes on in any police department."

The chief considered it. "Pete Bowman. He's been here even longer than I have. He knows everything that goes on, either on the surface or beneath it. I'll have to follow that up, though. To him, you're an outsider."

"Chief, are you certain you want him involved?"

"Now you suspect *him?*"

"There have been only a few key players involved in this investigation. Bowman is one, McKibben is another. Then there's you and I, Benjamin and a few other tribal officers."

"Pete and I go back a long way. I trust him implicitly. You might as well get used to that."

"I have no objections. I just thought this was something I should call to your attention."

"Have you stopped to consider the likelihood that no one in

my department is involved? What has happened might be co-incidence, or the result of good timing and careful planning.''

She held his gaze for a moment. ''You don't believe it's coincidence any more than I do.''

''No,'' he admitted grudgingly. ''But I know my men. And I know McKibben, too. He's not the most diplomatic guy around, but he's a good cop. He worked his way up in the Sheriff's Department, and he's now close to retirement. He wouldn't mess things up for himself this close to the finish line.''

''The possibility that someone in this department is involved exists,'' she answered in a soft voice. ''Until we prove otherwise, I suggest you keep your back to the wall and think twice about trusting anyone.''

''I intend to do that,'' he said, then glanced at the door as Bowman entered.

Julia stood up. ''I'd appreciate it if you'd keep me posted on your progress.''

''*Now* you want our cooperation?'' Bowman retorted angrily.

''It's okay—relax,'' Roanhorse said, then gestured Bowman to a chair.

Julia followed Benjamin out, closing the door behind her.

As they entered the outer office, Benjamin went over to the secretary's desk. *''Buenas tardes, Teresa,''* he said, glancing at the nameplate on her desk. *''Tienes un momentito?''*

The woman slipped off her glasses and abruptly stopped her typing. ''Your Spanish is just beautiful! And yes, I do have a moment. What can I do for you?''

He smiled. ''I would appreciate if you would help us by answering a few questions.''

''People in your position often see what others miss, because your job demands you stay in tune with everything around you,'' Julia added.

''That's the truth,'' she agreed, turning to Julia. ''And I can assure you of one thing. Chief Roanhorse would never betray the trust the people have placed in him.''

"We know that," Benjamin answered gently, "but someone is trying very hard to convince us otherwise and make things difficult for the chief. We need to find a trail that will lead us to the guilty ones. Can you tell me who might be able to enter the chief's office unnoticed when he is not there?"

"No one, except me. And I'm here all day. These offices are never left unattended."

A thought formed in Julia's mind. "There were two doors in addition to the entrance inside the chief's office. Are they both closets?" she asked.

"No, the one opposite his desk leads to a small adjoining office. But that door is kept locked all the time."

"Is the office on the other side vacant?" she asked.

"No. Captain McKibben of the Sheriff's Department uses it. He comes in three times a week to update us on county law-enforcement activities and needs a place to fill out reports. If you want a look, all you have to do is go around the hall. It's the first doorway after the watercooler. There's nothing in there except a desk, so it's kept open."

Julia went down the hall and entered the small office. It was stark, with just a desk, a chair and a framed Sheriff's Department seal on the wall. Julia walked to the adjoining door and turned the knob soundlessly. It was locked, as the secretary had said. She could hear the men on the other side. Not wanting to interrupt them, she crouched and studied the locking mechanism. After a few minutes, she returned and joined Benjamin, who was still involved in a conversation with Teresa.

Benjamin said goodbye and went out into the hall with Julia. "She had no more information we could use. What did you accomplish?"

"I took a look inside McKibben's office. With the right tools, I could defeat that passage lock in five minutes or less. Admittedly, I didn't see any overt signs of tampering, but that isn't conclusive. We could be dealing with a skillful thief or someone who has access to a set of skeleton keys. That's not hard for anyone in law enforcement."

"So getting hold of the chief's keys wouldn't have been as

difficult as we've been led to believe.'' Benjamin lapsed into a thoughtful silence.

"It would have been easiest for McKibben,'' Julia said, "but anyone around here could have done it. Take Pete Bowman, for instance. He comes and goes freely. He could have walked in and out without anyone ever knowing about it. He might have even counted on McKibben being blamed if the keys were discovered missing.''

"The deputy chief also has one advantage that McKibben does not,'' Benjamin added. "The chief counts Bowman as a friend and an ally, and Bowman knows it.''

"Both McKibben and Bowman have been in on all our communications right from the beginning. Either one could have set up the ambush, and both have tactical training,'' Julia observed.

"We know where Bowman is now, but I think we need to track down McKibben,'' Benjamin said.

As they turned the corner, Julia saw Chief Roanhorse at the water fountain. "Chief, I haven't seen Captain McKibben around for a while. Do you know where I could find him?''

"He was planning to take a trip up to Window Rock today, so he'll probably be out of contact. Most county radios are old and unreliable across terrain like ours. If you want to try and reach him, you might leave word at the east roadblock on Highway 666. That's right outside the reservation, and he'll have to pass by there when he returns to Farmington.''

"Okay, thanks. I'll drop by there.'' She paused, considering the best way to say what was on her mind.

His eyes narrowed. "Something else is bothering you. What is it? This is the first time I've ever seen you hesitate,'' Chief Roanhorse observed.

"I know Pete Bowman is your friend, but the time has come to monitor his activities,'' she said.

"That's absurd.''

"Chief, you're probably right, but if we're going to identify the inside man, we have to rule Bowman out. Why don't you put a tail on him for twenty-four hours, starting tonight?''

"And the reason you're trying to find McKibben is so you can tail him?"

"Yeah, that's my plan," she answered.

"All right. I'll keep an eye on Pete myself, then. I know where he goes every evening."

"Where's that?"

"Home, to his wife and four sons," the chief spat out. "But I'll still keep watch all night, don't worry. Are you prepared to trust my word?"

"As much as you'll trust mine," Julia answered, her smile softening the impact of her words. "It works both ways, Chief. We've got to trust each other. There's no other way if we plan on ever closing this case."

## Chapter Eighteen

Silence stretched out between Roanhorse, Benjamin and her as they walked past the squad room. It wasn't until they entered an empty hallway that Roanhorse finally spoke.

"I assume you'll want to secure an emergency channel to stay in contact." Roanhorse glanced at her, saw her nod and continued. "I have two portables that can use the Bureau's tactical frequencies. I'll give you one and I'll use the other. The only people who could listen in are other Feds."

"We'll communicate only when necessary, but that's a good backup in case something urgent or unexpected comes up."

"I'll also have a unit drive up to take a look at McKibben's ranch later on this evening, in case there's been trouble or a problem with the radios."

"Okay. But have one do a drive-by on your location, too. Word it any way you like, but don't leave yourself open to surprises."

He nodded, a scowl on his face. "I'll handle it."

"I'll need directions to McKibben's ranch, Chief. Do you know how to find it?"

He pulled a notebook from his shirt pocket and scribbled a quick map. "Keep your eyes open, or you'll drive right past the dirt track that'll take you to it. It's technically off the res-ervation, but we cover the place for the county because the only access road is from the reservation side." He marked a spot on the sketch. "This hillside overlooks the ranch. I think it'll be the ideal surveillance point."

"Thanks, Chief."

Julia and Benjamin stopped by Roanhorse's office. In his locked closet were the tactical radios, which they quickly tested and placed at their belts. "One more thing. A replacement vehicle arrived for you today from the Bureau office in Albuquerque." Roanhorse gave her the keys, and she returned those for the tribal car she'd been using.

Moments later, they were in her new vehicle and underway.

"What's next?" Benjamin asked.

"I want to learn more about McKibben from his men. I'd like to know how they see him. Then I'll try to find out if they can give us his precise location."

It took them twenty-five minutes to reach the roadblock on the eastern reservation borders. Two county sheriff's deputies armed with shotguns as well as sidearms watched as she pulled off the road.

Julia produced her gold shield, holding it up high and in clear view as one of the sheriff's deputies drew near. The officer checked it, then moved back as she stepped out of the vehicle. "Can we help you with something specific, Agent Stevens?"

"How's it going out here for you? Any trouble?"

"No, ma'am. Things are pretty much under control." He eyed Benjamin with open suspicion, but said nothing.

The older officer came out from behind the cars. "It's really boring most of the time, if you want the truth."

"Most of these roadblock assignments are, don't you think?" she said with a friendly smile.

"Yeah, I suppose. But the way it was laid out for us, I really thought we'd see some action by now."

"Stay sharp. The operation's not over yet," she cautioned. "Who's been doing the briefings for the county officers on roadblock duty?"

"Captain McKibben. He said that the tribal cops were having a problem rounding up a gang of white people running wild. We're to be ready for when the ones still at large make a break for it.''

"None of us expected them to hole up," Julia answered. "Waiting them out has been tough on all of us."

"Maybe they slipped through before we were even notified to set up." He glanced at Benjamin. "Most Indians seem to be laid-back when it comes to time."

She saw Benjamin tense up and didn't blame him. The man's comment and tone had been intended to provoke a reaction. "I think you should try to be a little more tolerant of other cultures, Officer," she said, biting back her temper.

"What I said is true."

"Look at it this way. You have orders to cooperate with the tribe. Statements like yours don't further that." She glanced at his name—Ernie Curtis—in case he gave them any more trouble.

"I hope you don't expect me to apologize," Curtis snapped back.

"Don't do it on my account," Benjamin answered calmly.

"Trust me, I wouldn't."

She had to get everyone to ease up. Tempers flared too quickly in one-hundred-degree heat. "Off the record, do you agree with the way Captain McKibben has set up the county's involvement in this operation?"

"He was doing just fine, until you Feds started making the decisions. These roadblocks wouldn't be necessary if the tribal police finished their job."

"The roadblocks are vital," she said flatly. "They send a very important message. The remaining gang members will search for any way to escape the reservation as we turn up the heat. You're here to make sure that doesn't happen."

"Yeah, and if anything does go wrong when they try to break out, it'll be the Sheriff's Department who'll end up shouldering the blame. McKibben's too good a cop not to know what you're trying to do."

"You're very loyal to him," she said, refusing to rise to the bait.

"I've known him all my life—he's my second cousin. But even if we weren't related, I'd still agree with him on this. Our department is getting shafted."

"You're mistaken," she said coolly. "You're just being asked to do your job." She refused to allow this to escalate. "When you have a chance to think about it, you'll see that the steps taken are appropriate under the circumstances." She started back to her car, then stopped and turned her head. "By the way, any idea where I can find Captain McKibben?" she asked in a deceptively casual tone. "I need to talk to him about some new developments, and no one on the reservation's seen him around today."

"We could relay a message," the youngest officer said, "if he's within range of the radio."

"She's got a radio, too. We're not errand boys," Ernie snapped.

Julia took a deep breath and walked directly up to Ernie Curtis's face. "What's your problem?" she challenged in a soft voice. "You've been on the offensive since we got here."

Curtis gave ground slightly, but refused to back down. "The facts are simple. Things have been going wrong for you ever since you started this investigation. You need results desperately. You've even paired up with this Indian guy, who's some kind of magician. If you don't catch the rest of the gang, you're going to want a scapegoat. I have a gut feeling it'll end up being the Sheriff's Department and my cousin."

"Your fears are groundless." Benjamin's voice came from behind Curtis. Although his tone was soft, the power behind it was deafening. "The truth will protect the innocent."

"You eavesdrop really well." Ernie Curtis whirled to push Benjamin back, but Benjamin moved aside at the last second. Curtis, off guard, lost his footing and staggered before recapturing his balance. "Are you assaulting an officer?" Curtis drawled. "Bad mistake."

"He didn't attack you—he moved aside. Chill out!" Julia snapped the order.

The officer, who'd taken a step toward Benjamin, froze in

his tracks. Benjamin stood his ground, arms at his side, as if nothing out of the ordinary had happened.

"You don't want to fight me," Benjamin said softly.

The officer's gaze locked with Benjamin's. "You need someone to teach you a lesson."

"A lesson in what? I've done nothing to you. Your anger is misdirected. We are not attacking your cousin, nor does he need defending. Do you disagree with that?"

The officer started to speak, then clamped his mouth shut as if he hadn't been able to figure out how to respond. "Just stay away from me," he said. Glancing at Julia, he added, "If you want to find Willy, leave a message at either of his offices. You could also try his home number, but he has a machine that intercepts his calls. You'll never know when, or if, he got your message. If you really have to talk to him as soon as possible, you'll have to go to his ranch. But I warn you, he hates to be disturbed there unless it's an outright emergency."

"Then I'll wait until tomorrow."

"Good choice," he muttered.

As they drove away, Julia gave Benjamin an admiring look. "You handled that well."

He shrugged. "He's a very angry young man. I don't think he was trying to defend his cousin—he was just tense and ready to let off steam. But I don't believe in fighting for that reason."

She followed the directions on the map the chief had given her. But the deeper they went into the desert, the more uneasy she felt. She wanted to solve the case and find the amulet, and she had a feeling she was close to accomplishing that. But when she did, she'd lose Benjamin forever. That knowledge tormented her, leaving her feeling vulnerable and achingly alone.

The worst part was knowing she could do nothing more to compel him to stay. Love—the kind that fulfilled both body and soul—honored another's freedom to choose what was right for them. Love couldn't exist centered on selfishness.

"You're very quiet all of a sudden," Benjamin observed.

"I'm just thinking ahead," Julia said in a businesslike tone. She wouldn't let him know he'd become her biggest heartache.

Benjamin reached across the seat and touched her cheek lightly in a caress. "It's all right, my beautiful woman. I share the hurt you feel." There was so much more he wanted to tell her, but the words wouldn't come.

The warmth of his touch lingered on her skin. It filled her with longing and left her aching for more. She struggled to keep her thoughts focused solely on business.

Silence hung heavy between them. By the time they found the dirt road that led to McKibben's ranch, it was nightfall. "I'm going to have to switch my headlights off," she said. "It's too much of a giveaway. Help me keep a lookout for potholes and sharp rocks."

"There's plenty of light. The moon is full."

"Well, there's not as much light as I need." She narrowed her eyes, hoping they'd adjust to the dark quickly. "There's supposed to be a starlight scope in the trunk. We can use that to keep watch on the farmhouse."

"Be careful. Move the car to the left. There's a big cactus straight ahead."

She followed his instructions, trying to get a clear glimpse as they approached the hazard. "Where is it? I don't see anything." She spotted the cactus a second later as she drove past it. "In this light, everything looks gray. How did you see it against the rocky ground?"

"How was it that you did not see the cactus?"

She sighed. "I'm going to park here, behind these rocks. We'll go up the rest of the way on foot."

Julia pulled to a stop. She opened the trunk and took out a scope-equipped rifle, loaded it, then checked her sidearm. "Okay, let's go." They scrambled up the ridge of rock and sand, arriving at the top minutes later. Staying low, they moved toward the edge of the mesa. She brought the rifle to bear, using the starlight scope to survey the ranch house below them. "Interesting. Why would McKibben have an armed man walking around his property?"

"May I take a look?"

She passed him the weapon. "Everything will have a greenish glow, but you'll be surprised how clear the images are."

He shouldered the rifle and lowered his eye to see through the scope. A few seconds later, he peered up in surprise. "It's almost like peering into a different world. One that looks familiar, yet isn't."

"But you've got to admit, it really improves visibility."

He took another look through it. "But not enough. I should go down and take a closer look. We need to know for sure if that man is one of the gang members."

"Do you think he is?"

Benjamin hesitated. "Yes, but that's only an impression based on the way he moves. This man has a clumsy, almost lumbering way of walking. He reminds me of one of the men who ambushed us after chasing us into the canyons. I remember watching him and thinking he should have been making even more noise than he was."

"Let's move in. I'll take the front, you go around the back. If any of the gang members are there, we'll radio the chief for backup and have him gather his men."

"It's possible this will turn out to be nothing," he cautioned. "McKibben may have hired someone to stand watch at night. He might fear the growing tension within the tribe. Everyone knows that the gang is comprised of whites."

"Good point. Let's go find out for sure."

They split up and slipped quietly down the hill toward the ranch house, remaining hidden as they advanced. Julia felt her nerves stretched taut. If the guard turned out to be a gang member, they'd have to try and verify the number of people inside the house. That information would be vital, yet getting it would also be incredibly risky.

She stopped every few feet, searching the ground for surprises. She wouldn't have put it past McKibben to lay out a few traps to greet intruders. Warily, she listened to the night sounds and realized how attuned she'd become to the desert. She wasn't a stranger to this land anymore.

Julia was closing in when she saw the guard near the side of the house stop to light a cigarette. In that brief flash, she saw his face and the bandage on his hand. She was almost certain it was the man who'd posed as the wounded policeman when they'd captured her. The guard's position made it impossible for her to draw any closer, but she'd seen enough to call for backup.

As she edged away, she suddenly realized that the guard's position made it easy for him to spot anyone coming down the road. So much for a surprise raid, unless everyone came in silently on foot. But there were few around who could move as quietly as Benjamin did, and that was precisely what it would require. Cursing under her breath, she headed back to the mesa.

She was nearly at the base of it when she heard Benjamin's familiar whisper. "I'm here," he said, emerging from behind an outcropping of rocks. "I believe that man is the one who was cut up after kidnapping you."

She nodded. "He looked familiar to me, too. Were you able to tell how many are inside the house?"

"Three at least, along with my agate Twin. I felt its presence strongly."

"We'll need backup, but I'm not sure how we can get them up here without alerting the gang." She explained the problem, then said, "It might be possible for a police team to drive up using a less direct route, but with all the dry arroyos around, any vehicle is going to find it slow, rough going."

He drew in a long, deep breath. "We cannot count on others now. If we bring in the tribal police, the amulet will be taken in as evidence—that is, if it survives. The criminals may decide to destroy anything that could incriminate them."

He didn't have to say it. They both knew that his life depended on the amulet's safety. Fear, more powerful than any she'd ever known, filled her. For a moment, her throat felt so tight that she didn't trust her voice. She swallowed, bracing herself. "It's settled, then. We'll handle this ourselves." Julia peered into the darkness pensively. "Our chances aren't that bad—we've certainly handled worse. I think we can pull it off, providing we catch them by surprise.''

''First, we'll have to get that guard out of the way.''

''I'll take care of that while you watch the rear exit.'' Julia handed him the rifle. ''Here. You might need some firepower. I have my pistol.''

He took the rifle and opened the bolt enough to verify that a shell was in the chamber. ''I remember what you taught me about this type of weapon. If it's necessary, I'll use it.''

''Remember not to shoot unless there's no way to avoid it. The moment we fire, we'll have everyone in there coming down on us.''

He nodded. ''What's your plan?''

''I'm going to sneak up on the guard and knock him out. Once he's out of the way, we'll take the ones inside the house.''

''If there's trouble, I'll be there. Remember that neither of us is alone in this.''

''I know.'' As she met his eyes, she felt an overwhelming wave of sadness. Soon Benjamin would be gone. Dear heaven, she wasn't sure how she would stand it! ''Let's get started,'' she managed in as even a tone as she could muster.

Julia crept forward silently. Fear spiraled throughout her, coiling her muscles and sharpening her instincts. Spotting the guard directly ahead of her, she slowed her steps. She waited for an eternity, scarcely breathing, making sure he hadn't sensed her presence. Minutes elapsed, but his attention remained on the canyon road, which was illuminated by the clear glow of the moon.

She moved toward him silently, aware of everything that surrounded her. She would have only one chance at this. Carefully, she turned her pistol, so she could use the butt as a club.

She was within three feet of the guard when he suddenly spun around. ''Took you long enough. I only heard you once, but it was enough to know you were there. I was hoping to draw you in. Loved the way you cooperated.'' He leered at her. ''Remember me from the house, beautiful?''

Julia remembered the voice and the snippets of conversation she'd heard. Though the sound had seemed a thousand miles away, their intent had been clear. Just thinking about it filled her with revulsion.

"Let's go inside," he said, gesturing with his gun. "I think the boys are going to be very glad you're here. We were getting bored. And this time we'll check around carefully for your Indian buddy. He's not going to take anyone by surprise again."

Before she could draw in a breath, she heard a dull thump. The man's gaze turned glassy and his mouth fell open. Something shiny and red jutted out from his neck. Then a soft gurgle escaped his lips, and blood trickled out. In an instant, he collapsed like a puppet whose strings had suddenly been cut. As his head struck the ground, there was a sharp metallic snap. The guard lay facedown, revealing the knife embedded in his neck. The blade had gone clear through him, severing the jugular and snapping in half when he hit the gravel surface.

She started to move the body, intending to hide it behind a stand of junipers, when she noticed Benjamin approaching from the shadows. He silently retrieved what remained of his broken knife, then helped her drag the body out of view of anyone inside the house.

"Another came out the back," he whispered. "He's alive, but securely tied and gagged."

She nodded, then silently gestured for him to return to the rear of the house. He moved like a ghost into the darkness, and she quickly lost sight of him.

As she went toward the front porch, she saw that the screen door was closed but the front door was open. If she could slip inside without alerting them, she might be able to make the arrest without ever firing a shot. She listened for voices and concluded that the men were somewhere past the living room.

Julia crept to the entrance, then waited, hoping to hear something that would give her an advantage. McKibben's voice boomed out clearly.

"Will you shut up and quit whining? I've kept my side of

the bargain. You guys are still out of jail, aren't you. All the money, except the thousand I stuck in Roanhorse's car, is still safe in a storage locker under a phony name. As soon as the roadblocks are lifted, you can take off without running the risk of getting caught with evidence that would incriminate all of us.''

"Yeah, sure, but how long are they going to keep those roadblocks up? At this rate, by the time we get out of here we'll be too old to enjoy the money."

"No chance. This can't go on for more than a few days, at most. The tribal police are already strained to the limit, and they've got to resume their regular patrols. And as far as my department goes, I've been letting a few rumors spread. Most of my deputies want off the roadblock detail. They figure it's a thankless job and one expressly designed to cover the Feds in case things go wrong."

"Once we split up the money, what's going to happen to you? Are you going to leave this hellhole, too?"

"Not right away. We laundered a large percentage of our money buying jewelry and artifacts, so I'll need to contact buyers and sell off that stuff. After I'm finished, I'll rendezvous with you three so we can split the profits."

"Wait a second," the man protested. "We also need to decide who'll hang on to the shares that belong to the guys who'll be serving time. That money is all that's keeping them from talking to the FBI."

"That, and knowing that they're dead meat if they say a word. They wouldn't have been caught in the first place if you incompetents had finished off that woman and her Indian pal. I kept telling you that they were a threat—they could second-guess us too accurately. But you guys blew it. Now quit stalling, Foster," McKibben concluded. "It's your turn. Get out there and relieve Martinez. His watch is over."

Julia quickly pushed herself flat against the wall. If he was McKibben's last companion, then all she'd have to do is clobber Foster when he came out and slip into the house. The odds were looking much better. Foster cleared the doorway, and in a flash, she smashed the butt of her pistol against the back of his neck. As Foster began to sag, she grabbed him by the middle, lowering him to the porch soundlessly.

Julia unfastened her belt, using it to tie the unconscious man to a pillar on the porch. She worked fast and noiselessly, then slipped inside the house. The only sound came from McKibben, who was in what she assumed to be the kitchen.

Her luck had held. She moved across the room quietly, heading for the kitchen door. Adrenaline poured into her bloodstream, making her senses more acute. Now it was time to press her advantage and finish what she'd started.

She rushed in low, but McKibben saw her immediately. In the blink of an eye, he dove toward the shotgun on the counter, hitting the ground and rolling through the doorway into the living room.

Julia snapped off a shot, but missed. McKibben's response was swift. The shotgun blast reverberated in the tiny room as he aimed for the light fixture. Glass shattered, and the room was blanketed in darkness as crystal shards rained down over her.

She kept perfectly still and heard him moving as the hardwood floor creaked. Uncertain of his exact location, Julia crept back behind the breakfast counter, giving her eyes a chance to adjust to the blackness that enveloped the house. Finally, images began to materialize in the darkness, and she peered out from cover. The room was as silent and still as a tomb. She moved up a little farther, struggling to see into the gray veil that enshrouded everything. Minutes dragged by.

Julia lay low, forcing herself to wait him out. Then, at long last, she caught the brief glimpse of a shadow against the far wall. She had him now.

She moved forward in a crouch, but just as she left cover, she saw the barrel of a shotgun swinging toward her from behind the television set. He'd used his reflection in a wall mirror to trick her! She dove out of the line of fire just as a blast screamed past, gouging chunks of plaster from the wall. Julia spun around quickly, bringing her pistol to bear.

Suddenly, there was a resounding crash and the skylight above her shattered into a million fragments. She saw a blur of motion ahead as she ducked, protecting herself from the glass cascading down.

# Chapter Nineteen

Julia shook the glass off. McKibben's errant blast must have hit the skylight. She started forward, when she saw the figure of a man coming straight toward her. Julia rolled aside instantly, bringing her gun up.

"Relax, it is me," Benjamin said. "McKibben has been knocked out."

She crawled out from behind cover and looked around. The hole in the roof, and McKibben's prone body, confirmed what had happened. Benjamin had jumped down through the skylight and knocked McKibben to the floor.

As Benjamin strode across the room toward her, McKibben rose to his feet. He sprinted unsteadily for the door, but Julia stepped in his path, throwing her best right cross. McKibben, clotheslined by the blow, slid backward, unconscious.

"That was some punch," Benjamin said softly.

"Actually, he did most of the work by running into my fist." She handcuffed McKibben quickly.

"The agate amulet is close by. I can feel it."

"If you need it, I have the turquoise Twin with me," she said, unsnapping her shirt pocket and touching it with the tip of her finger.

"Can't you sense the presence of the other one? It calls to us," Benjamin asked in a hushed tone.

"Not to me, but I'll search McKibben while you look through the room."

As Benjamin moved away, Julia rolled the sheriff onto his back, grateful that the big man was out cold, and frisked him. A moment later, she pulled a small object wrapped in cloth from his pants pocket. She untied the string, revealing what was inside. "I've got it."

He stared at the amulet in the moonlight filtering through the window. "So the time has finally come." His voice was an anguished whisper in the silence of the room.

Pain laced through her as she met his gaze. It wasn't fair, but if she truly loved him, she now had to let him go. Forcing herself to look away, she unsnapped her shirt pocket and took the turquoise amulet out.

Choked by a wave of regret, she placed both amulets in the center of her palm. Her heart felt heavy as she stared at the Twin effigies that had brought the man she loved into her life— and would now take him away.

As she held them out to him, the turquoise and agate Twins touched. Suddenly, a dense shadow overwhelmed the room. Wind swept around them, coming out of nowhere, for all the doors and windows were closed. The temperature soared, turning impossibly hot in a few seconds.

Julia quickly separated the two amulets, placing one in each hand. "Run, Benjamin! Their fight is not with me. I'll be okay. Get away before they destroy you!"

"No, I won't leave you to face this alone."

The darkness thinned slightly, and a voice suddenly boomed from across the room. "Running won't do you any good, you stinkin' renegade. You and I have a score to settle."

He didn't sound like a god to Julia. It was more like one very angry human. She stared into the shadows, trying to make out the shape in the darkness. "Who are you?" she demanded, unconsciously dropping one of the amulets as she instinctively drew her pistol.

"I'm Capt. Alger Thayer, ma'am, and you are very right, my fight is not with you. Leave now, while you can still do so safely."

"I'm a federal police officer, mister, and I don't barter for lives, including my own. Whatever your problem is, we'll work it out in a calm and peaceful manner.''

''No, ma'am. That is not possible.''

''What are you doing here, Green Eyes?'' Benjamin's voice seemed to come from everywhere.

Julia tried to pinpoint Benjamin's location, but was unable to do so. Though the captain was on the move and making full use of the darkness, his voice was marginally easier to track. But his shadow remained elusive, shifting continually and barely discernible. Julia suppressed a shudder and kept her gun ready.

''I was no volunteer, renegade. This was your handiwork. You trapped me in that accursed stone. When they touched before, the spell weakened, allowing one of us to pass through. Your witchcraft was your salvation, and I remained trapped. From that moment on, it was worse than before. For days, ever since you got away, I've been within a hairbreadth of escaping. I almost went mad. I could hear and see everything around the damnable turquoise, but I just couldn't leave that purgatory.

''Quick as a whistle I remembered the whole thing—being pulled kicking and hollering into the stone. I knew it was you that had tricked me, but I still couldn't get my hands on your heathen throat. Shortly after you were released, I discovered I could get into your enemies' thinking, especially the one who had the amulet. I made them hate you as much as I did. I told the lot of them you needed killing. They failed, and eventually my kin found me. But now righteousness has prevailed, and here I am. Nothing will save you now.''

''What happened to you was an accident,'' Benjamin said. ''My chant compelled the amulet to make me, its owner, one with its power. But the turquoise Twin was by then yours, and I did not take that into account. Your entrapment was an unwitting mistake. Despite that, I welcome your presence, Green Eyes. You betrayed my people. You will pay for what you have done.''

''One of us will die, but it will not be me.''

Julia heard a footstep, then suddenly felt the cold steel of a barrel against her back and a powerful hand on her wrist. "And you, my own flesh and blood, have dishonored me by siding with this Indian. Your gun, please." Before she could pull away, Thayer wrested the pistol from her grip.

"Leave her out of this." Benjamin's voice echoed from somewhere in the room. "The death of a dozen or more Navajo women and children is on your hands. Are you so afraid of fighting a warrior man-to-man?"

Moonlight finally managed to penetrate the room, and Julia was beginning to see more clearly. Her heart froze as she watched Benjamin come out into view, trying to goad the cavalry officer into action.

Julia pushed away fast, escaping Thayer's grasp. But as she did, she dropped the other amulet. She stood back, watching the men and waiting for the chance to retrieve both amulets.

Thayer glanced at her, but then turned toward Benjamin again. Crouching, he slid her pistol out into the middle of the floor. "I'm giving you more of a chance than you gave me," Thayer growled. "Reach for that gun before I kill you like a dog."

"What happened is over with," Julia argued. "Over a century has passed."

"This score must be settled," Thayer answered.

"There's no victory in death," Julia insisted, struggling to make them see reason.

"Look at it this way, Julia Stevens. There is no other way for justice to be done," Thayer said, his gaze on Benjamin.

The tall, powerfully built officer, clad in his dark blue uniform and black riding boots, seemed invincible. "Benjamin doesn't have a chance, and you know it," Julia said. "You can squeeze the trigger before he even touches the pistol."

"He has a slim chance, I'll admit, but it's there." He stared hard at Benjamin. "If you don't move, I'll kill you, anyway."

Julia looked at one man, then the other, trying to think of something—anything—to prevent them from carrying out their deadly plans.

Suddenly, the shadow of a huge bear appeared to Thayer's

right, and a vicious growl engulfed the room. Thayer reacted instinctively and fired at the image.

As the bullet blew out a chunk from the wall, the shadow dissipated instantly. Realizing it was a trick, Thayer whirled around to face Benjamin, who was diving for the gun. Just as Benjamin's fingers reached it, Thayer kicked the pistol away. "No more magic, renegade. Your time to die has come."

Julia groped blindly for the gun in the darkened room. In a desperate move, Benjamin lashed out with his broken blade, catching the officer in the thigh.

Bellowing in anger and pain, Thayer unsheathed his saber from its scabbard. He swung wildly at Benjamin, who barely managed to deflect the blow with the knife handle.

Spinning, Thayer struck out at Julia, who had almost reached the pistol. She jerked her arm back and rolled away as the blade flashed down. It struck the floor with an angry ring, an inch from her head, showering her with chips of tile.

Thayer raised his saber quickly to strike again, but in a flash, Benjamin was on him. Face-to-face with his enemy, he grabbed both of Thayer's wrists, twisting and turning his hands inward, forcing both gun and saber together. The officer tried to pull away, but Benjamin hung on to his hands so Thayer could neither aim his pistol nor swing down with the blade. "Get out of here, Julia! This isn't your fight," Benjamin managed as he struggled.

"Worry about yourself!" she shouted back, trying to locate her pistol again.

Seconds later, she spotted it underneath the men, who were locked tightly in battle. She started crawling forward, ready to reach out for it, when she saw the amulets. Both were on the floor inches from her gun. She'd have to do something fast, or they'd be crushed under the captain's heavy boots.

Just then, Thayer kicked out viciously, catching Benjamin in the chest. Benjamin fell back, but his grip on Thayer's arm remained firm. Benjamin hit the floor, bringing Thayer down, too. The saber slipped from Thayer's grip, the handle lodging against Ben's thigh.

As Thayer fell face forward, the long blade impaled him, emerging out the back of his jacket as crimson steel. He let out a long gasp, then was silent.

Benjamin felt the crushing weight of the dead man upon him. Choking back his aversion to the body, he pushed the corpse away and managed to stand shakily.

He was silent for a moment, catching his breath before speaking. "It is finished. You fought for me, as I did for you. And what we have done together has restored the balance of justice." He gathered her into his arms. "You are mine. I will stand beside you always."

She rested her head against his chest, but the warmth of his body suddenly began to fade. The solid feel of Benjamin's chest gave way to wispy tendrils of icy air, as a chilling breeze swirled around them. Fear slammed into her as she stepped back and saw Benjamin losing substance and fading before her eyes. In a few seconds, he'd become more ghost than man. "No! You said you wouldn't go back!"

Benjamin glanced down at himself, then raised his nearly transparent hands before his face. "I won't return! I don't belong there anymore." His gaze fastened on the amulets, and he saw that the captain's blood had streamed across the floor, engulfing the Twins. "Smash the amulets, *sawe*. It's our only chance!" His voice was distant and distorted.

"But you said that could destroy you!"

"If you want me, you must break both Twins. It's all or nothing now. There is no other way."

His voice was so faint she could barely hear it, even in the silent room. Her whole body ached with despair. She wanted him more than anything, but not at the expense of his life!

"Goodbye then, *sawe*." His whisper was laden with sadness. "You've made your decision. I will go back by your hand."

She couldn't let him go. He didn't belong in 1864! He belonged with her! She looked at the turquoise figure she'd cherished for so long. It no longer mattered to her. Knowing it had housed the enemy of the man she loved made it almost repulsive. Trusting her instincts, she smashed the butt of her pistol against both stone figures until only fragments remained.

Looking up, she searched frantically for Benjamin, but his image had faded into nothingness. Julia choked back a sob as a part of herself died. Tears streamed down her face. She'd waited too long—she'd failed him. "Don't leave me!" she whispered to the emptiness that surrounded her. "Fight, Benjamin Two Eagle!" Navajos believed names had power, and she knew of no better time to invoke all the help she could. "Stay with me. I need you!"

When nothing happened, a suffocating grief engulfed her. She tried to tell herself that memories would be enough, but the ache knifing through her told her a different truth.

Suddenly, a searing gust of wind ripped through the room. She heard an odd, crackling noise behind her and turned quickly to look. The cavalry officer's body began dissolving into dark gray smoke. In seconds, it vanished completely from her sight.

The next instant, Benjamin's image sparked the air, forming in wispy curls of smoke that lacked clear definition. Hope flared within her, brilliant as a rainbow in a cloudless sky. "Yes! Come back to me, Benjamin Two Eagle!"

A heartbeat later, Benjamin stood before her, whole once again. He pulled Julia against him tightly. "I knew you wouldn't let me go."

"I couldn't." Tears of happiness fell down her cheeks. "You need me far too much," she added, pressing herself against his solid form.

"You're a stubborn and irritating woman. But you're *my* woman," he growled, taking her mouth in an endless kiss.

## *About the Author*

Aimée Thurlo is a nationally known bestselling author. She's written forty-one novels and is published in at least twenty countries worldwide. She has been nominated for the Reviewer's Choice Award and the Career Achievement Award by *Romantic Times* magazine.

She also co-writes the Ella Clah mainstream mystery series, which debuted with a starred review in *Publishers Weekly* and has been optioned by CBS.

Aimée was born in Havana, Cuba, and lives with her husband of thirty years in Corrales, New Mexico. Her husband, David, was raised on the Navajo Indian Reservation.

If you enjoyed what you just read,
then we've got an offer you can't resist!

# Take 2 bestselling
# love stories FREE!
# Plus get a FREE surprise gift!

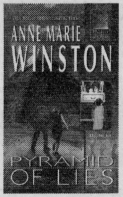